Death By His Grace

Also by the author

The Inspector Darko Dawson Mysteries
Wife of the Gods
Children of the Street
Murder at Cape Three Points
Gold of Our Fathers

Death at the Voyager Hotel
Kamila

Death By His Grace

Kwei Quartey

Published by
Soho Press, Inc.
853 Broadway
New York, NY 10003

Library of Congress Cataloging-in-Publication Data
Quartey, Kwei.
Death by his grace / Kwei Quartey.
A Darko Dawson mystery ; 5

ISBN 978-1-61695-708-7
eISBN 978-1-61695-709-4

1. Police—Ghana—Fiction. 2. Murder—Investigation—Fiction. I. Title
PS3617.U37 D45 2017 813'.6—dc23 2016057007

Interior design by Janine Agro, Soho Press, Inc.

Printed in the United States of America

10 9 8 7 6 5 4 3 2 1

To Joana

What shall we say then? Are we to continue in sin that grace may abound?

—Romans 6:1

Death By His Grace

PART ONE

CHAPTER ONE

KATHERINE WOULD NEVER FORGET the day she married Solomon. The wedding was immense, glorious, and the talk of Accra. Solomon's father, Ezekiel Vanderpuye, a wealthy ex-member of parliament, spared no expense. Clem Howard-Mills, one of Ghana's most prominent bishops, officiated the service at the Power of God Ministry Church in La Paz on the outskirts of Accra.

Four hundred guests flocked to Unique Floral Palace for the reception. The enormous space dazzled in white and gold, with Queen Anne's lace, white calla lilies, and pink gardenias decorating the guests' tables. Lights cascaded from ceiling to floor, sparkling like a South African diamond.

Caterers in crisp white uniforms served up a large spread of food, from palm nut soup to kung-pao chicken. Champagne, wine, beer, and hard liquor flowed while the DJ played loud hip-life. Weddings and funerals—no difference: eat till stuffed; imbibe till drunk. And the first commandment: thou shalt not run out of food or drink, or you will tarnish your name forever.

Solomon and Katherine observed traditional Ghanaian nuptial customs the day after. With gifts of alcohol and yards of cloth, Solomon's family paid an official visit to Katherine's.

The elders on both sides poured libation and performed the necessary rites.

Katherine felt joy and pride whenever she looked at Solomon, so slim and tall in a dark, embroidered smock. Already, she could picture her future life with her husband and two or three kids in a happy home. Katherine wanted a little girl first. After that, she would be perfectly happy with either gender.

For a moment, Katherine watched her parents, Nana and Ransford. She could tell how elated they were. Both of them liked Solomon and admired his intelligence and educational accomplishments. He was a young, up-and-coming lawyer. Ezekiel, Solomon's father, was also pleased. Every so often, he beamed at Katherine and his eyes moistened behind his spectacles.

Solomon's mother, Maude, was a different matter. She had welcomed Katherine into her family with reluctance. Status was critical to Maude. *Vanderpuye*, her husband's name, had been tied to the Ghanaian upper class for generations, since the seventeenth century when Dutch colonists and indigenous people produced mixed offspring. Katherine's Yeboah family, on the other hand, was of working class stock, and in Maude's view, fell below a certain "essential" threshold. But to Katherine, her mother-in-law's preoccupation with caste was a pointless contrivance.

Always at Maude's right hand was her daughter, Georgina. She looked and behaved like her mother—down almost to the gesture—and sided with Maude over everything. The two women felt Solomon had rushed into marriage. He had met Katherine a few months before he went off to the University of Virginia to study Business Administration. While away from Ghana, Solomon kept in touch with Katherine by phone, WhatsApp, and Skype. They were in love. Some nights Katherine would stay up until three or four in the morning talking to Solomon. Not long after his return to Ghana, he proposed to Katherine. Thrilled, she accepted.

Maude and Georgina had been dead set against Solomon's

engagement to Katherine, but Ezekiel had prevailed over his wife and daughter. He told them Solomon had every right to marry the woman he loved.

In the midst of the laughter, drinking, and dancing of the after-wedding party, Katherine stole a glance at her mother-in-law. Maude's mouth was hard, her jaw set, and her eyes cold.

CHAPTER TWO

LATE ONE WEDNESDAY AFTERNOON in February when the rush of the wedding had subsided and the Harmattan weather had become insufferable, Katherine and Nana were preparing a meal in the kitchen.

"So will I be a grandmother soon?" Nana asked her daughter with a sidelong glance.

"Mama, it's only been a month since the wedding," Katherine said with a short laugh.

Nana searched her face. "I hope you're not waiting, are you?"

"Waiting? What do you mean?"

"Well, you know," Nana said, wrinkling her nose, "your generation sometimes has a notion to wait awhile before having children, for whatever reason."

"My generation?" Katherine said with some amusement. She shook her head. "Not us. Solomon and I want kids as soon as possible, and we're not wasting any time getting to it." She hesitated. "In fact, I thought maybe I was pregnant last weekend, but the test was negative."

"That sometimes happens at the beginning," Nana reassured her. "Don't worry. As long as you and Solomon continue trying to conceive, I'm sure it won't be long now."

"I'm not worried, Mama," Katherine said. She added more salt to the pepper stew that would accompany the rice, which the guests would enjoy later on in the evening after Bible study.

Katherine had made it a tradition to provide a meal whenever she and Nana hosted a *bussell* session. It was Bishop Howard-Mills who had introduced the concept of *bussells* to his congregants. Held in the homes of church members, these meetings provided an opportunity to worship the Lord if and when one could not make it to church. This was especially helpful to working professionals.

Katherine and Solomon had been participating in the *bussell* program since before their marriage. No more than ten members attended a session, and although the proceedings were less formal than regular church, the Bible discussions still needed some direction. That duty usually fell to one of the junior ministers. Young Reverend Atiemo had customarily officiated at the *bussells* Katherine and Solomon hosted, and Bishop Howard-Mills's assistant, John Papafio, often accompanied the reverend to notify members about upcoming community events.

AROUND EIGHT, THE first of the church members began to file in. Katherine greeted them with hugs and kisses. She was profoundly happy, with enough love and warmth to fill an ocean as far as the horizon. After thirty minutes or so, Reverend Atiemo led the group of seven in prayer, following it with a discussion of Psalm 139: "'I can never escape from your spirit! I can never get away from your presence.'"

John arrived late, slipping in as quietly as he could. Solomon pulled up a chair for him.

"Welcome, John," Atiemo said.

John flashed an easy smile. In his late twenties, he had a boyish face and a relaxed manner. He was tall but rather round and soft. Efficient, he seemed to pull off church events with little effort, and his sense of humor could belie his competence. Once the discussion was over, John made a few announcements, and then it was time for the best part: the meal.

After dinner, the church members talked and laughed among themselves as they straggled out to the courtyard. Gabriel, the faithful little watchman who had worked for the Yeboahs for years and who was related to them in some way, was at the front gate ready to bid the guests good night.

As Reverend Atiemo was preparing to leave, Katherine pulled him aside and asked if he would stay for a few minutes. He joined Nana, Katherine, and Solomon in the sitting room. Glancing at Solomon every so often, Katherine asked the reverend to pray for them as they sought to conceive a child together. Atiemo listened with patience and understanding, and then the group joined hands and bowed their heads as the reverend led them in a heartfelt prayer.

"I FELT BLESSED as he prayed for us," Katherine confided to Solomon later as they were getting into bed. "Did you feel it too?"

"I did," he said.

"He's a caring soul, Reverend Atiemo," she observed. "Everyone in the church is—the bishop, the reverend, even John."

"John thinks the world of you," Solomon said, as Katherine snuggled up to him. "You should see the way he stares at you sometimes."

"Oh, come on," Katherine said.

"I'm not kidding."

She lifted her head off his chest to look at Solomon with a smile. "Are you jealous?"

He snorted. "Not at all. John has a pure heart."

"He does seem to," Katherine agreed.

"So, when you become tired of me," Solomon joked, "you'll know where you can turn and to whom."

Katherine gave him a mock slap. "Silly boy."

He laughed.

"Honey?" she said after a moment. "I think we'll be successful tonight. I can feel it." She reached down to touch him. "Seems like you do as well."

• • •

AFTERWARD, SOLOMON TURNED over and went to sleep, never one to cuddle. Katherine always felt lonely after sex when he moved away from her like that. But it mattered less to her tonight because she was confident that this time, a tiny Vanderpuye was about to form within her.

CHAPTER THREE

One year later

THE NURSE SHOWED Katherine into the obstetrician's consultation room. She sat in front of a large, polished desk and gazed at the framed degrees and diplomas on the wall.

She turned as the obstetrician entered from a side door. He was a short, graying, bespectacled man who reminded Katherine of one of her professors in college. After taking his seat on the opposite side of the desk, he got straight to the point with barely a social pleasantry.

"I believe you may have polycystic ovary syndrome," he told Katherine.

Katherine stiffened. She had spent hours on the Internet reading up on causes of infertility, and PCOS was one she feared most.

"Besides your irregular menstrual periods," the obstetrician continued, "you get pimples and facial hair every once in a while. These may be manifestations of excess androgens from polycystic ovaries."

"But what causes that, Doctor?"

"Causes what?" he said with a hint of impatience.

"The polycystic ovary syndrome."

"The details are a bit complicated," he said, "but the condition can cause anovulation, which means the egg doesn't come out of the ovary. I'm quite confident that's why you're not getting pregnant."

"What can we do about it?"

"First, you need an ultrasound to confirm my suspicion. I know you brought images from the doctor you saw before, but the study is suboptimal, and we need to repeat it."

Katherine was annoyed. The obstetric and fertility specialists she had been consulting for several months were all in private practice. Their fees were hefty, as was the price of the specialized blood and ultrasound tests. Every exam or procedure on her internal organs had been uncomfortable or downright painful, especially the hysterosalpingogram she had had two months prior. It tested whether her fallopian tubes were patent, and according to the doctor who had performed it, they were.

Katherine wished Solomon were there with her, but listening to "all that female stuff" got him squeamish. She was always alone at medical appointments. Somehow, that didn't seem fair.

WHEN HE CAME home from work that evening, Solomon was dead tired. He threw his briefcase onto the armchair in the sitting room and wrenched off his tie. Katherine made space for him on the sofa, and he plopped down beside her.

"Busy day?" she asked.

"Very. My client load is picking up—at last. And you? How was your day?"

"I went to the doctor."

"Oh," he said, surprised. "Which one is this—Doctor Opare?"

"No, that was the last. The one I saw this morning is Doctor Engman. He's supposed to be one of the best."

Solomon slumped back, eyes to the ceiling. "That's what you said about the other six or seven specialists."

"Four," Katherine corrected.

"Seems like more," Solomon said, sitting up. His jawline hardened. "What did this one say?"

"He thinks I have polycystic ovary syndrome," Katherine said.

Solomon wrinkled his brow. "What is that?"

"It's a bit complicated," Katherine said, echoing Engman's answer. "But it causes infertility. So the doctor wants to do an ultrasound."

"But didn't you have one before?"

"He says I need a new one."

"These doctors must think money grows on trees," Solomon said.

"Kind of like you lawyers?" she quipped.

They both laughed, although Solomon grew serious quickly. "I'll have to borrow some more from Daddy because I'm broke. So many expenses in setting up the practice."

Already, Ezekiel had given them the down payment on the house as a wedding gift. After the wedding, Katherine and Solomon had moved into their new home in Dzorwulu, one of Accra's upper middle-class neighborhoods.

"I'm sorry to be causing you trouble," Katherine said, her voice trembling. "If I had become pregnant, we wouldn't be going through all this."

He leaned toward her and pulled her to him. "Don't be silly. We're in this together, right?" He hugged her and wiped the tears from her cheeks.

"We've tried everything, Solo," she said in despair. "I've had procedures with names I can't even pronounce. The only thing left is in vitro, but we just can't afford it—even if we go to India."

"I hear you," Solomon said. "This is not easy for either of us or our families."

She searched his face. "Your mom is upset, isn't she? What has she been saying about me?"

"Oh, no," he said, his eyes skipping away from hers. "Nothing like that. Don't worry about Mama. Everything is fine."

But Katherine wasn't entirely reassured.

"When I get back from Takoradi on Thursday," he said, "we'll sit down together and plan out what we should do next, okay?"

"You're going to Takoradi?" she asked in surprise.

"Honey, I told you last week. I'm talking to someone about setting up an office there."

"You did? I don't remember."

"Because you're stressed out. What I say to you goes in one ear and out the other."

She laughed. "Silly." She kissed him on the cheek. "I love you."

He stood up without reciprocating. "I'm going to take a shower. What have you made for dinner?"

"I bought *kenkey* on the way home, and I fried some fish the way you like it."

He brightened. "Great. I won't be long."

As she got the meal ready, Katherine felt strange. Had Solomon seemed cold just now when she kissed him, or had she imagined it?

CHAPTER FOUR

AFTER SOLOMON HAD LEFT early Tuesday morning to catch the first flight out to Takoradi, Katherine dressed for work and ran out of the house to the car, hoping to beat the worst of Accra's rush hour. If she could get on the road by 6:15, she would be okay. Even so, the commute to the Ring Road Provident Towers, where she was a junior accountant, turned out to be nerve-wracking.

When she got up to the insurance offices on the third floor, Katherine found two of her female coworkers scrolling through phone pictures. Katherine knew what they were gushing over.

"Come and look at Ama's baby," Ernestina called out.

Katherine felt her heart twist like wrung towel.

Ama swiped through dozens of images of her adorable, smiling infant.

"He's such a cute baby" Katherine said.

"And I know you'll have one soon," Ama said.

"Oh, yes," Katherine said.

"Baby on the way?" Ernestina asked her.

"I'm sure." Katherine turned away and went to the office. Out of sight of the other two women, she leaned against the wall feeling ill. Her insides writhed and she thought she would throw up. Oh no, not here, please God. She hurried to the ladies' room out in the hallway and locked herself in one of the stalls. Her hands on her thighs, she bent forward and waited. Nothing happened, and her nausea cleared.

Maybe I'm pregnant. Katherine's heart leaped.

SHE TOOK A pregnancy test as soon as she got home from work. While she waited the required two minutes for the result, her heart beat like a jackhammer. If only. If she were pregnant, she would have loved to have had Solomon there for this moment.

She squinted at the test, trying to will the second line to appear. It didn't. She hurled the strip into the toilet bowl and leaned on the bathroom counter with her head down.

She looked up at the sound of knocking. When she opened the door, Christine Dawson was standing on the other side. The instant Katherine saw her cousin, she burst into tears and collapsed into her arms.

ON THE SOFA, the two women held hands and Katherine took comfort from Christine.

"You've been through an awful time so far this year," Christine said, her face full of sympathy. "Both you and Solo."

Katherine nodded. She thought Christine was lovely, with her short, unprocessed hair and her dark, soft eyes. She was slim but well-built with marvelous broad shoulders.

"Is Solo still at work?" Christine asked.

Katherine hesitated, looking down. "He went to Takoradi this morning for a couple of days."

Christine lifted her chin. "What's going on?"

"Nothing," she denied.

"Come on," Christine said. "Remember I've known you forever."

Katherine gave a little laugh. "That's true. Well, I'm scared . . . I'm afraid Solomon will leave me if I don't get pregnant soon."

Christine showed her surprise. "Kate! Why do you think that?"

"He seemed distant last night and this morning. And this trip to Takoradi—well I don't remember him telling me about it in advance, although he says he did."

"He probably did," Christine said. "Don't imagine the worst. We women are always doing that to ourselves."

Someone knocked on the door for the second time that evening. Katherine got up to find Maude and Georgina on the doorstep.

"Mama?" Katherine said. "Good evening."

Maude's hair was perfect without an errant strand in sight. "We want to speak to you," she said.

They entered in awkward silence. Not a social visit, Katherine thought. Something was wrong.

"Oh, hello," Maude said as she saw Katherine had company.

"You remember my cousin Christine?" Katherine said.

"Yes, I do," Maude said, managing a smile.

She and Georgina sat down and exchanged a few words of painful, polite small talk with Katherine.

Christine cleared her throat and sat forward, "I must take my leave."

"Oh, so soon?" Katherine said, dismayed. "Please, stay."

"We need to discuss family affairs," Maude said.

"Oh," Katherine said. "All right. Then I'll see you out, Christine."

Outside, Katherine whispered, "This is trouble. I can smell it. For them to come to see me while Solo is not here? Not good."

Christine squeezed her hand. "Call me later, okay? I wish I could stay to give your moral support, but—"

"No, Chrissy, it's okay."

They hugged each other, and Christine left. Katherine returned to Maude and Georgina, who were talking in hushed tones. They stopped as Katherine sat down and faced them.

"We have come to see you about an important matter," Maude said.

Katherine swallowed. "Yes?"

"Solomon is away," Maude continued, "so Georgina and I have chosen this occasion to speak to you. He did not ask us to come. We are here independently."

Katherine frowned. "Okay, but what is this all about?"

"The marriage between you and him is not working," Maude said.

"Not working?" Katherine said. "What are you talking about?"

"Solomon wants a baby," Georgina said. "And so do we—his family."

"Why are you thwarting Solo's efforts to impregnate you?" Maude demanded.

Katherine pulled back. "Me? How could I be doing that?"

Maude leaned forward. "You have to tell us. Has someone cursed you to be barren? Is that what has happened to you?"

Katherine was rigid. "This is nonsense."

Georgina got to her feet and leaned over Katherine with a finger in her face. "What are you doing to my brother, you witch?"

"I'm a witch?" Katherine pointed to herself. "*Me?*"

"Do you see me talking to someone else? Of course, you!"

Katherine jumped up and shoved Georgina away. She staggered back, recovered, and advanced on her sister-in-law for a full-blown fight.

Maude stepped between the two younger women. "No!" she shouted. "Stop! Sit down, both of you."

They did so, glaring at each other. Maude returned to her chair. "Katherine," she said, "we know you have been going to a lot of specialists. You've had all kinds of procedures and tests for your infertility, but nothing is working. Have you consulted a traditional healer or fetish priest?"

"No, and I'm not going to," Katherine said. "I don't believe in that."

"But you've exhausted all the modern medicine options," Maude said, gesturing in frustration. "What harm could come from trying a traditional healer?"

Katherine shook her head. "Solo and I will continue to seek professional medical advice. This other stuff you're suggesting is a waste of time."

"Because you don't want to bless my brother with a child," Georgina said with finality. "I knew it."

"Shut up," Katherine snapped. "You hate me, Georgina; that's all there is to it. Because you and Solo are so close, you've always felt I took him away from you."

Georgina flapped her hand backward and sat back with her arms folded.

"Did Solomon ask you to come to tell me this?" Katherine demanded.

"Didn't I already say he didn't?"

"Then I don't need to hear any more," Katherine said, striding to the door. She held it open. "Goodbye to you both."

Maude picked up her purse, shaking her head. "Such disrespect. You're a disgrace."

She and her daughter marched out to the Benz waiting outside. Georgina shot one glance backward that seemed to say, "This is not over."

CHAPTER FIVE

As soon as Maude and Georgina had left, Katherine tried to call Solomon, but he didn't pick up. Her heart was racing. She was confused and felt hot around the face and neck.

She called Christine to tell her what had just occurred.

"What infuriates me is how they've used Solomon's absence as an opportunity to attack me," Katherine said.

"Have you called him about it?"

"I tried—no answer. I'll try again as soon as . . . Oh, that's Solo on the line right now. I'll call you back."

She clicked to Solomon. "Have you spoken to your mother today?" she asked.

"This morning, yes. Why?"

Katherine told him what had just transpired.

"I don't know what's going on," he muttered.

She found his subdued response strange. "But how dare they speak to me like that, Solo?" she said, trying to coax more indignation out of him. "Accusing me of being a witch, or somehow preventing the pregnancy from taking place? Don't they understand what a difficult time this is for me as well? I mean, I'm beyond insulted. I want an apology from both of them."

Solomon cleared his throat. "Well, that might be difficult, but I'll talk to them."

Why was he so cool about this? "Solo—did you know they were coming to see me?"

"No, of course not! Why would you think that?"

"Because you don't sound angry or upset. As though this is nothing."

"We already know about the tension between you and my mother."

"Tension is one thing; insults are quite another."

"Like I said, I will talk to them."

"Hurry home. I miss you."

"I miss you too. I'll do my best to leave Takoradi early in the day."

"I love you," she said.

But he had already ended the call.

Katherine felt a sudden chill, as though malaria had struck her for an instant. What had Solomon's flat, monotone voice meant?

That night, she dreamed about Maude, Georgina, and witches. Katherine heard every creak in the house and kept imagining a prowler outside. But she had no reason to be anxious. The front gate was secure, bolted, and padlocked, and besides, faithful Gabriel was on night duty keeping Katherine and her home safe.

AFTER WORK THE next day, Katherine went to Kaneshie Market to get food and supplies. By the time she returned home, Accra's chaotic rush hour traffic had sapped her like a wilting plant. But she perked up in the kitchen as she cleaned the fish she had bought and washed off the *garden eggs*, *okros*, onions, and tomatoes in readiness for Solomon's favorite meal the following evening.

IN THE MORNING, she woke up with the eagerness of a child at Christmastime. Solo was coming home today. She had asked her boss if she could leave work early if she came in at 6:30 A.M., and he had agreed. At around three o'clock, she left for home. Solomon's flight was scheduled to get in at five, and he would take a taxi home. With any luck, in rush hour, he would get home by seven.

Katherine put the finishing touches on the *okro* stew, which smelled delicious. Esi, the house girl, was starting on the *banku*. At 5:35, Solomon called Katherine to say he had just arrived and would head home shortly.

Less than an hour later, he called again. Maude was ill, so he would take a detour to check on her at home. Katherine barely swallowed her anger. Solo's mother was probably doing just fine. All she was doing was diverting her son away from his wife.

The minutes mounted to an hour, and then two. Katherine called Solomon's number, but he didn't pick up. What was going on?

It was almost ten when his taxi pulled up. Katherine heard the horn blow, and she hurried outside, where Gabriel was opening up the gate.

"Oh, I'm so happy to see you!" Katherine exclaimed as she embraced Solomon.

"You, too," he said, laughing. "I'm sorry I'm late."

Gabriel carried his bags into the house. Katherine and Solomon followed holding hands.

"You must be exhausted," Katherine said.

"I am," he said, kicking off his shoes and undoing his tie. He was about to slump into his favorite chair.

"No," Katherine said, pulling him back. "You know you're going to fall asleep. Come straight to table. I've prepared your favorite."

"I'm not that hungry," he said.

"Come on, you're always hungry," she retorted.

Esi put the meal and a basin of water on the table.

Katherine released her for the night. "Thank you for staying late."

"Yes, madam." Esi, so petite she was sometimes mistaken for a young girl, curtseyed and left.

Katherine served Solomon up two balls of *banku* and plenty of stew to go with it. "I missed you, honey," she said, beaming at him.

"I missed you too," he said. "Share half of the *banku* with me."

"You're only going to eat half of it?" she asked, surprised. "That's not like you."

"I ate something at Mom's," he confessed. "Sorry, I was hungry."

"Oh," Katherine said, disappointed. "Okay. Is she all right?"

"Her back has been troubling her," Solomon said, rinsing off his hands in the basin as he prepared to eat the traditional way.

"So, nothing serious," she said, sitting down. "Why did you take so long there?"

"We were talking." He shrugged. "You know how she is."

"Did you talk about what took place the other night when she and Georgina came to see me?"

"Not so much," he muttered.

"What does 'not so much' mean?"

"Kate, please," Solomon said. "We'll discuss it tomorrow. I'm just too tired for that right now."

"Sorry," she said, changing the subject. "Did you get everything done in Takoradi?"

"Just about," he said.

A brief silence followed as Solomon began eating. As they chatted, Katherine noticed something peculiar. He seemed to be passing each handful of food past his nose before putting it into his mouth.

"Honey," she said. "What's wrong? Why are you eating like that?"

"Like what?"

"As if you're smelling the food," she said, with a half-laugh.

"No, I'm not," he scoffed.

He appeared self-conscious, so she stopped staring, looked away, and tried to make some other conversation.

After a few minutes, he stopped eating. "Wow, I'm full already."

He hadn't cleaned his plate the way he typically did.

"Don't you like it?" she asked him.

"Of course, I do," he assured her. "It's delicious. You know your *banku* is the best."

She cleared the table while he went to take a shower before bed. She didn't want to admit to herself something was wrong, but the feeling hung around like a pesky fly.

She had hoped that his shower would reinvigorate him, but he was fast asleep even before she got into bed beside him. She had been looking forward to a little cuddling, maybe even intercourse. She had prepared herself for it, and she was fresh and clean. She hadn't wanted to waste any time before trying for a baby again, but perhaps it was just as well. A tired man meant ineffective sperm.

She couldn't stop her mind from straying to the worst possible scenario that Solomon had a Takoradi mistress who had drained him sexually and left him exhausted.

Katherine's head told her not to be ridiculous, but her heart said otherwise.

CHAPTER SIX

THE NEXT DAY, A surprise awaited Katherine when she returned home from work. Solomon was in the bedroom fast asleep with the AC on full tilt. He rarely beat Katherine home, and his sleeping at this early hour—six-thirty—made her worry that her husband was ill. She thought it best to let him sleep awhile.

Katherine got dinner ready—simple *gari* and sardines. She hummed an absent-minded tune, thinking she should check on Solomon soon. As she turned to reach for a dish on the counter, she caught a glimpse of someone standing behind her and jumped out of her skin. She whirled around.

"Oh, my goodness, Solo!" she gasped, putting her hand on her chest. "You scared me!"

He was still in his work clothes, but his shirttails were out, and he was barefoot.

"Solo, what's wrong?" Katherine whispered.

"I'm sick," he said, rubbing his belly. "Pains in my stomach. That's why I came home early to sleep."

"Oh, I'm sorry, love. Do you have a fever?" She took two steps to put her hand on his forehead, but he backed away from her as if she had Ebola.

"What are you doing to me?" he whispered.

She froze. "What?"

"Are you trying to poison me?" His eyes burned bright and sick.

"The food last night. No wonder it tasted strange. You put poison in it."

Her heart stopped for a moment. He must be delirious with malarial fever.

"I understand everything now," he continued. "The baby—how you've been killing it in your womb instead of allowing it to be born."

Katherine went rigid. "You're frightening me, Solo. What's wrong?"

He began to back away. "You and your fellow witches. That's what you all do, isn't it? Kill people, destroy children."

"Stop," she said. "Please, Solo. Stop saying these things."

"I can't eat your food," he said, now turning his back on her and walking to the bedroom. "I can't stay here either. I don't want to be around you."

Katherine followed him. Stunned, she watched him stuffing a suitcase with his clothes.

"Solo, you know I love you," she said. "Not even love—I adore you. And you know I want a child more than anything. Maybe even more than you do. None of what you're saying is true."

He hesitated as though processing what she had just said, but then he resumed packing. He went to the bathroom for his shaving things. "I have to be alone for a while to think about what I should do," he said, zipping up the case. "I'll let you know."

He walked past her into the sitting room.

"Solo!" she cried out as he reached the door. "Please, Solo!" She ran after him. "You mustn't believe the things people have been saying about me."

In the courtyard, Solomon opened the trunk of his car and threw in his bag. Katherine reached for his arm, but he snatched it away and went to open the front gate. He got in his Jaguar and reversed into the street.

Weeping, Katherine called her mother.

"Wait for me," Nana said. "I'll be there as soon as possible."

Katherine hung up and sat shivering with shock until Nana arrived.

"He'll come back," Nana said, wrapping her arms around her daughter and rocking her. "This is just some temporary thing. He'll come to his senses soon. I'm sure of it."

"But it must be his mother who is feeding him all this stuff about witchcraft," Katherine said. "And you know how much he hangs on her every word. She'll continue to prejudice his mind against me—I know it."

"Everything will be okay," Nana soothed. "It will all turn out right."

THAT WEEK, RANSFORD received a call from his sister Gifty, Christine Dawson's mother. She was distressed about the ominous developments between Katherine and Solomon and his family. The marriage was in danger of unraveling like a flimsy ball of twine.

"We can't allow this catastrophe to progress," Gifty said. "We have to do something and do it fast, or the wounds will deepen."

After talking to his sister, Ransford was deep in thought when Nana came into the room.

"Who was that?" she asked.

"Gifty," Ransford said. "She's worried about Katherine and Solo. She wants us to take action."

"But what, exactly?" Nana sat down beside him.

"I've been thinking about it," Ransford said. "What about setting up a meeting between our two families?"

"It's a good thought," Nana said, "but I'm afraid any discussion will deteriorate into bickering. You know Ghanaians."

"You're right," he agreed, "but a good mediator between the parties might prevent that situation from developing."

"A lawyer?" Nana asked.

"Good gracious, no. Solomon is a lawyer, so that won't go down well at all. I was thinking more of a minister."

"Yes," Nana said, snapping her fingers. "What about Bishop Howard-Mills? He married Kate and Solomon, after all."

"He's well respected," Ransford agreed, "and everyone will be on his or her best behavior. But do you think the bishop can do it? He's always busy."

"I'll ask him," Nana said. "If he's not going out of town, I know he will be willing to step in. He's always cared a lot about Katherine. If he agrees, we can coordinate the meeting with John—assuming of course, that Maude acquiesces to it. She can be difficult."

WORKING IN THE antechamber of Clem Howard-Mills's office, John acted as the bishop's gatekeeper, fielding calls, greeting guests, setting up appointments, and organizing events.

He hugged Nana when she came in. "Please have a seat, Madam Nana," he said. "Bishop should be done in a few minutes."

While she waited to see Howard-Mills, Nana made pleasant conversation with John as he went about his work. She could hear the bishop chatting on the phone from behind the closed door of his office. He emerged about ten minutes later in his custom-made outfit of a thigh-length embroidered tunic with matching trousers.

"My dear Madam Nana," he said, holding his arms apart. "How have you been?" He embraced her. "It's such a long time since the wedding. Look at how marvelous you look. How is it you never age, eh? What is your secret?"

Nana laughed, pleased. "Thank you, Bishop. You always know how to make a lady feel good."

He laughed. "Please, come in. Tell me all about yourself and the family."

Howard-Mills showed her in, closing the door behind them. Chilled by the air conditioner, the office could have been in the Arctic Circle. The bishop and Nana sat across from each other in comfortable leather armchairs. He was a tall, handsome man in his early forties, with copper-colored skin as smooth as an infant's. His hair was wavy and neat as if someone had spun it to perfection on a loom. His female congregants must lust after him the way the Chinese want Ghana gold, Nana thought. But Howard-Mills was married—happily, it was reported—with three gorgeous children.

They chitchatted for a while. Nana segued to Katherine's woes. The bishop expressed regret that the blissful marriage had turned into something so hurtful and toxic "Of course," he said. "I would be only too glad to help bring peace between Katherine and Solomon, and between the families."

"Thank you so much, Bishop."

"One other thing I might suggest," Howard-Mills said. "Every Sunday afternoon, I hold private counseling for married couples."

Nana was thrilled. "That's an excellent idea, Bishop. I'll suggest it to Katherine."

"Good," Howard-Mills said. "I know she participates in the *bussell* network with Reverend Atiemo, but she and Solomon are also welcome to my regular services on Tuesday and Thursday evenings."

Nana felt tremendous relief, like a *kayaye* girl getting rid of the punishing load on her head. She left the bishop's office with her heart singing.

THREE WEEKS LATER, after much discussion, the meeting of the Yeboah and Vanderpuye families took place. By that time, Nana's patience with Maude was at breaking point. Whereas Ezekiel had agreed to the get-together as soon as Ransford had called him, Maude kept inventing complicated reasons why the meeting could not take place on this or that day. She also wanted some impossible preconditions in place beforehand.

Finally, on a Thursday evening, Nana, Ransford, Maude, Ezekiel, Katherine, Solomon, and Georgina met with the bishop in his office. John brought in soft drinks and biscuits, which helped relieve some of the tension in the room.

Howard-Mills made it clear he didn't expect them to solve everything in one session, but he got everyone to agree to some basic ground rules.

All name-calling had to stop, including referring to Katherine as a witch.

The in-laws would keep lines of cordial communication open.

Solomon would move back into the house with Kate, and they would try again to conceive. Solomon, who had up till now been unwilling to get his sperm tested, must have it done.

Kate and Solomon would meet with the bishop at least once a week for counseling, discussion, and prayers.

At the end of the meeting, the bishop asked everyone to bow heads. "Let us pray. Our Father . . ."

They joined in the Lord's Prayer.

CHAPTER SEVEN

KATHERINE AND SOLOMON MET with Bishop Howard-Mills several times over the next two months. Solomon was mostly silent and brooding during the sessions. When the bishop tried to engage him, he shrank away like a snail pulling into its shell. Katherine cried several times, expressing her angst over her inability to get pregnant. She blamed herself and repeated how sorry she was. Now that the lab had tested Solomon's semen and found his spermatozoa more than adequate in quality and quantity, it was pretty certain the deficiency, whatever it was, lay with Katherine.

At home, the relationship between the two became more strained by the day. At first, they tried to sleep in the same bed, but they didn't get close to each other, let alone have sex. The night she reached out to touch his arm, he flinched, went rigid, and held his breath like a kid trying to be invisible. Then he rose and went to the sitting room to watch TV for a while. Katherine hoped he would return to bed, but he never did. In the morning, she pretended to be asleep as she heard him dressing. He left without a word.

That week in early April, Solomon didn't show up for the session with the bishop.

"How are you feeling?" Howard-Mills asked Katherine.

She sat still, head down and hands crossed in her lap. "Numb," she said.

"Things are no better at home?"

She shook her head. "Worse."

"Take strength from the Lord."

Katherine began to weep. Howard-Mills scooted his chair over to hers and put his arms around her. She cried into his chest.

"Has God forgotten about me?" she asked, looking up at him.

"No, *no*," Howard-Mills murmured, smoothing her tears away. "Remember Psalm twenty-three? The Lord is your Shepherd, Kate. When Jesus, God's only begotten son, was upon the cross, he cried out, 'My God, my God, why have you forsaken me?' It was Jesus's worst hour. He was in terrible pain, and he was dying. He thought all was lost. But after death, he rose again. And you too shall rise."

"Thank you, Bishop." She moved out of his arms, and he offered her a box of tissues. She wiped her eyes and blew her nose.

"There, you see?" Howard-Mills said with a gentle smile. "Psalm thirty says, 'Weeping may last through the night, but joy comes with the morning.'"

"Amen."

"I've made you a list of Bible passages on which you can meditate and draw strength," the Bishop said, giving her a thick manila envelope. She thanked him and smiled anew, like the sun coming out from behind dark clouds. She felt a thousand times better. The bishop was her rock at the moment, and she could not overexpress how grateful she was to him.

"Now," he said, "let's pray."

She bowed her head, closed her eyes and put her hands together with her fingers interlaced. The bishop prayed that Katherine and Solomon would reunite in Jesus's name, and he asked God to bless the couple with a child.

"WHY DIDN'T YOU join me for counseling with the bishop today?" Katherine asked Solomon. On the sofa with his feet up on the center table, he was clicking through TV channels, which irritated Katherine more than the repetitive plop of a leaking tap.

He didn't answer for a few moments. "Because he's taking your side, that's why."

"What do you mean, 'my side?' This isn't a boxing match."

"The counseling is not helping us," he said. "The only reason you go is that you like him."

"Oh, please," Katherine said, sucking her teeth. "That's ridiculous."

"Okay, say it's ridiculous and keep on going to him. You'll see."

She raised her eyebrows. "Are you threatening me?"

"I'm not threatening anyone," he replied with a grim smile. "I'm just letting you know."

The following day, Solomon didn't come home from work. Katherine called and texted him multiple times, but he never responded. Finally, she called Maude.

"Is Solo with you?" Katherine asked her.

"Yes, he is," Maude replied. "What do you want?"

"Please, may I speak to Solo?"

"He's busy right now."

"Why won't he speak to me?"

"I'll give him the message you called," Maude said. "He'll return the call if he sees fit."

"It's you who's scaring him, isn't it, Maude? Brainwashing him against me?"

"That's your imagination," she replied. "Sorry, I have to go now."

It was after midnight, and Katherine was unable to sleep. She lay staring at the ceiling in the dark; then she rolled from side to side, trying to find a position of comfort. Her phone rang, and she snatched it from the side table. The screen showed an unknown number, and Katherine's first thought was Solomon could be calling her with a different sim card.

"Hello?" she said.

Silence, except for the sound of someone breathing.

"Solo, is that you?"

Silence.

"Please, talk to me, Solo," she said. "I know what we've been going through has been tough, but we can get through it together."

"Witch!" a voice said.

Katherine stiffened. "Who is this? Hello? Who is this?"

The caller hung up. Katherine called back immediately, but no one answered. A chill ran through her. Who could it have been? It had been a harsh whisper, like the rustle of parched brush in the dry season, and Katherine could not tell whether the voice had been male or female.

IN THE NEXT few days, she didn't hear from Solomon. At first, she called and texted him multiple times, but like a candle dying out, her energy waned, and she made fewer and fewer attempts to reach him. Nana, Christine, and Aunty Gifty called Katherine almost every day, sometimes conversing for an hour or more.

Vowing that this would be the last time, Katherine tried to text Solomon again one evening. She was no longer in begging mode. She had begun to get angry. Standing at the kitchen counter, she wrote, "Don't I deserve at least an explanation for your silence?" Then, less confrontational and more persuasive, "I've kept your clothes and everything just the way you left them."

Her heart surged as she saw Solomon was typing a message. Dear Lord, let it be that he wants to come back home.

But no. "All my things can wait until you've left," he wrote. "Please pack up all your belongings and vacate the house by next Sunday."

With a gasp of disbelief, Katherine sat down on the barstool in front of the wine cabinet. "I'm calling you right now," she texted. "Please pick up."

He did. "Hello."

"Solo, what are you talking about, I should leave the house?"

A long silence before he spoke again. "You're barren. You're a bad omen for my family and me—a curse. You are saturating the house with evil, and so you have to go."

"You can't make me do that," Katherine said. "The house belongs to both of us."

"No, it doesn't," he responded. "Not anymore. Your name is no longer on the house deed."

"What? I signed the loan documents with you, remember?"

"The names have been changed."

"Changed," she repeated. "What do you mean?""

"The only two signatories now are my mother and me."

Katherine was perplexed. "But who changed it?"

"I had it changed," he said.

Katherine's reaction was turning from alarm to anger. "How can you do that? That's not even lawful."

"It's legal," Solomon said. "And it's been done."

"I need to see proof," Katherine challenged.

"I'll take a photo of the signature pages and text it to you."

"Why are you doing this?" Katherine cried, her voice shaking. "It's your mother feeding you nonsense about me being a curse and a witch, isn't it?"

"Keep her out of this."

"How can I, when she's already so involved?"

"I have to go," he said.

"Wait!"

But he had ended the call. Katherine almost dashed her phone to the floor in fury. She stood up and emitted an anguished, guttural scream.

IN THE MORNING she called Nana from work to relate what Solomon had said to her.

"This is insanity," Nana said.

"I'm not moving from this house," Katherine said. "He can't kick me out."

"Kate," Nana said, her voice reflecting anxiety, "I don't think that's a good idea."

"Why?"

"I'm not saying Solomon is a violent man, but it's not safe to be in that house all by yourself. Stay with me for the time being, and meanwhile get a lawyer."

"I don't want a legal battle with Solomon, Mama."

"How can you avoid it? Solomon is a lawyer himself."

Katherine felt she was losing control and her mother was driving the agenda. "Mama, I have to go," she said. "I have a meeting."

BUT NANA DIDN'T let it go at that. She called Katherine back soon after lunch. "I don't want to be a pest, sweetie," she said, "but you have to get a lawyer to protect your rights, and I know just the one."

"Who?"

"James Bentsi-Enchill."

"Mama! James is an old flame. To go to him would be a flagrant conflict of interest."

"You're adults now," Nana said. "The two of you were an item, but that was a long time ago, and both of you realize that."

It was the last sentence that alerted Katherine. "Mama, have you already called James?"

Nana cleared her throat. "I might have."

Katherine was angry. "In other words, you have. Why did you do that?"

"Kate, I only want the best for you, and James is a superb lawyer. He told me he'd be able to take the case and discount his regular fee for us. Come on, Kate. Do this for yourself. You've suffered enough."

Katherine felt frustrated and trapped. Whereas she wanted to avoid the conflict of interest, James was indeed a good lawyer, and he would understand the case because he knew the players well. "All right," Katherine said. "I'll call him."

"Em, will you be able leave work by five?" Nana asked.

"Yes, why?"

"Well, James said he'd be available by six."

"I should have known," Katherine said with resignation. "You made me an appointment as well."

"While I had him on the phone, I thought I might as well. So you can go this evening?"

"Yes, *yes*," Katherine said irritably, and then in a more accommodating tone, "I will, thanks."

CHAPTER EIGHT

JAMES HAD CHANGED QUITE a bit from the good old days of senior high school. He had a belly now, and his salt-and-pepper hairline was receding like a depleted forest. If you looked beyond those deficits, however, you could discern the ghost of the handsomeness.

"Kate!" he exclaimed as she came through the door of his office. "Great to see you!" He came to her with arms open wide, and they embraced.

"And you as well," she said, smiling.

"You look as lovely as ever, I must say."

"Well, thank you."

"Listen, I want us to talk, but I'm so famished I'd like to do it over dinner. What do you think?"

"Oh, why not?" Katherine said. She was quite hungry herself.

"Excellent. I had Il Cavaliere at the Polo Club in mind. Have you ever been there?"

"No, I haven't."

"Then it will be my treat."

KATHERINE HAD FORGOTTEN how funny and entertaining James could be, and although they had talked about the case while dining, they had discussed other matters—everything except the James-Katherine-Solomon love triangle. At the end of the evening, Katherine felt confident James had grasped the facts. "No, of course not!" he had said. "Solomon cannot erase your name from the house deed without your permission and without going through the appropriate legal channels."

When Katherine told the bishop about engaging James's services, she didn't mention he had taken her to a sumptuous dinner at Il Cavaliere. The bishop seemed concerned. "I don't want to pry," he said, "but I hope there'll be no issues dealing with James? Given your past with him, I mean."

"Yes, I understand," Katherine said, feeling uncomfortable. "But he is okay, Bishop. We will be professional with each other."

"All right," he said. He gazed at Katherine and then smiled. "Please, call me Clem. We've known each other long enough, don't you think?"

"Thank you. That will feel a little strange, but I suppose I could get used to it. But only when we're together alone. Not out in public."

"Yes, of course," he agreed, looking at her with an inviting, engulfing softness. "Like now."

She felt her heart skip a couple of beats and warmth rising from her neck into her face. "I must get going," she said. "Thank you for seeing me, Bishop, uh, Clem."

"You're very welcome."

KATHERINE CAME OUT of the Bishop's office to find John writing in a notebook. She went a little closer. "You write poetry?"

"A little bit," he said with a bashful smile.

"I had no idea," Katherine said. "May I take a look?"

Standing next to John, Katherine read some of the pieces. She thought he wrote very well and she was attracted in particular to one of the poems called "Hibiscus Fever." Katherine recited it. "That's beautiful," she said.

"Really? You like it?" John was pleased. "Thank you."

"It's refreshing to see poetry from our young folk," Katherine said. "Rather than the usual rap music."

"It's true," John agreed. "Can I text the poem to you?"

"But of course," she said. "That's very kind."

Katherine thought back to what Solomon had once told her about John. *He thinks the world of you*. Perhaps Solomon had been right.

John hesitated as he looked up at her. "Madam—"

"It's okay to call me Kate."

"Thank you, Kate." John cleared his throat. "I know you've been having some troubles of late, you know, with Solomon and so on. Maybe it's not my place to say anything to you about it, but I wanted to tell you I'm sorry this has happened to you. You don't deserve it, and you have all my support."

Kate was touched. "Thank you." She squeezed his hand. "What you've said means a lot to me."

WHEN KATHERINE GOT home, she stood in the middle of the bedroom and looked around with a feeling of heaviness and fear. What legal wrestling match was about to take place between Solomon and her? What was her future? Would she *ever* become pregnant? How, why, had this catastrophe befallen her? She thought of Jesus crying out in despair to his Father.

CHAPTER NINE

AT 11 P.M. ON her last Friday night at home, Katherine reassured Christine and Nana she could finish packing up on her own. In the morning, Christine would return with a truck to load up the boxes, and Katherine would finally leave the home she had shared with Solomon.

For a while, she gazed at the wedding picture in which she reached up to Solomon and gave him a delicate kiss on the cheek as he gave her a mischievous, sidelong glance. In the past, she might have shed tears, but photographs representing the love between Solomon and her now provoked a mixture of bitterness and sadness.

She felt the same conflict over this home, where she had once anchored her dreams of a happy marriage and a loving family. A part of Katherine didn't want to leave, but now, every corner and every object in the house reminded her of some aspect of marital rancor. So, yes, in the end she had come to agree with her mother that departing was the only option.

She went to Solomon's side of the closet to touch his crisp, starched business shirts and his suits. Leaving them behind seemed strange because his clothes had become part of her. Most of the time it had been Katherine who had taken his dress shirts and pants to the cleaners. She had shopped for clothes for him as well. Katherine slid the closet door shut with a sudden stab of anger and turned away.

She wanted to go to bed, but first, she had to wash the day's dirt and sweat away. In the middle of her shower, the electricity went off. Accra's power cuts were tiresome. Practically every neighborhood was on an unendurable 12-hour on, 24-hour off schedule that everyone called "*dumsor, dumsor*," meaning, "off-on, off-on."

Because an external electric pump maintained water pressure, the shower slowed to a trickle. Katherine waited for Gabriel to start up the generator outside. As it roared into action, the lights flickered on, the air conditioners hummed again, and the shower restored itself. Katherine rinsed and toweled off.

IN BED, HER mind flitted from thought to troubled thought. She felt herself drifting off to sleep, and she stayed suspended somewhere between drowsiness and slumber. In a dream, someone was knocking on the window. She woke with a start and propped herself up on one elbow to see who was there. No one.

Katherine listened. The knocking was from the front door, so it must have been Gabriel. What did he want this time of night?

She slid her feet into her house slippers and padded to the front. "What is it, Gabriel?" she said through the door.

But it was someone else who responded. Katherine raised her eyebrows in surprise. So he's come after all, she thought. He hadn't taken no for an answer. She felt an intangible thrill of both excitement and apprehension.

Katherine hesitated, torn. "Okay," she said with uncertainty. "Okay, come in." And she unlocked the door.

PART TWO

CHAPTER TEN

AT 6:05 ON THE Saturday of the big move, Christine Dawson left Darko and their two sons at home and set out to Katherine's house in a borrowed Toyota pickup truck. Christine's heart was heavy with regret that Kate's marriage to Solomon had turned so disastrous. As cousins, Christine and Kate were close and always had been. Before the wedding, Christine had approved of Solomon. At one point when Kate was having doubts, Christine had encouraged Kate to stay the course, but now, all had changed. Christine was firmly on her cousin's side against Solomon.

Whereas Christine was involved with the Kate saga, Darko had distanced himself from it. Christine knew he had challenges of his own with his father, Jacob, who was becoming more demented by the day, but she wished her husband would lend more moral support to her than he did. Sometimes, his detachment seemed callous.

Christine turned off Nkrumah Highway and drove toward Dzorwulu, an upper middle-class and burgeoning part of town, a product of Accra's exuberant urban sprawl. Houses sprouted like mushrooms, but it didn't mean paved roads came with them. New Town Road, a major street with auto repair shops, billboards, and mobile phone outlets, was broad and surfaced, but Katherine's street, Tetteh Owusu Road, was bumpy and unpaved. The dirt vehicles kicked up throughout Accra made it the dusty city it was.

Christine passed a stone-colored, a beige, and an orange

house—all generous in size with satellite dishes mounted like giant ears—before Katherine's sunset-yellow house came into view.

Christine frowned in puzzlement as she saw a group of about fifteen people hanging around Kate's front gate. For a brief, silly moment Christine thought the neighborhood had turned out to wish Kate goodbye. Dismissing that thought, Christine pulled over on the opposite side of the street in front of an unfinished home.

She approached the cluster of people, recognizing one—Kate's next-door neighbor, Yaa. She was a tall woman with a long, graceful neck and a colorful head wrap.

"Morning, Yaa," Christine said. "What's going on?"

"Good morning." Yaa looked shocked. "Oh, Christine! Gabriel, Kate's watchman, is dead!"

Christine gasped. "*What?*"

"Esi, the house girl, came in for work around five this morning and found him dead on the ground in the courtyard. His head was almost cut off."

"*Ao!*" Christine cried out, staggering back. "When we left him last night, he was safe and sound. Have you talked to Kate about it yet? Have you seen her?"

"*No!*" Yaa said, looking apprehensive. "I didn't see her come outside. Maybe she's not even home? People were crowding around to stare at the dead body. And then the police arrived and went inside the house. They locked the gate, and they won't let anyone in or tell us anything except they're investigating the murder."

Christine dialed Katherine's number at once. When it went to voicemail, Christine tried texting. Still no response. Her thoughts were crashing and spinning like a body thrown down a ravine. Where was Kate? Was she inside with the police? Were they suspecting her of Gabriel's murder? Was she home? If Kate was home, was she okay? Christine felt dizzy and sick.

"Oh, God," Yaa whispered, her hand over her mouth. "This is a terrible, terrible day."

Christine pushed her way through the group, which had started to grow into a crowd, and reached the tall, solid dark-blue cast-iron gate topped with razor wire. She banged on the door with her fist.

"Hello! *Hello!*" She looked through the small gap between the gate and its post. She could just see Kate's white Kia under the carport. She must be home, surely. "Open the gate, please!" she called out.

She saw a policeman in dark blue approaching, and she stepped back a little as he undid the bolt lock and opened the gate partway. He was a young guy with a broad, flat face—probably Ashanti, Christine guessed—and he was angry. "*Heh!*" he yelled. "Who is shouting like that? Is it you?" He glared at Christine.

"Yes, officer—"

"Why are you disturbing, eh?" he demanded. "Like, I will arrest you just now if you don't take care! Can't you see we are busy?"

"But do you know who I am?" Christine snapped.

"Who are you?" the officer challenged.

"I'm Christine Dawson, cousin of the woman who lives here, Katherine Vanderpuye—"

"And so what? In Ghana, everyone is somebody's cousin."

Christine ignored the people who tittered behind her and decided to pull rank. "Do you know Chief Inspector Darko Dawson?" she shot at the officer. "He's my husband. What is your name? I will report you to him. As a matter of fact, let me take a picture of your badge and I'll text the photo to him right now."

She dug into her purse looking for her phone. That got the policeman's attention. "Wait one moment, please. I'm coming." He banged the gate shut.

Christine waited, arms folded, forehead sweating from stress and the already burning sun.

The gate opened again and a different person peeped out. Plain clothed, he was much older than the first man. "Are you the one who said you're Chief Inspector Dawson's wife?" he asked.

"Yes, I am."

"Good morning, madam. I know your husband. I'm Detective Inspector Twum-Barima."

"Morning, sir," Christine said. "Please, I would like to know what is happening. Is my cousin Katherine inside?"

"Madam, I—" He looked at her as if lost for words. Christine's stomach plunged as she saw a deep sadness come over the detective's expression. Something was awfully wrong. "Please, madam, if you can wait for just a few moments, then I can talk to you. I beg you, oh. Is it okay? Please."

Christine pressed her lips together. "All right. But still, I'm going to call Chief Inspector Dawson."

Rather than appearing threatened or insulted, Twum-Barima's face brightened. "Thank you, madam."

Christine stepped to one side. Yaa joined her. "What did he say?"

Christine shook her head. "Nothing. I'm calling my husband." As she did, she noticed a man in green and black standing on the veranda of the unfinished home across the street. He stared at her without moving, his eyes bloodshot as if he hadn't slept or had been smoking *wee*, or both. His hair and full beard were unkempt, like the wild brush on hinterland roadways. Christine shivered and turned away.

CHAPTER ELEVEN

DARKO DAWSON HAD WOKEN up early to prepare a lecture for police academy recruits: *How to Interview a Suspect.* He knew how to conduct an interview. Teaching the skill was another matter. Ever since he had become chief inspector the year before, his superiors had been delegating these types of tasks to him.

From his small desk in the sitting room, he glanced over at his two sons, Hosiah and Sly, on the sofa watching cartoons. At nine years old, Hosiah took after his father, and not only in appearance. The boy was as observant of people and their behavior as Darko had been at that age. You couldn't get a lie past Hosiah. Like his father also, he appeared to have a form of synesthesia, which was a type of crossing of the senses.

Sly, eleven, was adopted—an uncommon practice in Ghana—and had been in the Darko family for three years. A lanky prankster, he had the gregariousness that Hosiah lacked somewhat. Darko loved them both to his bone marrow, as he did his wife.

The two let out a loud groan of protest as the power went off, ending their TV entertainment for the morning. In an exaggerated gesture, Hosiah threw himself on the floor and writhed in angst. Unfortunately, the Dawsons didn't have a generator, and electricity wasn't scheduled to return until around six that evening.

The blackouts were a well-established part of life in Ghana, with the duration of the outages appearing to lengthen every week. The exceptions to that were the upscale neighborhoods of Labone, Cantonments, Airport Residential, and the like. They rarely experienced the blackouts because, as an official once said, "they are the customers who pay for their electricity." It was true that in poor areas, theft of electricity from the main cables was common.

"In any case, that's enough TV for today," Darko said, getting up from the laptop. "It's time for breakfast, and then you have football practice."

His sons beat him to the kitchen, which, after all, was no more than a few meters away in this small house the family was outgrowing. Both of the boys were shooting up in height and eating staggering amounts of food.

No doubt, the Dawsons could have done with more spacious accommodations, but the price of housing in Accra was prohibitive. For the time being, they had a relatively stable rent from Christine's Uncle Ransford, who loved his niece and had taken family ties into consideration.

Christine's father was dead, but he had had several brothers. The only one with whom Darko had any familiarity was Uncle Ransford. His daughter, Katherine, was Christine's favorite cousin, and Darko liked her too. Through Christine, Darko knew about Katherine's infertility and her marriage problems, but he had stayed clear of getting involved. In Ghana, the family was all-important, but it could turn ugly and brutal as well.

"Mama left porridge," Sly said, lifting the lid off the pot on the stove. He and Hosiah served themselves generous helpings. As usual, Sly ate quickly while Hosiah chatted nonstop and dawdled over the meal.

"Eat up," Darko prodded him. "You're going to be late."

"Daddy, are you going to Grandpa's house today?" Sly asked.

"Yes. After football, you go straight to Grandma's house, understood?"

They chorused their "yes." Grandma Gifty was Christine's mother.

"Please, may I be excused?" Sly asked.

Darko nodded. "Yes, you may. Get your backpack for practice."

"I'm going to do that now," Sly said, putting his plate in the sink.

"Hosiah—" Darko began.

"Yes, Daddy," the boy said, "I'm hurrying. But Mama always says I should eat slowly."

"Right," Darko said, getting up to the sink, "but not when you're late."

"Oh," Hosiah said. Seconds later. "There. Finished!"

CHAPTER TWELVE

DARKO GUIDED HIS FATHER into the bathroom, positioning him in front of the toilet. Jacob began to sit down.

"Wait, Daddy," Darko snapped, and then regretted sounding so impatient. "We have to take your shorts down first. Otherwise, we'll have a mess on our hands. Mostly on mine."

"Okay, okay," the old man said. He was losing weight, refusing to eat much of anything.

Once Jacob's shorts were down, Darko straightened up. "Grab hold of my arms."

"Don't let me fall," Jacob said, voice quavering.

"I'm not going to."

His father began to cry out in fear of falling as Darko helped him lower onto the toilet seat. Darko shook his head and blew his breath out. Every morning the same old *wahala*.

With Jacob secure, Darko stood next to him, his hand resting lightly on his father's shoulder, should he begin to topple over.

"What am I doing here?" Jacob asked, looking up at his son.

"You know what you're here for, Daddy," Darko said with a slight smile. "Don't pretend you don't."

Jacob grinned—most of his teeth were gone—and then cackled like a guinea hen. Darko laughed with him, but his father trailed off. "What am I doing here?" he asked with childlike panic.

"You have to go poo-poo," Darko said.

"I can't," Jacob protested.

"Yes, you can. You go every morning. Now do it."

Darko tried to banish his emotions, but he felt a mixture of revulsion and deep regret as he waited for his father to finish defecating. The disgust rendered Darko guilty, and the pity he felt for Jacob wasn't the right kind either. This man, who now could not shit on his own, once regularly beat Darko and his older brother, Cairo, when they were kids—especially Darko, the less athletic and gregarious of the two siblings. For the smallest mistake or a minor disobedience—a sound beating. And now look at him, Darko thought. A quivering, frightened man with brains like *fufu*.

While Jacob had been mentally competent, he had managed quite well living alone in this house, but as he slid into dementia, it became clear to Darko and Cairo that their father needed help. At first, it had been a little bit of assistance, but one day when Darko looked in on Jacob, he had found him disoriented, dressed only in soiled underpants and peeing on the bedroom floor. The truth and urgency of Jacob's condition stunned Darko.

"He has to live with us, then," Cairo had said, as soon as he heard the story. "He can't manage on his own."

Darko had taken a deep breath. "If we remove him from the environment he knows, he'll just . . ." He shrugged, shaking his head. "I think he'll go crazy."

Cairo wrinkled his forehead. "Do we have a choice?"

Cairo had been a quadriplegic since the age of twelve and at one point had become overweight from spending so many hours in his wheelchair. But he had managed to trim down and develop tremendous upper body strength from training regularly in the backyard. He chewed on his cheek, reflecting. "We've done this all wrong, haven't we? We should have tried to get him to move in with one of us before now. Then he would have become accustomed to the new surroundings."

"I doubt he would have moved," Darko said. "He's too stubborn."

Faced with a growing crisis, the Dawson brothers had patched together a plan. Franklin, a nephew who had arrived in Accra from Takoradi looking for employment after the oil boom crashed, agreed to help take care of Jacob. For a decent pay, Franklin would stay with Jacob during the week and take some time off during the weekends, when Cairo and Darko would manage somehow. Meanwhile, Cairo was getting an extension built onto the side of his house to create a bedroom for his father.

Franklin had left about thirty minutes ago to enjoy his Saturday off. Jacob announced he had finished his business, and Darko steeled himself to the task of wiping his father off and taking him to the bath cubicle to help him shower. Darko had a sense of great accomplishment once he had dressed Jacob in fresh clothes, combed his hair and clipped his fingernails. It was time for his walk around the backyard. Jacob held onto his son's arm and shuffled along, trying to keep up the pace. As they completed the second lap, Darko's phone rang. It was Christine.

"What's up, love?" he answered.

She was breathing as if she had run a mile. "Why haven't you been answering your phone?" she cried.

"Oh! I'm sorry—I didn't hear it. I was helping Daddy. What's wrong?"

"Gabriel—Katherine's watchman—is dead."

"The old guy who's worked for her family for ages? What happened?"

"Murdered." Her voice quivered like a rubber band. "They say his head was nearly chopped off."

"Jesus," Darko said before he could check himself. Christine didn't like him using the Lord's name in vain. "That's a terrible shame. Was he at his home?"

"No, at Katherine's, while he was on watch. The house girl came to work this morning about five and found the body in the courtyard. I'm at the house right now. But I don't know where Katherine is, Dark." Her voice shook.

Darko frowned. "Come again?"

"The police are inside the house; they won't say if Katherine is there, but her car is in the usual spot; she's not responding to my calls or texts."

Christine was hyperventilating. "Dark, I'm scared. I don't know what to do."

"Okay, listen," he said, "I need you to calm your breathing, okay? I'll get there as soon as I can."

Darko speed-dialed Cairo.

CHAPTER THIRTEEN

DARKO GOT ON HIS motorcycle and tore off as soon as he had reached Cairo, who said he would take over Jacob's care.

Darko rode a motorcycle instead of driving a car to get where he was going fast. Not bothering with the busy Nsawam Road until its terminal portion, Darko took back and side streets, some too narrow to accommodate two cars alongside each other. From the N1 Highway, it was a straight shot to Dzorwulu. Darko made quick work of it.

Twenty or so onlookers stood around outside Katherine's front gate as if waiting for a store to open. Christine ran up as Darko parked his bike against the wall. Her eyes were puffy.

"Any news?" Darko asked.

"No." Her face looked like it might crumble, and when he put his arm around her shoulders, it did.

"Okay, okay," he soothed her. "I'm here now."

She nodded resolutely and collected herself. "I'm good."

"Wait for me a moment while I find out what's going on, okay?"

Skirting the audience, Darko strode up to Katherine's gate, rapped on it, and waited a few moments until a voice from the other side called out, "Who is there?"

"Chief Inspector Dawson."

The gate opened, and a uniformed policeman appeared. "Good morning, sir."

"Morning."

The policeman, whose ID badge said MENSAH, was a constable. He stepped aside to allow Darko through.

"My wife called me," Darko said. "She's the cousin of the woman who lives here."

"Yes, sir," Mensah said, appearing nervous. "Please, let me get my boss, Inspector Twum-Barima, to report."

Mensah hurried into the house as Dawson looked around. The concrete courtyard was spacious. As Christine had mentioned, Kate's white Kia was under the carport left of the house, which had a front porch with a small table and two chairs. A squat yellow generator sat in the corner of the yard on Darko's left, and on his right, next to a small sentry kiosk, a soiled gray tarp lay on top of a human shape, dried blood surrounding it like a crimson halo.

Careful where he planted his feet, Darko lifted the cloth and tensed as he saw what was underneath. Gabriel lay crumpled in a lifeless heap. He had deep gashes to his arms and torso, and the cut in his neck was so deep that Gabriel's head seemed to be hanging onto his body by a mere thread. Who would do that to this poor little man? Darko thought, shaking his head. He turned at footsteps behind him. Detective Inspector Twum-Barima was about forty, slight in physique, and wore a red-and-blue checkered shirt with khaki pants. He was grim and soaked with sweat.

"Glad to see you, sir," Twum-Barima said, as they shook hands. "I know all about you."

"Thank you."

"You have seen the first murder of two," Twum-Barima said. "The second one is inside."

"Who is it?" Darko asked, afraid of the answer while knowing what it would be.

"Katherine Vanderpuye."

Darko winced as if a steel-tipped spear had jabbed his side.

"I apologize, sir," Twum-Barima said. "I know your wife wanted to go in. But I just couldn't let her see. It's terrible, sir."

Darko swallowed. "As terrible as that?" He gestured toward Gabriel.

"Worse," Twum-Barima replied. A small muscle in his cheek twitched.

Darko felt cold. His usually reasonable detective mind was tumbling down a chasm of confusion and dread. Katherine, the woman Christine loved like a sister, was dead.

"To me, it looks like the murderer eliminated the watchman to get access to Mrs. Vanderpuye," Twum-Barima said. "What he did to her is . . . Well, you'll see for yourself."

"I understand the house girl was the first witness to come across the body?" Darko said.

"That we know of, yes, sir. Esi was in as usual at five this morning."

"Did she also go inside the house?"

Twum-Barima shook his head. "Didn't get that far."

"Where is Esi now?" Darko asked.

"At the station. We had to get her away from here before she went into a state of total collapse. She and Gabriel were good friends. In fact, everyone in the neighborhood loved Gabriel."

Darko nodded. "That's what my wife always said about him."

"Shall we go inside, sir?" Twum-Barima asked.

Darko steeled himself, which he often did before entering a crime scene, but this occasion was different. He was steadying his emotions as much as his intellect.

Constable Mensah was standing guard at the front door, which was ajar.

"No forced entry that we can see," Twum-Barima said.

"And none at the front gate, either?" Darko asked.

"Correct," the inspector said. "It seems likely that Gabriel and Mrs. Vanderpuye knew the killer, and they didn't see him as a threat."

Darko reserved comment. He didn't know enough yet.

Before they stepped into the sitting room, the inspector paused and pointed down. "Careful here, sir. Blood."

A trail of crimson began at the doorstep with satellite blotches that widened to a large pool of semi-dried blood. Taking care not to step in any of it, Darko paused, hands on his knees, to study the blood streaks. From the large puddle, they traveled in an untidy smear across the floor toward the hallway. He must have dragged her, Darko thought. And she was bleeding all the way.

Darko saw a purple house slipper lying sole-side up next to the blood trail; the other half of the pair was to the right of the doorway at the opposite end of the room.

The hallway was semi-dark. Twum-Barima illuminated the path of dark red streaks and splotches with his phone light.

"We have to come this way," the inspector said, pressing his back against the wall and walking sideways to avoid stepping in blood.

"The bedroom, sir," the inspector said, stopping in its doorway.

Darko gasped and took a step back. He was looking at an abattoir. Blood soiled the floor, walls, and the window. The air smelled of blood and raw meat.

The bed hugged the far wall of the room.

Darko was searching for Kate. "Where is . . ." He saw it at the same instant that Twum-Barima pointed: a foot sticking up between the mattress and the wall.

"She is behind the bed," the inspector said. "You can come this way where there is less blood."

He took the lead, staying more or less against the wall closest to them and approaching the head of the bed in a half circle. The bedside table and its lamp were overturned, suggestive of a violent struggle. The covers on the bed were tangled, disheveled, and blood-soaked.

Darko was close enough to view all of Kate's body now. Her back was to the wall, and Darko had a vivid impression of her murderer stuffing her headfirst down the side of the bed. A broad smear of blood, trailing down the wall like a river delta, seemed to confirm that.

Darko stared in disbelief. "Oh, God," he whispered.

She had long, thick, brutal gouges in her legs, thighs, torso, and neck. Her head was turned upward and nearly detached by a profound wound from ear to ear, like a jagged grin. Darko recognized Kate all right, but at the same time, she didn't seem real. Her skin had taken on an awful gray hue. Parts of the nightdress she had been wearing adhered to her body with dried blood. Her left arm extended slightly upward. Possibly a defense posture, Darko thought, and disliked the inner detective that had crept out of some cranny of his mind.

"Terrible," Twum-Barima whispered. "See here, sir."

Darko bent down to look where the inspector was aiming his phone light underneath the bed. Now he could see the side-down portion of Kate's body. Her right arm appeared to be broken at the elbow as if it had snapped under the pressure as the murderer shoved her down. Any blood left in her by the time she had been dragged to the bedroom had pooled on the floor, flowing along the wall away from the head of the bed.

The murderer had stabbed or cut Kate once, perhaps twice, at the front door with a knife or machete, Darko speculated. Then he had dragged her in here and begun to chop her up. As Darko looked around the room, he saw spots of blood high up on the wall and even on the ceiling. He could see the murderer bringing up the machete in preparation for another cruel blow and the blood on the blade being cast off to hit horizontal and vertical surfaces.

Why such brutality?

In one corner of the room, a fine blood spray had sprinkled six stacked boxes waiting for the house move Kate had been about to make. Darko's eyes welled, which had never happened to him at a crime scene. He started as he heard Mensah's voice from outside shouting, "Madam, stop! Please, madam, you can't go in!"

Holding his palms up toward the bedroom door, Twum-Barima yelled, "No, no, no!"

Darko snapped his head around and saw Christine.

"I have to see, Dark," she begged him. "I can't bear it any longer. I have to see what's happened to my Kate."

He reached her in two bounds. "No, love," he said, putting his arms around her and pulling her away from the door. "Christine, no, you mustn't—"

Her face changed, a new horror overtaking it and wrenching it to one side. "Is that her?" she asked, her voice cracking. She pointed. "Is that her foot, Dark?"

He lifted her up and carried her away, and for the first time in their life together, she fought against him, trying to break from his grasp while screaming, "Is that her foot? Is that her foot? Dark, tell me, please. Is that her foot?"

CHAPTER FOURTEEN

DARKO CAME OUT OF the house with Christine sobbing in his arms. A mortified Mensah followed, apologizing. "Please, sir, I'm sorry. I beg you. She climbed over the wall; I didn't see her until it was too late. I'm sorry."

"Go away!" Darko shouted at him. "Go and be useless somewhere else."

Darko struggled with Christine, trying to get her out of sight, to the shade of a jasmine tree at the side of the house. She was limp with shock and difficult to hold up. He was afraid she was about to faint. Darko gave up trying to keep Christine upright. He collapsed with her in an ungraceful heap.

"Why?" Christine asked, weeping. "*Why?*" Her voice splintered like wood cracking in the Harmattan. Her tears wet Darko's chest through his shirt. He knew she was running Kate's slaughter through her mind like a video, and it was too ghastly to watch. Darko knew Kate *had* suffered, and he didn't try to persuade his wife otherwise. Patronizing her never worked.

Darko shifted his weight and pulled her up into a more comfortable position. He rubbed her back and cradled her head, trying to soothe her. After a while, she became silent except for the intermittent whimper or soft moan.

"Kate loved this tree," Christine murmured, looking up at the jasmine flowers in bloom. "At night, it perfumes the air."

She sat up, hugging her knees to her chest. "I'll be okay," she said shakily.

"You want to go back to the car?" Darko asked her.

Christine nodded, biting her upper lip. She stood up straight, pulled back her shoulders, and lifted her chin.

As they emerged from the gate, some of the curiosity seekers had left, but Yaa from next door was still there. Christine introduced her to Darko, who got a brief account from her about how she had come running out as she heard Esi's screams. Darko took Yaa's phone number just in case.

A blue crime scene unit van pulled up to the gate, which Mensah opened so the van could drive into the courtyard. Three men and a woman carrying a forensic bag got out. The woman was Dr. Phyllis Kwapong, the nation's only trained forensic pathologist. In Ghana, academic and hospital pathologists without specialized forensic training handled both hospital and wrongful deaths. Dr. Kwapong had just been tasked by the president of Ghana to develop the first forensic medicine training program at the Korle Bu Medical School.

Darko's heart leaped, not only because it was the first time he had ever encountered a bona fide forensic pathologist at the scene of a crime, but because this meant the case would be handled correctly almost from the very beginning. Darko and his wife needed that, and justice demanded it.

"Are you okay, love?" Darko asked Christine. "I need to talk to the CSU folks."

"I'll be okay." Darko watched her as she walked away to the car with her head down.

Darko had never seen Dr. Kwapong dressed in weekend casuals: black jeans, a yellow and blue striped top, and black tennis shoes.

"Good morning, Doc," Darko said, approaching with arm extended. "I'm very glad to see you."

"How are you, Chief Inspector?" she said with a broad smile as they shook hands. She was tall for a woman, and her overall confidence reminded Darko of his mother. "You were called to the case?"

"Yes, and no," Darko said, going on to explain what had happened.

Dr. Kwapong's expression changed as Darko related Christine's call, the bloodbath he had come to find, and how Christine had just witnessed the crime scene.

"I'm very sorry for your loss, Chief Inspector. And for Christine to see the body at the scene—I can't even imagine how terrible that was." Kwapong frowned. "How did she get in? Wasn't the crime scene being safeguarded?"

"It wasn't supposed to happen," Darko said, frustrated that Christine had climbed over the wall. She should have waited outside as he had instructed.

"May I express my condolences to her?" Kwapong asked.

"Of course, Doc."

He walked with her to the truck where Christine sat in the driver's seat with her head down. He could tell she was crying. Seeing her like that wounded Darko's heart.

After he had introduced the two women to each other, he stepped away because when Dr. Kwapong took Christine's hands in hers and began to talk to her, Darko grew teary-eyed, and he had to stop such a show of emotion in its tracks.

Mensah, who was shutting the gate again, looked away as Darko approached him.

"It's okay, eh?" Darko told the constable. "These things happen."

"God bless you, sir," Mensah said gratefully. "Forgive me. Thank you, sir."

"From now on, be careful," Darko admonished. "If anyone wants to come in, check with me first."

"Yes, sir. No problem, sir."

Twum-Barima was with Joseph the CSU photographer, who was using a Samsung tablet to take shots of the outside of the door and its jamb, neither of which revealed evidence of forced entry. Amos, the fingerprints man, began work on the door.

Dr. Kwapong didn't want to see the body and bedroom scene immediately because she felt it would prejudice her judgment to work backward from the murder. On the other hand, she wanted to get to the body as quickly as possible to minimize its decomposition. African weather had no mercy on the dead.

Kwapong looked around the room first. "It's a beautiful home," she commented, walking over to the closer purple slipper of the two. It had light bloodstains in addition to faux gems on the straps. Kwapong knelt down and rummaged through her bag for her LED flashlight, which she shone on the blood staining the floor. The first stain was about six inches long and irregularly shaped, with a pattern of radiating streaks that made it look like a bizarre bird with erect feathers.

"It appears this is where and when she began to bleed from the assault." Kwapong moved laterally on her haunches. "Here's a cluster of tiny spots, like a spray . . ." She moved down again. "The bleeding is heavier here—big splotches with a radiating pattern, the way kids draw the sun. You see?"

"Yes," Darko said.

They followed the smear trail as it curved, and there to the right side, just before the beginning of the short hallway, lay the second slipper. Soaked with blood, it told a different story from its counterpart.

"By now, she has profuse bleeding," Kwapong said. She sighed. "Sorry, Kate. Awful."

Darko watched as she moved into the hallway proper.

Kwapong contemplated the congealed blood on the tiles for a moment while shaking her head. "I apologize, Chief Inspector. I am remiss." She went back into the sitting room. "We should have looked for cast-off blood. Drops of blood thrown off the weapon as the assailant raised it in the air to strike her."

Twum-Barima had just joined them as Darko and Kwapong looked upward, searching. Close to the front doorway, Darko spotted multiple oval-shaped drops of blood on the surface of the ceiling. "There," he said, pointing.

"You have good eyes," Kwapong said. "And I've just spotted a few more bloodstains on the wall. See them?"

"I do now," Darko said.

They went closer to the wall and peered at the blood spatter.

Kwapong removed a laser pointer from her bag. "See here? These bloodstains are not as random as they might seem. They form a pattern"

With the pointer, she traced a more or less straight line formed by several spots of blood along the wall. "These were cast off from the weapon after the first strike. Then, a second strike here. This time, the blood travels farther and hits the ceiling, as you can see by the curvilinear pattern of the elongated bloodstains." She indicated them with her pointer and asked Joseph to come over and take some photographs.

"So we have a sharp weapon like a knife or machete inflicting at least two blows on Kate when she was at or close to the doorway," Kwapong said. "My guess is that she sustained those blows to the throat. She collapses, bleeding heavily. He drags her along the floor to the bedroom."

"Why?" Darko wondered aloud. "Why not finish the job here?"

"Sexual component?" Kwapong suggested. "I can't be sure. Just a thought. So, let's review. No sign of forced entry. The perpetrator pushes the door open after she opens it partway; or she voluntarily lets him in, he strikes her twice with the weapon, let's say a machete—probably to the head and or neck. She might have sustained a wound to the forearm as she raised her hand instinctively to defend herself. Are you with me?"

Darko nodded.

"She falls, blood dripping down over her chest and back and into her clothing. She loses one slipper here"—Kwapong paused—"as he picks her up and drags her to the hallway. Just before they get there, she loses the second slipper. Right?"

"Yes."

"And then into the hallway to the bedroom," Kwapong continued, moving to the side and walking sideways in the same manner as her predecessors. When she got to the bedroom, Kwapong stopped as if she had slammed into a wall as she stared at the carnage.

"God help us," she said.

CHAPTER FIFTEEN

BY THE TIME DR. Kwapong and the CSU crew were finishing up, the smell of Kate's hacked flesh lingered as much in Darko's brain as in his nostrils. The house had become, hot, stuffy, and foul.

The chest of drawers in the bedroom was mostly empty. Gloved up, Darko went through it carefully. He found a few items of Solomon's underwear, socks, and T-shirts.

Mid to small-size droplets of blood had splattered the wardrobe mirrors. Darko slid open one door and found Solomon's suits in bold blues, darks, smooth tans, and sophisticated olives. Darko didn't have even one suit as well-made as these. He peeked at a couple of labels. Italian, of course.

Darko went through the pocket of each jacket and pair of pants, but he didn't find anything more significant than business cards. He swept the top of the shelves in the wardrobe. He wasn't sure what he was looking for, but he would be when he saw it.

Darko opened the drawers of the bedside table and found a couple of romance novels, a box of tissues, hand lotion, sunglasses, loose change, and some keys. The bottom drawer was locked. Darko tried the keys lying in the top drawer and found one of them worked for the bottom one. It was empty. Might Katherine have kept something private or valuable in it?

Darko headed to the bathroom and examined the labels on the bottles of Solomon's fragrances stacked on shelves on either side of the basin. The shower cubicle was one of the largest Darko had ever seen, with a wide, chrome-plated showerhead and slate-gray tiling.

Back in the sitting room, Darko found more boxes stacked in a corner for the move. He didn't plan on going through them right then, but he would in the next day or two.

Mensah put his head in the door. "Massa," he said, "please, a man and a woman are outside. They say they are Mr. and Mrs. Yeboah, the parents of the victim."

Darko's stomach plunged. Talking to them about their daughter would be wrenching. "I'm coming," he said to the constable.

Darko followed Mensah, who unlatched the gate and opened it wide enough to admit Uncle Ransford and Aunty Nana. She had been crying and was wiping her puffy eyes and nose with a wet, disintegrating tissue. Her outfit wasn't black, but it was dark. In Ghana, mourning begins promptly.

Ransford, a big man with a heavy midsection, looked at Darko with dread, his spectacles tilted on his face. "Is it true, Dawson?" he asked, voice trembling.

"Uncle Ransford," Darko said, "Aunty Nana. I'm very sorry. Kate is dead."

Nana let out a harsh cry and collapsed. Her husband caught her before she hit the ground, holding on to her as she wept. His face crumpled like a ball of paper in a fist, cleared for an instant and crumpled again.

Darko signaled to Mensah to bring Nana a chair from the porch. She continued to sob as she dropped into the seat, and Ransford knelt down to hold her in his arms. Darko stood next to her with his hand resting on her shoulder. He felt useless.

Nana's sobbing gradually subsided, but she continued to have involuntary spasms as she buried her face in her husband's shoulder.

"When can we see her?" Ransford asked Darko after a moment.

"Later—at the morgue," Darko said. "We're still working on the crime scene."

Nana looked up at him. "Did she suffer?"

Constable Mensah appeared at that instant, saving Darko from having to face Nana's question.

"Please, sir," Mensah said, "one Bishop Mills is outside and says he wants to enter."

Darko was about to say no, but before he could, Nana leaped to her feet, startling him. "Bishop!" she cried, her voice cracking with emotion. She ran to the gate, shouting, "Bishop! Praise God!"

She wrestled with the gate's sliding bolt until Constable Mensah came to sort it out for her. Nana burst out and fell into the arms of Bishop Howard-Mills. Darko had never seen him in person—only his likeness on giant billboards advertising upcoming Pentecostal and evangelist events, which drew crowds in the thousands. Howard-Mills was a handsome man, probably in his early forties, tall, and light-skinned with wavy hair. He was also a millionaire with churches throughout Ghana and Nigeria.

With the bishop comforting her, Nana unleashed a new round of sobbing and tears. "God bless you, Bishop," she managed to get out. "How did you hear?"

"Aunty Nana," he said, "someone called to let me know, so I came as soon as I could. I'm heartbroken. I want to express to you and Ransford how sorry I am. So very sorry, Aunty."

After a while, Howard-Mills released her and sent an inquiring look at Darko, who was standing to the side. "Good morning, sir. You are?"

"Chief Inspector Dawson."

"Of course!" he said, shaking Darko's hand with a firm grip and a direct, sincere gaze. "Christine has told me about you. Praise be to God you are here to render your service and expertise. By His grace, you will get to the bottom of this."

"Thank you," Darko said, still wondering who had alerted the bishop. Not Christine, surely? She knew Howard-Mills from attending his services from time to time, but it wouldn't be like her to impose on him. Darko glanced to his left where Christine's truck was parked, but she wasn't there. He texted her, WHERE R U?

Howard-Mills was embracing Ransford now, murmuring words of comfort and encouragement. "God be with you and give you strength," he said.

Darko raised his eyebrows at a man a couple of meters away. He was in his late twenties, about as tall as Howard-Mills but softer and rounder. He came over to Darko. "Good morning, Inspector. I'm John Papafio, the bishop's assistant. Please, are you the one in charge of the investigation?"

"For the moment, yes," Darko said. "Did you know Mrs. Vanderpuye?"

"Yes, sir," John said. "Bishop Howard-Mills and I knew her very well. She was a lovely person, and we cared about her." John looked stricken.

"When was the last time you saw her?"

"On Wednesday evening. Reverend Atiemo and I were at her home for a prayer meeting."

"Who is Reverend Atiemo?" Darko asked.

"He's one of the bishop's junior ministers. He often ran the Bible discussions at Katherine's home. We call them *bussells*. Katherine hosted one every month on Wednesdays."

"I see," Darko said. "How did Mrs. Vanderpuye seem to you on Wednesday? Was she troubled in any way?"

John thought about it for a moment. "You know, she had been experiencing difficulties in her marriage, and of late she had been very sorrowful. But her spirits always came up during the prayer meetings and Bible discussions. She and Mr. Vanderpuye were having counseling sessions with Bishop Howard-Mills."

"Because of their marital problems."

"Yes, please," John said.

"Where you between about eleven P.M. last night and five A.M. this morning?"

"I was with the bishop for the prayer vigil overnight at the

Baden Powell Memorial Hall on High Street, Inspector. I was still there at six this morning, helping with the cleanup."

"Bishop Howard-Mills was also present at that time?" Darko asked.

"No, he left around four. For safety reasons, a driver takes him home after the vigils. We don't want the bishop to fall asleep at the wheel after a long night."

Darko nodded. "Thank you, John. Please, may I have your number in case I need to call you?"

"But of course, Inspector."

"Oh, one other thing," Darko said as he entered John's number into his phone, "was Solomon Vanderpuye at the last *bussell* with his wife?"

John folded his lips between his teeth and shook his head. "Mr. Vanderpuye hasn't been participating in the Bible studies for the past a month or so—not since February or March."

Bishop Howard-Mills had brought Ransford and Nana together with his arms around their shoulders. "My dear family in Christ. A cloud has come over our lives, but by the grace of God, it will pass. 'Yea, though I walk through the valley of the shadow of death, I will fear no evil: for thou *art* with me; thy rod and thy staff they comfort me.' Now, let's pray."

After almost every sentence of Howard-Mills's lengthy prayer, Ransford and Nana murmured their acknowledgment.

Darko turned at the sound of the ambulance arriving. Mensah opened both sides of the gate, and the vehicle backed into the courtyard next to the CSU van. Darko returned to the house to find Dr. Kwapong finishing up. Katherine's body had been removed from between the bed and the wall and covered with a drop cloth. Darko felt relief. He had no desire to see more than he had already.

"Is the ambulance here?" Kwapong asked.

"Yes," Darko replied. "If you're ready, I'll let them know."

"We are. The rest of the work I'll do on postmortem." Sweat poured down Kwapong's brow and soaked the top of her mask.

Darko went back outside to let the ambulance crew know they

were set to go. He spotted Christine again by herself watching from a distance and went over to her. "Where were you?" he asked, taking her hand.

"I went around the corner for some quiet," she said. "I needed a few minutes to myself."

"Did Bishop Howard-Mills talk to you?"

She nodded. "Yes—just before he went to the gate and Aunty Nana came out to meet him. We prayed together."

"Good," Darko said. "Do you feel a little better?"

"A little, yes."

Two ambulance attendants brought out Katherine's covered body on a stretcher. The now substantial crowd of spectators watched the attendants lift her inside the ambulance, and the doors closed behind her. Darko squeezed Christine's hand. She stared at the vehicle as it started up and rumbled away. He scrutinized her for a moment. She seemed numb and tired.

Darko took out his phone to call his brother with the news. Cairo's reaction was shock, followed by anger. "Who would do that to Katherine?" he demanded. "*Why?* You have to get this guy, Darko. Whoever he is, you must catch him."

"Yes," Darko agreed.

"I feel sorry for Christine," Cairo continued. "How terrible this must be for her."

"It is," Darko said. "I need someone to pick her up because she's not fit to drive or be alone. I have to stay here for a while."

"Audrey can come for her," Cairo said. "It's no problem."

"Thank you, big brah." Darko hung up and turned to Christine. "Audrey will come to get you. I'll stay with you while you wait."

Christine didn't seem to have heard him. She was gazing at the house. "I'll never see her again," she murmured.

He put his arms around her shoulders and pulled her close. He sensed she was too spent to weep at the moment, but he knew tears would flow again soon.

"You should go," Christine said. "You have investigating to do."

"It can wait," Darko said.

"No, it can't," she said, lifting his arm off her shoulders and ducking away. "Time is precious when you're hunting down a murderer. Now go."

CHAPTER SIXTEEN

DARKO SENT INSPECTOR TWUM-BARIMA and Constable Mensah out to canvass the neighborhood. "We want to know if anyone saw or heard anything even the slightest bit suspicious," Darko told them. "Call me if you have questions. I'll be here looking through Mrs. Vanderpuye's personal effects."

When the inspector and constable had left, Darko stood in the sitting room contemplating the ten boxes Kate had categorized by content: clothing and purses, jewelry, shoes, DVDs, stationery, toiletries and perfumes, laptop/electrical cables, pots and pans and dishes, vital documents. The few items that had gone unpacked were three mobile phones, a Michael Kors purse, a pair of sunglasses, and the jeans, T-shirt, and tennis shoes she must have been planning to wear for the move.

Darko turned on the phones. They were all password or fingerprint protected, and one was less than ten percent charged. He would let the IT guys at CID handle those. On the other hand, for faster service, Darko could take it to any one of many *Sakawa* boys, the notorious Internet fraudsters who invoked magical powers to fuel their success.

Darko pulled down the laptop box and opened it up. The computer did turn on, but it, too, required a password.

He rummaged through the documents box and found loan and mortgage disclosure papers with Katherine's and Solomon's signatures. Christine had told Darko about how Solomon had arranged for his mother's name to replace Katherine's. Darko was no real estate lawyer, but he couldn't see how that maneuver could be lawful. In Ghana, though, that had little to do with whether it was *possible*.

None of the other packages contained anything of interest to Darko. He called Inspector Twum-Barima, who reported that he and Mensah had drawn a blank in their canvassing. No one had seen or heard anything unusual. That was no surprise. An Accra residential area like Katherine's was typically dead quiet at night except for the odd dog barking.

Darko waited for Twum-Barima to bring a spare padlock from the station to secure Katherine's front gate. The property wasn't ready for release to the family yet.

"Please, sir," the inspector said to Darko, "will you be in charge of the investigation from now on?"

Darko hesitated. "No, I don't think so. It's still under Dzorwulu jurisdiction."

"Very good, sir."

Darko sensed some uncertainty on Twum-Barima's part. "Are you comfortable with that?" he asked the inspector.

"No problem at all."

Darko was experiencing conflict. Typically, he would have allowed the cumbersome CID machinery to determine how a homicide would be assigned, but this time the murder victim was a family member. Should he lobby to be the chief investigator? The answer wasn't that clear-cut for Darko.

LATE THAT AFTERNOON, he sat at the edge of the bed and roused Christine. When she was depressed, she slept too much. When Darko was depressed, he slept too little or not at all.

Christine lifted her head and blinked at him, eyes bleary and puffy. For a moment, she seemed to wonder why she was in bed at this time of day. When she remembered, she wilted and dropped her head back with a soft gasp of anguish.

"Come on," Darko said. He helped Christine sit up and swing her feet to the floor. "Okay?"

She nodded.

"Your mother's here," Darko said. "She wanted to see you, but I asked her to let you sleep a little longer."

Christine stood up, weary even after several hours of sleep. "Okay, I'm coming," she said, her voice thick. "Let me wash my face."

Darko left her and returned to the sitting room where Gifty, Christine's mother, sat on the sofa waiting. Earlier on, Hosiah and Sly had gone to stay with her for a couple of hours after soccer practice, but once Gifty had received the awful news about Kate, she had kept the boys with her longer.

This was another of several occasions in which Gifty being there to take care of the children at short notice had been a welcome solution for Darko and Christine in a pinch. Gifty was eager to participate in the life of the Dawsons and particularly when it came to the children. Sometimes, Darko felt she went too far.

Earlier in Hosiah's young life, he had suffered from a congenital heart defect. Without the permission of either Darko or Christine, Gifty took the boy to a traditional healer. During the encounter, Hosiah slipped and cut his scalp on the edge of the pan into which the healer was trying to force the boy as part of the ritual. In addition to being outraged over his son's injury, Darko was furious with his mother-in-law for what he considered her gross overstepping of boundaries.

Darko would probably never understand why Gifty often tried to control the lives of her grandchildren, but on a psychological level, perhaps her thinking was, "You took my daughter away from me, and so I'll take your children in exchange."

Or maybe Gifty was on a constant quest to disparage her son-in-law. Darko felt she had never liked him much. Her notion of an ideal marriage for Christine had been one to a lawyer or physician, not the policeman Darko was. Every so often, out of sheer meanness, he thought, Gifty would make a snide comment about Darko's profession.

"She'll be out in a minute," Darko told her, as he sat down opposite Gifty and noted how attractive she was in a pink and white outfit. Christine got her good looks from Gifty, but certainly not her personality.

"How is she faring after her rest?" Gifty asked.

"She hasn't said much," Darko said. "I hope she's feeling better, but the shock is still brutal."

Christine emerged from the bedroom. Gifty stood up to embrace her, and they both began to cry. Darko looked away. He had never been comfortable with crying.

Mother and daughter sat down opposite Darko, hugging and rocking each other for several minutes.

"All will be well, my love," Gifty whispered.

Christine sat back, staring at the floor.

"Okay?" Gifty asked, squeezing her daughter's hand.

Christine nodded and looked up. "Where are the boys?"

"Playing with the kids down the road," Darko said. "You need to eat something. I made some *jollof* rice."

She didn't seem to hear him. "Who would do that to Kate?" she said. "How is it possible?"

"I think it was a burglary," Gifty declared. "He got into the house and tried to steal something; Kate caught him, and he attacked her."

"Burglars try to get away as quickly as possible, Mama," Christine murmured. "They don't want to stay long enough to butcher you to death. Isn't that correct, Darko?"

"More or less," he said.

"Are you saying it's personal? Someone Kate knew?"

"Could be," Christine said.

Gifty looked at Darko. "So the official investigation begins on Monday?"

"It began when we were at the crime scene," Darko said.

"Yes, of course," Gifty said, recovering. "I meant when you assemble your team and so on."

Darko frowned. "How do you mean?"

Gifty looked surprised. "You're heading the investigation, aren't you?"

"I was in charge at the crime scene only because I outranked the first officers," he explained, "but the case is still officially with the Dzorwulu police."

"Do you think Dzorwulu police even know how to conduct a murder investigation?" Gifty asked with disdain.

"The detective I met at Kate's house seemed competent," Darko said.

"It's only if they transfer the case to CID Headquarters that Darko will get it," Christine explained to her mother.

Darko cleared his throat. "Even then, it's not a sure thing that they would assign it to me."

"But you will push for it," Gifty said keenly.

"It's really out of my hands."

Gifty's eyes narrowed. "A family member has been murdered, and yet you seem quite unconcerned."

"On the contrary, I'm very concerned," Darko said. "And I'm worried about how impartial I would be investigating the murder of someone in the family."

"How so?" Gifty said.

"For instance," Darko offered, "how awkward would it be if I found out Kate was having an affair."

Gifty raised her eyebrows. "*Was* she?"

"*No!*" Christine said, her voice shaking. "She wasn't that kind of woman! Why would that even enter your mind, Dark? Are you trying to tarnish her?"

"It was just an *example*," Darko protested. "Okay, sorry; it was a poor choice, but you see my point? You're upset that I said that, but these kinds of revelations come to light all the time when you're investigating a murder. Would I be comfortable sharing them with you? Maybe not. And that would get in the way of my asking probing questions."

The two women were silent for a moment. Christine seemed irritated she had just helped Darko prove his argument.

"Well, in any case," Gifty went on, "ask anyone who was in close contact with her—Reverend Atiemo, the bishop, anyone—and I'm certain they will vouch for Kate's integrity."

"Exactly how much contact did she have with Bishop Howard-Mills?" Darko asked. "His assistant told me about the *bussell* meetings at Kate's house. Did the bishop attend those?"

Christine shook her head. "He assigned the junior ministers to them, but rarely went to them himself. Kate's close connection with Bishop Howard-Mills—I mean beyond ordinary churchgoing—began around late January this year after Aunty Nana went to him to appeal for his help. By that time, things were getting out of control."

"Meaning what?" Darko asked.

"By then, Solomon was leaving Kate alone for days at a time to stay with his parents," Christine expounded. "Maude and Georgina even went to see Kate while Solomon was away and said awful things to her face. They accused her of being a witch! And then someone started calling Kate anonymously to say the same thing.

"So after Aunty Nana consulted the bishop, he held a meeting between the two families and started seeing Kate and Solomon together for counseling. After some time, though, Solomon stopped going, which left Kate to go by herself."

"I see," Darko said, forming a clearer picture of events.

"Kate took comfort and strength from the bishop," Gifty said. "Don't you agree, Chrissy?"

She nodded. "He's a caring man, and I must say I was glad to see him this morning."

Darko sat up. "I've been wondering who called him to inform him Katherine was dead."

"It certainly wasn't me," Christine said. "What are you thinking?"

"Could be important." Darko shrugged. "But maybe not." He stood up. "I'm going to fetch Hosiah and Sly."

CHAPTER SEVENTEEN

DARKO CROSSED DIAGONALLY AT the junction of Nim Tree Road and Nathan Quao Road. The early evening was warm and clinging with barely a breeze. A *tro-tro* rattled by with the driver's mate half hanging out of the door singing out the destination in a robot-like voice. In the yard of the auto repair shop Darko was passing, four men wrestled with an engine block, while just outside St. Theresa's Catholic Church, a seller had just begun frying *kelewele* for the evening. The delicious aroma wafted over to Darko, and he decided he would buy some to take home.

He approached the house where Hosiah and Sly were practicing soccer moves with their friends in the front yard. The tenants, Mr. and Mrs. Tackie, had three sons around the ages of the Dawson boys. For a moment, Darko stood just out of sight to watch them take turns at being the goalie. Sly wasn't with them, however.

"Hi, boys," Darko said, coming in through the squeaky gate.

They chorused their greeting.

"Where is Sly?" Darko asked.

"I don't know, Daddy," Hosiah said. "He went somewhere. Watch me."

Darko counted as his son kept the ball in the air kicking from one foot to the other ten successive times before he at last lost it to the ground. "Well done!" Darko praised him. "But where's Sly? Didn't you see where he went?"

"Please, I think he went to buy something at Joy's," one of Hosiah's friends said.

Joy's was a small, all-purpose store around the corner. Darko looked up and down the pavement. Seconds later, Sly came into view running up the pavement—not from the direction of Joy's, however. He arrived panting and sweating. "Hello, Daddy."

"Hi. Where did you go?"

"Just to buy something," Sly said, heading toward his playmates.

"Wait," Darko said, pulling him back and wiping off his forehead with a face towel he kept handy to tackle heavy perspiration—many in Ghana did the same. "To buy what?"

"Malta." Sly had developed a fondness for the rich, sweet beverage Darko favored. But it was an expensive item for the boy to buy with the minuscule pocket money Darko gave him.

"You can't afford Malta," Darko said.

"Yes, that's why I didn't buy it," Sly said with a smile. He had straight, thick eyebrows and warm, deep-set, eyes. He was more athletic than many boys older than him.

"I thought you went to Joy's," Darko said, frowning.

"Oh, yah—no, I was going to, Daddy, but decided to go to the shop down there."

"What shop?"

"The one near the church."

"I see," Darko said, studying Hosiah's face. His eyes didn't quite meet Darko's. "Anyway, cool down. We're leaving soon, but let me go inside to greet Mr. Tackie."

He knocked on the door, and Tackie, wearing an undershirt that didn't quite cover his beer belly, came out to the porch. He had been watching TV. A big soccer game was about to begin. Darko chatted with him for a minute as they debated Chelsea versus Manchester City.

But Darko was troubled that Sly had just lied to him. Darko had synesthesia, which caused his senses to cross. Sometimes, when someone told a lie, and his vocal quality changed, Darko detected it as a sensation in his left palm.

The instant Sly had said, "Just to buy something," a quick, short stab radiated in Darko's palm like the bite of a small, annoying dog.

He bid Mr. Tackie goodbye and summoned Hosiah and Sly. Outside on the street, Darko stopped and turned to them, resting his hands on their shoulders. "I have some sad news to tell you."

"What, Daddy?" Hosiah said, his face laced with anxiety.

"You remember Aunty Kate was going to move this morning, and Mama went to help her?"

"Yes?"

"The police found her dead at home."

Hosiah's eyes widened to twice their normal size.

Sly's mouth dropped open. "Daddy, what happened to her?"

"Someone killed her. We don't know who."

Hosiah's face clouded. "Why would anyone do that to her, Daddy?"

"That's what the police are going to find out."

"But *you'll* find out, won't you, Daddy?" Hosiah said.

"Maybe it will be me, or maybe it will be someone else."

Hosiah nodded, his eyes wet.

Darko pulled him close. "Are you okay?"

The boy nodded, biting his bottom lip.

"So Mama is sorrowful today," Darko said. "I want you to be especially nice to her and help her to cheer up, all right? You know what I was thinking? She loves *kelewele*, so let's buy some, and we can all eat it tonight."

Hosiah's mood transformed and he let out a cheer of approval. *Kelewele* was a favorite of his as well.

Darko dug into his pocket for his wallet and gave a few *cedis* to his younger son. "Run down to the corner and buy some. We'll wait for you here."

Money in hand, Hosiah ran in big, happy steps down the street to the vendor and waited his turn behind two other customers.

Darko looked at Sly and cupped his hand at the back of the boy's neck. "What's going on? You told me you had gone to buy something, but I know you didn't. You went to do something else. What was it?"

Looking down and tracing a toe in the dirt of the unpaved sidewalk, Sly muttered, "But Daddy, I did go to buy something."

"Sly." Darko brought his face close. "Look at me. I don't like lies. I'm a detective, so people try to lie to me every day. You went to meet someone. Tell me the truth, now."

Sly cleared his throat. "Just some friends."

"Which friends? From school?"

"Yes," Sly said. "I mean, one of them is. The other two are not."

"Do I know any of them?"

"Yes—the one we call Kiddo. On the school team?"

"Yes, I remember him," Darko said. Kiddo was about fifteen and a consummate athlete. He was a showoff, with a bevy of male and female admirers who hung on his every word. "Why did you go to meet him and his friends?"

"They said . . . they said I should come to . . ."

Darko glanced down the street. Hosiah had the *kelewele* in a plastic bag and was paying the seller. "To what? *Stop delaying*. To what?"

"To smoke weed."

Darko went cold. For a moment his vision left him, and he felt like he was swaying like a palm tree in the wind. "And so you went to smoke weed with them?" he said sharply.

Sly looked distressed. "They were teasing me that I've never smoked, so . . ."

"So you went there to prove yourself?"

Sly nodded miserably.

"Did you smoke any?" he asked Sly.

"I was going to, but I know you don't want me to do that, so I told them I had to leave, and I ran away. Daddy, I'm very sorry."

Darko nodded. "You did the right thing." From the corner of his eye, he could see Hosiah was on his way back. "I need you to promise me not to mix with those kind of guys again. Hear me?"

Sly nodded. "Yes, Daddy."

Hosiah came running up to Darko's side, a plastic bag of *kelewele* in hand. "I got it!"

"Thank you." Darko poked his nose into the bag to get a whiff of the heavenly, spicy aroma.

"Can I have a ride, Daddy?"

"Okay." Darko stooped down and his son, beaming with delight, clambered up on his father's shoulders.

Darko grunted as he stood up. "Hosiah, you're not a small boy anymore, you know? You're getting too heavy for me now."

The boy laughed.

Darko loved having his sons close, but this episode with the older one had been unnerving. Sly had been a street child before Darko and Christine had adopted him. He still had a kernel of attraction to what was a little wild and adventurous. That in itself was fine, but not if it was going to lead him to drugs. Should Darko tell Christine about this? No—not now, anyway. She was already dealing with her cousin's death. That was enough to handle. And as for Sly, Darko would have to be more watchful of him from now on.

CHAPTER EIGHTEEN

CHRISTINE WAS SLUGGISH WHEN she woke up Sunday morning. Darko joined her as she sat on the edge of the bed.

"How are you doing?" he asked her.

She shook her head. "Numb. It doesn't seem real."

He nodded, rubbing her back.

Her phone rang, and she looked at the screen. "It's Mama." She answered. "Hello, Mama. No, I don't feel like going to church this morning—"

Darko caught bits of his mother-in-law coaxing her daughter to go.

Christine tried to argue, but to no avail. She heaved a sigh. "All right. We'll meet there, then."

"What's going on?" Darko asked her as she put her phone down.

"Mama says I should go to Bishop Clem's sermon this morning; that it will uplift me and give me strength. She says I shouldn't let the anger fester."

"Fester?" Darko said. "You've barely had time to grieve, and she's talking about festering,"

"Dark," she said with reproach. "You know what she means."

"No, I don't," he said, shaking his head. "I never do."

"Would you come with me to church?" Christine asked him. "Please? I'll go if you accompany me."

Darko was surprised. He rarely went to church. He hadn't found one he liked—not that he was looking. Sermons often left him cold, and the amount of money pastors made on the backs of their congregations offended him.

"I'll feel better if you're with me," she pressed.

"Okay," he said. "But first, let me see if Cairo will be home this morning so we can drop Sly off there, and then we'll take Hosiah to Sunday school."

Typically, while Christine was at church and Hosiah at Sunday school, Darko stayed home with Sly, who was Muslim.

Darko called Cairo, who said he had been thinking of going to church but would forego it for this week to watch Sly.

BISHOP CLEM HOWARD-MILLS'S congregation gathered at a large venue in a lovely, still underdeveloped area within view of Weija Lake. Huge Howard-Mills billboards lined the unpaved route to the site.

As they approached the car park, Darko gave a soft whistle. Scores of white buses were carting in the congregation. A parking official guided Darko into an available space, and he alighted with Christine and Gifty.

At least three thousand people sat under a massive white tent with overflows on each side. Facing them was the stage on which Bishop Howard-Mills would appear. For the moment, a large choir and a female soloist, all dressed in blue-and-white outfits, were performing an ear-piercing song in Twi all about following Jesus.

About two-thirds of the distance from the back of the crowd, videographers on a mounted stage were filming the show, no doubt to post later to YouTube and Howard-Mills's podcast. Darko thought of this event as a show rather than a church service. First, the enormity of the gathering was a spectacle in itself; second, the entertainment aspect: the choir's singing and dancing performances; third, the star quality of the man this crowd had gathered to see with the anticipation of a child on his birthday.

A female usher in blue with a white sash around her waist guided Gifty, Christine, and Darko to available seats a few rows in from the periphery of the congregation. Darko let the two women go in before him, and he took the chair on the aisle.

After two performances from the choir, a Reverend Tagoe came to the podium and asked the congregants to stand for a prayer. As they did so, many closed their eyes and raised their palms skyward as they swayed from side to side. Gifty did the same, but Christine only bowed her head. Darko was on the fence about these actions and didn't participate. Tagoe went on for quite a while and then told the congregation to sit down for his sermon on how to clothe oneself in the armor of the Lord.

"Satan lurks at every corner of the street, in every room in your home and office," Tagoe said. "He throws distractions and temptations at you to make you stumble and fall off the path in which God wants you to walk."

After another song by the choir, Tagoe introduced Bishop Howard-Mills and welcomed him to the stage amidst thunderous, ecstatic applause from the standing congregation. The bishop took in his ovation, looking back and forth over the crowd, waving in acknowledgment. He wore his trademark long blue top with a thin gold stripe running down the side and a mini-microphone on the collar. He had no swagger, but he was confident and composed, imparting reassurance. Stepping to the lectern, he placed his Bible on it. "Thank you, dearest brothers and sisters in Christ. Father, guide us by your mighty spirit today. In Jesus's name, amen."

"Amen!" the congregation chorused.

"You may be seated." His voice seemed deeper than Darko remembered from when he had met the bishop at Kate's crime scene, and the slight echo effect from the sound system rendered his tone Godlike and commanding.

Darko heard not a whisper or stir as everyone waited for the first word from Howard-Mills. "'You shall not murder,'" he began. "'You shall not murder.' That is what the Sixth Commandment tells us." He sauntered along the edge of the stage. "Very simple. You shall not murder. And yet, murderers are among us."

The crowd shifted uncomfortably.

"Oh, yes!" the bishop said with a hint of a smile. "I know what's happening." He switched to Twi for a moment. "Without moving your lips, you are trying to tell the person next to you that maybe the bishop has gone mad."

The congregation burst into collective laughter.

Christine looked at Darko, who smiled, acknowledging that Howard-Mills knew how to deliver a line.

"But now, let us be serious," the bishop continued. "Why do I say murderers sit among us? Do you remember the story of Cain and Abel?"

The people murmured their assent.

Howard-Mills returned to the lectern. "Open your Bibles to Genesis, chapter four."

Those with Bibles flipped to the page, and a prolonged rustle went through the crowd like cornstalks in the wind.

The bishop continued. "Genesis chapter four says, 'The Lord looked with favor on Abel and his offering, but on Cain and his offering he did not look with favor. So Cain was very angry, and his face was downcast.'" Howard-Mills looked up. "Yes, Cain was furious. He had *rage* in his heart. Cain wasn't just annoyed like when you miss the bus or the line at the bank is too long. He was *enraged*. And what else was he feeling besides anger?" The bishop's finger searched the crowd. "Anybody? Yes, you over there. What else was Cain feeling?"

A young man about halfway back in the tent stood up. "Jealousy!" he called out.

"Ah, yes!" Howard-Mills pivoted on his feet a quarter circle. "Correct. Give that gentleman a hand."

The congregation clapped, some of them smiling at the young man.

"Anger," Howard-Mills continued. "*Jealousy*. These terrible feelings had taken over Cain's body. They had occupied him like a monster, and now they were devouring him from the inside. But brothers and sisters in Christ, what are anger and jealousy but tools of the devil?" He raised his voice. "Blessed Jesus, descend upon this gathering and banish Satan. *Banish him!*"

The congregation leaped to its feet shouting, "*Amen!*"

"Verse six," Howard-Mills continued when everyone had sat down and become quiet again. "'Then the LORD said to Cain, *Why are you angry? Why is your face downcast? If you do what is right, will you not be accepted? But if you do not do what is right, sin is crouching at your door; it desires to have you, but you must rule over it.*' Listen to the Lord, my brothers and sisters! He says, '*Sin is crouching at your door. It desires to have you.*' Yes, sin—Satan—desires to have *you.* It wants to jump out at you the moment you leave yourself open. Listen to the Lord, hallelujah!"

"*Hallelujah!*"

"The Lord says, '*Sin desires to have you, but you must rule over it.*'" Howard-Mills growled the last part, and his followers jumped up shouting, cheering, and praising the Lord and his beloved bishop. Darko saw a good few tearful with emotion.

Howard-Mills looked joyful, even radiant. "You see, before Cain planned to kill his brother, he wasn't even aware he was going to commit murder. Proverbs 25:28 says, 'A man without self-control is like a city broken into and left without walls.' Those walls are supposed to keep Satan out, but now they are broken, and this is how he finds his way into your soul and leads you into temptation and all manner of evil."

Howard-Mills came down from the stage, in keeping with his custom of mixing with the congregation. Security guards on each side of the flight of steps kept a wary eye out. Darko supposed the bishop had had his share of fanatic followers throwing themselves at him and getting out of control.

"All manner of evil," he repeated, beginning to walk down the aisle one over from where Darko sat. "Like Cain, that evil can even lead to murder. And I have something sorrowful to tell you today as we gather to worship the Lord. Yesterday one of our very own beloved followers of Christ became a victim of murder, and therefore, my heart is heavy. Her name is Katherine Vanderpuye."

A gasp went through the congregation. Christine stiffened and sat up. Darko looked at her as if to say, *Did you know he was going to mention this?* She shook her head.

Howard-Mills went on. "Many of you knew her for her beautiful smile and her generous soul. We will pray for her today, and I ask you to remember her and her dear family in your prayers this entire week."

The bishop took one of the transverse rows to Darko's aisle, down which he continued to walk away from the stage. "We don't know who did this terrible thing to our precious Kate," he said, his tone soft now. "We ask God to guide the police in their investigations and bring this man, this monster who committed this terrible crime, to justice. Amen."

"Amen."

Christine's face clouded, and Darko was afraid she might break down. He took her hand surreptitiously and squeezed it.

"Proverbs 15:29 says," Howard-Mills continued, "'The LORD is far from the wicked, but he hears the prayer of the righteous.' So pray for Kate, and pray for the one who murdered her, that he or she may come forward and confess."

Darko heard a stir in the row on the other side of the aisle, and both Darko and Christine glanced over. A man in his late twenties dressed in a dark green shirt and black pants was leaving, and fellow congregants were making way for him, looking a little irritated at why the guy had to depart this minute.

Darko didn't give the disturbance much attention, but he noticed Christine was watching the man with a look of shock.

"What's wrong?" he whispered to her.

"I saw him opposite Kate's house yesterday," she told Darko in his ear. "He stood there staring at me."

"Really?" Darko said, looking at the man again. He didn't remember him. "Are you sure?"

Christine nodded. "Same clothes."

Darko shrugged. "Could be a neighbor."

Christine shook her head. "I don't think so."

The man left by a side exit. Still distracted, Christine returned to listening to the bishop, who had almost arrived at their spot.

"Hey!" one of the security guards in the rear shouted. Everyone turned. The strange guy in the dark green had returned and was running up to the bishop with the guard in pursuit. Howard-Mills, unruffled as the man kneeled before him, waved the guard away.

Members of the congregation stirred, leaned in to the aisle to stare, or stood up in their seats, wondering what was happening. Darko came forward to the edge of his seat.

The man spoke. "'*Thou shalt not kill*," he said. "*But vengeance is mine, I will repay*, says the Lord.'"

"Please," Howard-Mills said into the microphone, raising his hand to quiet the crowd. "My brother here says, 'Thou shalt not kill, but vengeance is mine, "I will repay," says the Lord." He was almost soothing as he knelt down beside the man. "My brother, what is troubling you? What have you done?"

As soon as the man raised a hand toward the bishop's neck, the security guards leaped forward to grab him. But his grip was powerful, and now it was evident that a struggle had broken out, with Howard-Mills fighting to get away from the man as the guards tried to pull him off. A scream rose from the crowd as people got to their feet and chairs began to scatter. Darko pulled Christine and Gifty into the aisle. "Get out of here!"

"What's happening?" Christine cried.

"I don't know," Darko shouted. "Just go!"

Christine took her mother's hand, and they made for the exit, looking back repeatedly.

Darko moved closer to the bishop. The tumult around him had grown. For an instant, a parting between the bishop and his assailant occurred, and Darko caught a glimpse of Howard-Mills. He wore a dazed, shocked expression as people dragged him away to safety. He touched the side of his neck where blood was pouring. He looked at his palm in disbelief. Then as a collective scream of horror rose from the congregation, his legs buckled, and he toppled sideways onto the ground.

Darko moved, shoving people aside as he made his way forward. He was trying to get to the bishop's attacker, not Howard-Mills. Ghanaian vigilante justice was about to take place, and if Christine was correct that this man had been present around Kate's home yesterday, Darko wanted him alive and conscious.

Someone had wrestled a knife away from the man, and people began to punch and kick him.

"*Stop!*" Darko yelled, trying to pull them back. He deflected some punches but took the brunt of others as he managed to get on top of the bishop's assailant. Confusion and screaming continued as Darko sustained the blows and kicks to his head meant for the man in the green shirt.

One of the guards managed to take control. "*Heh!*" he shouted at the crowd. "Get back!"

The mob pulled away, but the chaos had not subsided yet.

"Don't move," Darko said into the man's ear. "What's your name?"

"Peter Amalba."

"Peter Amalba, my name is Chief Inspector Dawson. You are under arrest."

CHAPTER NINETEEN

DARKO SAT ON THE toilet lid as Christine examined his bruised torso. Hosiah and Sly leaned against the bathroom doorjamb watching.

"Daddy, your ribs are swollen," Sly observed with concern.

"They are," Christine agreed. "I think they might have broken a couple of them."

"I don't think so," Darko said lightly. "I can move quite okay."

He nonchalantly did a body twist but stopped with a gasp as pain shot through his side.

"Yes, quite okay, I see," Christine said. "Be careful! You have to take it easy the next few days."

"I'll just be aware of the pain more if I do that," Darko said, gingerly touching his puffy right cheek struck during the commotion.

"Animals!" Christine said. "They could have killed you. Let me do that cut on your face. *Be still*, Dark!"

He squirmed as she cleaned the wound.

Hosiah came closer, putting his hand on his father's knee. "Sorry, Daddy," he said, looking pained. "Does it hurt?"

"It's not too bad, son. Don't worry."

"Will you put a *plaster* on it, Mama?" Hosiah asked Christine.

"Yes."

"Oh, can I put it on?" Hosiah asked eagerly.

"Okay, but wash your hands first."

Once he had done that, Christine gave him the *plaster* and

showed him how to apply it to his father's cheek without contaminating the inside surface.

"Thank you, Hosiah," Darko said.

"No, *Doctor* Hosiah," he said, laughing.

"Oh, I beg your pardon, Doctor."

"Can me and Sly go outside to play?"

"Sly and I," Darko corrected. "Yes, you may."

The two boys disappeared, jostling each other.

"So what happens next now that you've charged Amalba?" Christine asked.

"I'll question him first thing in the morning," Darko said. "But I need to know you're certain that's the guy you saw yesterday in front of Kate's house."

"I've told you twice—yes, I am. I can't forget that expression in the guy's bloodshot eyes. He seemed to be staring right through me."

"Did he seem agitated?"

"No, calm. Or maybe he was agitated inside; I don't know."

"Did you notice any red or brown spots on the man's skin or clothing—anything that might have been blood?"

"No, I didn't. His top and pants were dark."

"And to your recollection, have you ever seen him anywhere else?"

She shook her head. "No."

Darko felt odd questioning her this way. He put his shirt back on, wincing whenever he made a bad move.

"So then you're taking the case?" Christine said.

"I'm not sure," Darko said irritably

"You just said you're going to interrogate the man tomorrow about the murder, didn't you?"

He sighed. "Yes, I did say that. Have you finished patching me up?"

"Yes, I think so."

They went back to the sitting room, where Gifty was on the sofa checking her phone.

"Any news on the bishop's condition?" Christine asked her.

"I just got a text from a friend. They say the stab wound wasn't that deep, and he's now stable at Korle Bu Hospital. Looks like he will be all right, thanks be to God."

"Praise Him," Christine agreed.

"Are you okay?" Gifty asked Darko.

"A few broken ribs, that's all," he said, easing into a chair.

"You should see a doctor," Gifty said. "I know someone who punctured her lungs when her ribs broke after a fall."

"Neither of those things is going to happen," Darko retorted. "I'm not going to the doctor, and my ribs are not going to puncture my lungs."

She grunted and crossed her legs with the message, *Don't say I didn't warn you.*

Christine sat down and put her head back. "What a weekend this has been."

Darko agreed. "Something I've been wondering. Did either of you know—or guess—Bishop Howard-Mills was going to talk about Kate's death this morning?"

"I didn't," Christine said. "It took me by surprise."

"How did you feel about it?" Darko asked.

"Conflicted," she said. "Bishop Howard-Mills was trying to honor her memory, but . . . But it was too soon."

"Well, maybe in talking about the murder, he was trying to coax Kate's killer out of the congregation," Gifty suggested. "Maybe it worked. The guy who attacked the bishop could be the same one who killed Kate."

"But why did he say, 'thou shalt not kill'?" Christine asked.

"He's a madman," Gifty said with a shrug. "He doesn't think in the same logical way as you or I would. His thinking is disordered."

So is yours, Darko thought.

Christine looked at Darko. "What's your opinion?"

"I don't have one at this point," he replied, gazing at the ceiling, where a water spot revealed a leak in the roof. He would have to mend it before the rains came around again. He sat up again.

"However, getting back to a question I asked earlier, Mama, did you suggest to the bishop that he should talk about the murder at church?"

She looked uncomfortable. "I might have mentioned it."

"In other words, you did," Darko said.

"I didn't *tell* him to," Gifty said. "I suggested it."

"When?" Darko asked.

"After he left Kate's house yesterday, I called him back, and we had a chat."

"You called him *back*?" Darko said.

"Pardon?"

"You said you called the bishop '*back*.' Meaning you had called him before."

Gifty had a guilty look. "No, no I didn't mean that."

Darko smiled. "Mama, after Christine called you with the news that Kate was dead, it was you who notified Mr. Howard-Mills, wasn't it?"

Gifty tightened her lips and folded her arms.

Christine drew in her breath. "Mama!"

Gifty turned to her daughter. "I felt you needed the bishop for comfort and support."

"Wait a minute," Darko said. "You called a man we barely know to comfort my *wife*?"

"*You* might not know him well," Gifty said, "because you don't go to church. If you did, you would know Bishop Howard-Mills as a gracious man of God who gives succor those who are experiencing great sorrow."

"I don't care what kind of person he is or whom he gives succor," Darko said. "This is my wife we're discussing. How dare you call this bishop to 'comfort' her?"

"She's also my daughter," Gifty shot back. "Or have you forgotten?"

"No, I haven't, because you manage to remind me several times a year."

"Darko," Christine murmured, "try to calm down."

"Listen," Gifty said, her eyes blazing at Darko, "at the time Christine called me, she was alone with no one's shoulder to cry on. She was weeping, *weeping*. And where were you? You were busy inside the house at the crime scene. I couldn't go there to hold her hand because I was babysitting the boys. Ransford and Nana were on the way there, but he was distraught as well. What could I do? We needed someone we trust who would have the right words to say. No matter what you think of the bishop, he is a man with a blessed soul who can lift up many a grieving person."

"I wish you two would stop bickering," Christine said. "There's enough stress as it is right now. Please?"

"Okay," Darko said sullenly. "Sorry." His ribs gave him a sharp jab. He felt a little light-headed.

"Are you okay?" Christine asked him, touching his shoulder.

"I'm all right," he said.

But he wasn't. The events of the past two days had shaken him, and now a discomfiting collision between his working and personal lives was unfolding.

CHAPTER TWENTY

ON THE WAY TO work Monday morning, Darko grabbed a copy of the *Daily Graphic* from one of Ring Road's itinerant street vendors, who ran alongside the moving motorcycle to hand Darko his change.

He parked in his favorite spot outside the Criminal Investigations Department and went through security at the entrance. The creaking, seven-story building had had a new coat of sunshine-yellow paint in an attempt to render it less gray and grim, but its age was unmistakable. The stairway was too narrow, and the stone steps were worn down with decades of constant foot traffic. Officers raced up and down, squeezing to the side if anyone was ascending or descending in the opposite direction.

Invariably, Mondays at CID were chaotic. Darko wanted to see his boss as early as possible, but when he reached the fifth floor, he paused for a moment in the corridor to look at the paper he had just bought. On the second page, the headline was BLOODY WEEKEND, underneath which was a picture of Gabriel's savaged body surrounded by dried blood. At least they had the decency to cover his face, Darko thought. Showing photographs of murder victims in the press was practically a Ghanaian tradition.

He knocked on the boss's door and entered to find Chief Superintendent Joseph Oppong at his desktop computer. At a snail's pace, the Ghana Police Service was relying more on electronic records, but the preponderance was still paper.

Oppong was a thin man with a shock of white hair and a lugubrious expression. He seldom smiled, but his eyes were kind. Maintaining impeccable standards, he wore a neat suit and tie.

"Good morning, sir," Darko said, stiffening upright briefly in salute.

"Morning, Dawson," he replied, gesturing toward a chair on the opposite side of his desk. He took in Darko's appearance. "You look awful."

"Thank you, sir," Darko said, sitting down with care. "It's better than yesterday."

"I'm glad. First of all, my condolences for your family's loss."

"Thank you, sir. My wife is suffering the most. She was close to Katherine."

"I quite understand. Please convey my sympathies to Christine. Now, regarding the events of yesterday, the charge officer briefed me when I passed by this morning. But I need to get the full version from you."

Darko described in detail the extraordinary events that had unfolded at the church, and how he had forced himself into the mob to protect Peter Amalba from injury or even death.

"I commend you for risking life and limb," Oppong said.

"Thank you, sir."

"But," the chief super continued, and, Darko thought, there's always a 'but,' "let's look at the reason you went in to save him in the first place. I gather your wife believes she might have observed this Mr. Amalba in the vicinity of her cousin's home on Saturday morning."

"Christine is confident that she saw him near an unfinished home opposite Kate's house," Darko said. "She didn't give it any thought until the man appeared at the church service."

"So this morning you will interrogate him and find out where we stand. What was he doing around Kate's house? Does he live nearby? Did he kill Kate, and for what motive? Why did he stab the bishop, and why did he utter those Bible quotations? We also have the possibility that this man is not right in the head, so we must be careful not to be coercive or over-suggestive to him, especially if he's a vulnerable individual." Oppong leaned forward. "What I was about to say is that the case won't stay at Dzorwulu. We are bringing it to Central."

"Oh," Darko said. "And the reason, sir?"

"Assistant Commissioner of Police Lartey called me this morning to inform me that we're getting the case. He didn't give a particular reason."

Darko was both startled and unsurprised. After Lartey's promotion to his present rank, he was no longer Darko's direct supervisor, but somehow Lartey's influence kept appearing like *juju*.

"Has the case been assigned, sir?" Darko asked.

"Yes. To you, of course."

"Please," Darko said, "if it's possible, can the case be given to someone else?"

Oppong frowned. "Why?"

"The murder involves a family member, and so I might not be impartial."

"You were the superior officer at the scene, and you've arrested a man in possible connection to the victim's death. How would it make sense to assign the case to someone else when you're practically investigating it already?"

"Sir—"

"You are an experienced investigator, Dawson," Oppong went on. "If bias is intruding, then get it out of the way. Stop arguing."

Darko clenched his jaw. "Yes, sir."

"So you start with the Amalba interview and move forward." Oppong said. "Also, you will be training a new transfer from Kumasi—a Detective Lance Corporal."

"His name, sir?"

"Not 'his.' *Her* name is Mabel Safo," Oppong said. "She is supposed to meet you in the detective's office by"—Oppong looked at his watch—"eight o'clock."

Darko had never worked closely with a female detective. Except for clerical jobs, women occupied a minority of the GPS posts. Darko missed his ex-partner, Detective Inspector Chikata, who had moved full time to the tactical Panther Unit. Over the years, he had become Darko's faithful right hand.

DETECTIVES RANKING INSPECTOR and below did all their work in the general, all-purpose room on CID's fourth floor, including interrogations. The commingling of suspects, witnesses and police officers made for a strange club. Darko went into the office, which was as noisy as Makola Market. He said hello to anyone who wasn't too busy filling out reports or arguing about soccer or politics. One of the other chief inspectors jokingly asked Darko if his bruised cheek had resulted from a fight with his wife.

"Yes," Darko replied. "She won."

He spotted someone new—a young woman sitting by herself in a corner with her head bent over her phone. She was lean, almost skinny, but taller than the average Ghanaian woman and dressed in a tan trouser suit and white blouse. Her flat shoes were frayed around the edges just a touch. She wore her hair pulled back.

She looked up as Darko approached and he could see her wondering if he was the person she was expecting.

"Mabel Safo?" he said.

"Yes, please." She sprang to her feet as though her chair had propelled her.

"I'm Chief Inspector Dawson. Welcome to CID." They shook hands. "Follow me. We can go to my office where it's quiet."

As they walked out, one of Darko's superior officers called out, "Dawson! Be kind to her, eh?" and burst out laughing.

"Always," Darko replied. "Don't mind him," he tried to reassure Safo as he caught a shadow of worry crossing her face. "I'm not all that bad."

She smiled diffidently but didn't say anything.

Darko's office was a couple of doors down the corridor. Inside, Chief Inspector Gove, with whom Darko shared the office, was eating a breakfast of rice and chicken stew. Darko introduced

Safo, and Gove nodded at the new female officer with a mixture of interest and amusement.

Darko asked Safo to take a seat on the chair just beside his desk. As he talked to her, he couldn't form a clear impression of whether Safo wanted to be there or not. She spoke with hesitation and without much emotion or enthusiasm. Twi was her mother tongue, so Darko tried switching to that to see if she would loosen up. He thought he saw her expression brighten slightly, but then she seemed to withdraw again. Was she shy or timid, perhaps?

As a corporal, Safo had worked at one of the district headquarters in the Western Region. To become a detective, she would have had to pass an exam, and most detectives were among the brightest of the police officer crop.

"You've come at the right time," he told Safo. "We have a suspect to interview this morning. It concerns a case that arose over the weekend."

Dawson gave her the particulars from the beginning. She listened, nodding from time to time but not making any comment until Darko came to the end of the story, and she said, "I'm sorry, sir. I mean about your wife's cousin."

"Thank you," Darko said, not wanting to dwell on it. He called down to the charge office and asked them to bring Peter Amalba up.

CHAPTER TWENTY-ONE

AMALBA'S INJURIES WERE WORSE than Darko's. His left eye was swollen shut, and he had lost a tooth in the melee. He walked with a limp and clutched his right flank.

Gove had left the office. After removing Amalba's cuffs, Darko had him take a seat on the other side of the desk. Safo sat beside Darko. Amalba bowed his head and rubbed his wrists. He was shorter than Darko with powerful arms and the physique of a sedentary Ghanaian man: thick around the waist with a slack belly.

With Safo watching, Darko made sure he did everything by the book. He recited the legal caution to Amalba before beginning any questioning. Darko didn't pretend that, just like his colleagues, he often didn't bother to caution petty criminals. Few suspects insisted on having a lawyer present because almost no one could afford it. Many prisoners didn't understand that right and the police sometimes took advantage.

Darko began with some basic questions for Amalba, who was intelligent and well-spoken. At thirty-six, he was around Darko's age and unmarried, but he had two children who lived exclusively with their mother. Amalba's father was from the Northern Region, while his mother hailed from the Volta Region. Amalba had run away from home as a teenager and come to Accra. He had finished secondary school and up until a few weeks ago, he had been an inventory manager at one of Accra's ubiquitous Max Mart supermarkets. At the moment, Amalba lived with his brother, Michael.

"Is your eye okay?" Darko asked him.

"It's fine, sir," Amalba said. "And yours?"

Darko smiled a little. "It's also fine."

"We thank God."

"Do you love God?" Darko asked.

Amalba seemed surprised by the question. "Yes, sir. Of course, I do. And I obey Him. Always."

"Did He ask you to hurt the bishop?"

"No, please. Our God is a loving one. What I did was my decision."

"Why did you do it?"

Amalba looked Darko in the eye without flinching. "Because Bishop Howard-Mills killed the woman I loved."

Darko hadn't anticipated that answer. "What do you mean? Killed whom?"

"Katherine Vanderpuye."

Darko stared at Amalba. What was he talking about? "How do you know the bishop killed Katherine Vanderpuye?"

"I saw him walking away from Kate's house early on Saturday morning, sir."

Darko noticed Amalba said "Kate" this time. That was the name only those closest to her used. "When was that?" Darko asked. "At what time?"

"About three o'clock."

"And then?"

"He drove away, fast. When the house girl came at five, she opened the gate to find Gabriel's dead body. She started screaming. After the neighbor had come over, the police arrived, and then the woman sitting with you at church yesterday. Is that your wife?"

Darko didn't respond. Leave her out of this, he thought.

"Then, later when I heard Kate was dead," Amalba continued, "I knew the bishop must have done it."

"You *assumed* so," Darko commented. "What were you doing around Kate's house at that hour of the morning?"

"Sometimes, I checked on her," Amalba said.

Darko was baffled. "Checked on her? What do you mean?"

"I couldn't stay with her—not yet, but I used to go to her place to make sure she was okay."

A stalker, Darko thought. "How?" he asked. "Did you knock on the gate? Did you call Kate to let you into the house? What?"

"No, I didn't want to disturb her. I just looked in through the side of the gate to make sure her car was there, and then watched her place for a while from that house that's being built across the street."

"Did Kate know you were doing this?"

"Of course. I was like a guardian angel for her until the day we would wed each other. We were in love."

Darko frowned. In love? "Where did you first meet her?" he asked Amalba.

"At the Qedesh, the bishop's church."

"Who knew about this love? Was Kate's husband Solomon aware?"

Amalba nodded. "Yes. He was sad, but resigned." He shifted his weight and sat forward. "All the family knew."

Darko tapped his fingertips on the table. "You are making this story up, Mr. Amalba. It's just a fantasy. Isn't that so?"

Amalba looked away, setting his jaw like concrete.

Darko tried a different approach. "How long had you been outside the house on Saturday morning when you saw the bishop?" he asked.

"He was leaving at the time I was arriving—walking very quick, almost running. And he was holding a machete."

How would Amalba know that detail? Darko sat up to full attention. "Continue."

"He looked around to make sure no one saw him, and then he ran to his car and left."

"What did you do then?"

"I stood at Katherine's gate and called out for the watchman, but no answer. I would have looked over the top, but it's too high, and it has razor wire. So I decided I would just wait a couple of hours at the empty building opposite Kate's place."

"Something doesn't make sense," Darko said. "If you were in love with Kate, you should have had her phone number, and you would have called her to make sure she was okay."

Amalba nodded. "It's true, but my phone battery was dead. The area where my brother and I live had been having a blackout for more than twenty-four hours, so there was no electricity to charge my phone."

Dead phones were a fact of life in Ghana with *dumsor*, so Darko accepted the excuse as plausible, but questions remained. "Why would Bishop Howard-Mills kill Katherine Vanderpuye?" he asked.

"He was trying to take her away from me," Amalba said. "He loved her, but she didn't want him. He always invited her to the office behind the church saying he needed to counsel her. And it was there he tried to do things to her."

"Things like what?"

"Dirty things," Amalba said, his expression flat. "The bishop is a fornicator, even though he preaches against it."

"So you're saying the bishop was fornicating with Kate," Darko said.

"Yes."

"Knowing that, and seeing Mr. Howard-Mills leaving the scene of Kate's murder, why didn't you report it to the police?"

Amalba raised his eyebrows. "Sir, would they believe me? They would arrest *me*. Even now, please excuse me for saying, sir, you don't seem to think I'm telling the truth."

He had a point. "So," Darko said, "you decided to take things into your hands and kill the bishop in revenge?"

"Yes, please. For the evil he perpetrated on Kate."

"Why did you choose to do it at the service in front of thousands of people?"

"I wasn't ashamed," Amalba said with a shrug. "Why should I hide it? And where else would I get him? His home is like a fortress."

"At the church," Darko said, "you quoted the Sixth Commandment, 'Thou shalt not kill,' and yet you were trying to murder the bishop."

"Yes, sir. That's why I also said, 'Vengeance is mine, says the Lord, I will repay.'"

"But in Romans twelve, verse nineteen," Safo objected, making Darko turn in surprise, "Peter tells us that we should not harm are enemies. God is telling us it is for Him to take vengeance, not *you.*"

Amalba stared at her for a moment, grunted softly and then looked away as if he couldn't be bothered.

"How do you respond to that, Mr. Amalba?" Darko prodded.

He stared blankly at Darko for a moment. "She is not correct," he said finally.

Darko could feel resentment coming from Safo for Amalba's dismissal of her comment, but she said nothing.

"Mr. Amalba," Darko said, "I put it to you that it's you who killed Katherine Vanderpuye because of her so-called affair with Bishop Howard-Mills, and that you also tried to murder the bishop for the same reason—fornication with Katherine. Isn't that true?"

"No, please." Amalba slumped like a loose sack of cocoyams. "This is what I said would happen. You don't believe me."

"No, sir," Darko said. "I don't."

Amalba appeared as dejected as an athlete who placed last. "Sorry, sir."

Darko wasn't sure where to go from there. "You said you live with your brother, Michael. Where?"

"Abelenkpe, sir."

Abelenkpe was not that far away from Dzorwulu, Kate's part of town.

"What work does Michael do?" Darko asked.

"He's a manager at the Ring Road Central branch of Standard Chartered Bank."

Christine had had a savings account for years at that branch.

Darko looked at Safo. "Anything to add? Questions?"

"No, sir," she said, her emotion gone again.

Darko handcuffed Amalba. The suspect had stated he had intended to kill Bishop Howard-Mills. He would be charged accordingly.

But the puzzle remained, who had killed Kate? Could it have been Bishop Howard-Mills? Was he having an affair with her as Amalba had suggested? Or was it in fact Amalba, who was now fabricating the story of witnessing the clergyman leaving Kate's home? Lastly, could it be true that Amalba and Kate were planning to get married after she divorced Solomon? Christine had never mentioned anything like that to Darko, and she would have known. But as peculiar as it sounded, Darko didn't dismiss it outright. He had seen stranger things happen.

CHAPTER TWENTY-TWO

"LET'S GO OVER THE interview with the suspect this morning," Darko said to Safo in the detectives' room. He had found a couple of empty chairs at a corner table. As always, the place was noisy, and Darko preferred the quiet of his office, but to forestall even the remotest possibility of gossip developing about him and the new female officer, he had decided he would not spend time alone with her in his office unless necessary. He was not attracted to her, but gossip doesn't listen to the truth.

"We start with Mr. Amalba's appearance," Darko said. "Please describe him."

"Well," she began, "his cheek was swollen."

"No—you start with the words, 'the suspect is a,' and if possible give the age, gender, height, estimated weight. Didn't they teach you that at the Academy?"

"Sorry, sir. I forgot."

"Continue."

"The suspect is a thirty-six-year-old male . . . dark in complexion, about two meters in height and ninety kilos."

"Good. Physique?"

"You mean—"

"Fat, thin, average?"

"I think, average. Yes, average."

"Yes. Did you notice any distinguishing marks?"

"No, please."

"What about the tribal mark on his face?"

Safo looked mortified. "I didn't see any—"

"Correct. He didn't have one. Hairstyle?"

"Shaved close to the scalp."

"Yes. Teeth?"

"Em, one was broken."

"Which one?"

"The . . . upper left front tooth."

"Good. What else?"

"His cheek was swollen."

"Which cheek?" Darko asked.

"The right."

"Whose right? Amalba's right?"

"Yes. No, I mean, left."

"Okay. Go on."

Safo put her hand on her forehead and wiped the sweat that had broken out.

Darko saw she was trembling. "Are you okay?"

"Yes, Daddy. I mean, sir."

Darko smiled. "Not your father, okay? Why are you shaking?"

She gulped, gripping the fingers of her left hand with her right.

"Am I scaring you?" Darko asked her, glancing around in some embarrassment. No one seemed to be paying attention.

Safo shook her head.

"Then stop shaking," Darko said. "I'm not bullying you. When you're in court, the defense lawyer will try to make you crack under pressure by challenging your description of his client. I want you to learn very early on to look at someone and get his or her image stuck in your head. Do you get me?"

"Yes, sir."

"Relax, okay? Now, let's discuss what Amalba had to say and how he answered my questions. One of the first things I noticed about him was the lack of emotion. For example, when he stated he and Kate had been in love, there was nothing in his face to reflect that. When he said the bishop was a fornicator, he didn't show obvious disgust or anger. What could account for this?"

Safo chewed on her upper lip as she considered her response. "He could be lying."

"Yes," Darko said, writing that down on a piece of scrap paper. "What else? Let's imagine he has a mental problem. In fact, he could believe the bishop is a fornicator even though he has no evidence for it."

"Delusional," she said.

"Good word. Well done."

Pleased, she smiled.

"Or maybe he's just a sociopath," Darko continued. "He doesn't feel emotion the way you and I do. He doesn't play by the usual social rules. Whatever the case, Mr. Amalba is dangerous. He tried to harm Bishop Howard-Mills, possibly kill him."

"I don't believe Amalba ever saw the bishop around Mrs. Vanderpuye's house," Safo said. "He made it all up to frame Mr. Howard-Mills."

"Yes," Darko said, lost in thought for a moment. "Because there's the question of the machete Amalba says he saw the bishop carrying. If I were the murderer, wouldn't I hide my weapon in a bag, or under my clothes?"

"Yes, sir," Safo agreed. "I think the reason why Amalba knows about the machete is that he used one to kill Kate."

An idea came to Darko. "One moment," he said, springing out of his chair. He trotted to his office, grabbed the copy of the *Daily Graphic* and opened it to the second page.

"Ah," he muttered, scanning the article.

Darko returned to the detectives' room and dropped the newspaper in front of Safo. "Read," he said.

She did, maybe even twice, then looked up. "Yes, sir?"

"Does the article describe the probable manner of death?"

"Yes, I think so."

"Read it," Darko said.

"Well, it says here, 'According to a police spokesman, a

machete was probably used to inflict the wounds sustained by the two victims, Katherine Vanderpuye and Gabriel Saleh.'"

"There it is in black and white," Darko said with a mixture of annoyance and resignation.

Safo's eyes lit up. "So Amalba could have read this."

"Correct," Darko said. "This is why I keep telling officers not to talk to the press—especially to this guy." With his index finger, Darko jabbed the name of the reporter with his finger. "Wisdom Nortey. He wants to pack as many facts, theories, and speculations into his articles as he can get. And this is how he can taint an investigation. He just doesn't care."

"I see," Safo said. "So you try never to talk to him?"

"I avoid him like Ebola."

"So shall we go back to Mr. Amalba now and confront him?"

Darko shook his head. "Not yet. He will deny seeing the article. Let him roast in jail a little; then we'll return to him when we have more ammunition. Right now, we must go to see the top three people Amalba mentioned: his brother, Michael, Solomon Vanderpuye; and Bishop Howard-Mills."

STANDARD CHARTERED BANK, or "StanChart," stood along the one-way street that ran for a short distance along Ring Road Central and terminated at its western end at the new multi-level Ring Road Interchange that had once been the simple Kwame Nkrumah Circle. StanChart was in good company with Stanbic, EcoBank, and Prudential along the same street. After drawing money from one of them, one could go next door to Samsung or duck into Aunty Jane's restaurant, which had some of the best *red-red* Darko had ever tasted. Not the cheapest, though. Jane's was a lunchtime haunt for wealthy financial types who squeezed their eight-cylinder SUVs into tight parking spaces in front of the restaurant under the guidance of a flag-waving watchman. Any business of worth in a high-traffic area of town had a traffic-guiding watchman.

Ring Road was only a four-lane highway when it needed to be at least eight to handle present traffic levels. Pedestrians often hopped over the large open drain on each side and ran across. It was surprising more people didn't get struck. Even the dusty, naked madman who frequented the area and sometimes dug around in the filthy gutter looking for scraps of food knew how to dash across Ring Road.

Since Darko was on his motorcycle and no department vehicle was available, he had given Safo some cash for the relatively short taxi ride from Headquarters to the bank. Transportation for Ghana's under-resourced police officers was a devil of a problem. Small police stations had no official vehicles at all, and even CID Headquarters had few to go around. In most cases, the police expected victims or their families to chip in for transportation costs or provide a vehicle. Darko and everyone else knew the system was being abused, however. What officers requested for "transportation" had become grossly inflated. The repercussions to a civilian not paying up were simple: foot-dragging on the case. Although Darko accepted offers of cash for transportation, he never demanded it, which was a source of annoyance to colleagues who considered him a saboteur of sorts.

He arrived before her and chatted for a few minutes with the aging watchman who had been at StanChart for as long as Darko could recall. The heat drew sweat off Darko's brow like a river delta. The cooling rains would arrive in another month, but for now, the temperatures were ferocious. He left the watchman for the cool of the bank's interior.

The baby-faced receptionist looked almost too young to work.

"Do you have a Michael Amalba?" Darko asked.

"Yes, please. Mr. Amalba is upstairs," the receptionist said. "Have a seat and I will call him. Your name, please?"

Darko told him, adding that he was waiting for someone else before talking to Michael.

Safo arrived perspiring. "Sorry, sir. The taxi broke down, so I ran the rest of the way."

"Sit down and catch your breath," Darko told her, signaling to the receptionist that he was ready to meet Michael.

The receptionist called, and Michael came down after about five minutes. He wore dark slacks, a white shirt, and plain black tie. He was shorter and fairer than his brother. His shaved scalp did little to hide the bald runway at the top of his head. Maybe he was Peter's half-brother or a close cousin whom Peter called "brother," which was common in Ghana. Darko introduced himself and Safo.

"You are here regarding what, please?" Michael asked warily, once he'd learned they were police officers.

"Can we talk in private, sir?" Darko said.

"Yes. Please come upstairs."

Michael's office was as sparse as the Sahara Desert. He sat behind his desk. Darko and Safo took seats on the other side.

"Your brother is Peter Amalba?" Darko asked.

"Yes, sir. Well, he's my half-brother. Is something wrong?"

"You haven't heard about his arrest?"

"Oh, no." Michael pulled back. "What has he done?"

"He assaulted a bishop yesterday at a Power of God Ministry Church service in La Paz."

"Bishop Clem Howard-Mills?"

"Yes. You know the bishop?"

"Not personally, but I know *of* him. Was he hurt? The bishop, I mean."

"He sustained a wound to the neck, but I understand he's recovering."

"*Awurade*," Peter said. "Who arrested Peter, please?"

"I did," Darko said. "I happened to be at the church."

Michael rested his brow in his palm as he closed his eyes and shook his head. "I've been afraid of something like this happening."

"What do you mean?"

Michael looked up. "For the past two months, Peter has been acting erratically, losing his temper often, getting angry about even the smallest things. He even got sacked from his job last week because people couldn't work with him anymore."

"He was working at a Max Mart, correct?"

"Yes, please." Michael shot a glum glance at Darko. "I don't think I can even tell my parents in the village back home that Peter has done this. It's a disgrace."

Darko waited a moment. "That doesn't make it any easier to bring up another matter," he went on. "Does the name Katherine Vanderpuye mean anything to you?"

"Yes, please," Michael said, fidgeting. "I read she was a victim of a terrible murder over the weekend."

"Yes," Darko said, squinting at Michael. "Are you okay? You're sweating."

"I'm all right," Michael said with a nervous laugh. He wiped his forehead with a handkerchief. "I think I might be coming down with a fever."

"I'm sorry to hear that. But returning to what I was saying, Peter was spotted around the scene of Katherine's murder—at her house, that is."

Michael looked startled and confused. "Meaning? Please, I don't understand."

"Katherine was killed between the hours of eleven on Friday night and five in the morning, Saturday. Peter was witnessed standing in the vicinity of her home around six-thirty Saturday morning."

"He was?" Michael said, surprised.

"Yes. Furthermore, Peter claims he went to Katherine's house at approximately three in the morning."

Michael appeared mystified. "But that isn't possible, Inspector. Peter was at home with me the whole night."

"Wait a minute," Darko said. "I want to be sure we're talking about the same night. I'm referring to the Friday and Saturday that have just passed—the twenty-eighth and twenty-ninth. Only two and three days ago."

Michael nodded. "Yes, that's what I mean too. Peter went to

sleep on Friday night before I did. Saturday morning I left at five-thirty to get to the bank early because now we open half days on Saturdays, and he was still in bed."

"Are you sure?"

Michael laughed. "Yes, Inspector, I'm positive. We sleep in the same room, not in a mansion where we can come and go without each other knowing. I can't afford a big house. Not in Accra."

Yes, Peter could have made it to Kate's house by the time Christine arrived, Darko thought, but he couldn't have been there at *three* when he claimed to have seen Bishop Howard-Mills. As Darko had suspected, Peter must have made up the story, borrowing the details of the machete and Esi's arrival from news reports.

But Darko needed to be sure. "Michael," he said, "is there someone else who can confirm you and your brother were home Friday night?"

Michael turned down the corners of his mouth with regret. "No, please. I'm very sorry for all this. Sometimes my brother fabricates."

"Any idea why he does that?"

Michael made a gesture of resignation. "Seems like all his life he's battled with his self-image and tried to make himself the center of attention whenever he can, and at times he does that by making up stories."

"Are you aware of his having an affair with Katherine Vanderpuye?"

Michael shook his head. "Peter never mentioned her to me. Is that what he told you?"

"Yes. He said they were in love with each other."

Michael sighed. "I'm embarrassed to keep apologizing, but that's another story he's telling you."

Darko's attention had strayed to the pictures on Michael's desk, about the only personalized item in the room. "Who are the other people in the photo with you?"

"My ex-wife and our daughter."

Darko saw a look of sadness pass across Michael's face. A messy divorce, no doubt. Darko thought of Katherine and Solomon.

"Your daughter is pretty," Darko said.

A smile lit up Michael's face. "She's the apple of my eye."

"Do you get to see her?"

"Two weekends in a month," Michael said.

Darko couldn't imagine seeing his boys so infrequently. He would wither and die. "You didn't see your daughter this weekend?"

"No, sir," Michael said. "So, please, what will happen to Peter now?"

"He'll be arraigned tomorrow morning for his attack on Bishop Howard-Mills," Darko said.

Michael's eyes beseeched Darko. "Please, I know Peter has done wrong, but he's not well. Please take care of him."

"I'll do whatever I can. But you should understand that once Peter is in prison custody, I'll have nothing to do with his case until it comes up for trial—which could take months or even years."

Michael became even more dejected. "Yes, sir."

"I'm sorry to bring you such bad news, Mr. Amalba." Darko stood up, and Safo followed. Michael saw them to the top of the stairs. As Darko was about to descend, he turned to Michael. "Do you go to church, Mr. Amalba?"

He smiled. "Yes, please. Methodist."

"Ah," Darko said. "Not one of the charismatics?"

"No, please. Peter was fond of them, but I like a quieter, more traditional service."

"Thank you, Mr. Amalba."

CHAPTER TWENTY-THREE

"WHAT DO YOU THINK?" Darko asked Safo as they left the bank.

"It must be that Peter is lying about what he saw," Safo said. "He wants to frame the bishop and justify assaulting him."

"Probably," Darko said, watching a *tro-tro* belching black exhaust as it sped by on Ring Road. "But how can we double-check Michael's story that he was home on Friday night?"

"Do you doubt him, sir?"

"I'm undecided," Darko admitted. "What we can do is go back to Peter tomorrow morning to challenge him with what his brother told us. If he breaks down and admits to the lie, that will settle it."

It was only about two in the afternoon, but Safo looked drained. Darko sent her home and told her to mentally and physically prepare for a full schedule the next day. He wasn't about to pass judgment on her yet, but he was concerned about her apparent fragility.

Darko was about to return to the office when a thought came to him. He hopped back on his motorcycle and headed in the opposite direction from CID, going through the overpass onto Ring Road West and right on Awudome Road, where the cemetery flanked him on either side.

From the Awudome roundabout, he got on Bubuashie Road. Sly's school, St. Theresa's, was on Darko's right, not that far from the Dawsons' favorite *kelewele* spot. Darko made a left and pulled up on the dusty shoulder of the road, where he parked. He had a clear view of the school and the kids as they streamed out at the end of the school day in their sharp red and yellow uniforms. Darko kept a look out for Sly but didn't see him anywhere.

Darko walked up Bubuashie several meters and turned right on Palace Road. Sly was standing near a food kiosk talking to two other boys Darko had never seen before. They were older than Sly, probably mid-teens, and they weren't in school uniform. One of them, a lanky boy astride a late-model motorcycle, had spiky hair, a T-shirt with the image of soccer superstar Ronaldo, burgundy jeans, and loafers without socks. The other sported his cap backward and wore a diamond earring and a thick gold necklace with a jewel-encrusted cross dangling over his partly exposed chest.

Darko ducked behind another kiosk close to him and walked along the bumpy terrain at the rear of several other retailers—a clothing store, an MTN phone card store, and a woman selling roasted plantain and groundnuts.

He appeared on the other side close to Sly, who jumped and froze when he saw his father. The other two boys stared at Darko.

"Who are these boys?" he demanded.

"My friends," Sly stammered, shocked at Darko's magical appearance.

The boys looked suspiciously from Sly to his father and took a couple of wary steps back. Darko asked them their names. "Where do you go to school?" he demanded.

They muttered something about Kaneshie High.

"Then why are you not there?" Darko asked them.

"Please, we are closed today," the lanky one called Nii Kwei said, his eyes looking away.

Darko pulled him close to him. "You're lying," he said. "I just passed by there, and the school is open." Darko sniffed Nii Kwei's shirt. "You've been smoking *wee*."

The boy bowed his head, squirming in physical and mental

discomfort under Darko's glare. Darko grabbed the other boy by the top of his shirt and yanked him alongside Nii Kwei.

"Listen to me," Darko said, switching to Ga, the boys' mother tongue. "If you want to be bad boys and spoil your lives instead of going to school and growing up to be real men, then it's your choice, and I don't care. But what I care about is that you stay away from Sly. I won't allow you to spoil *him*. Do you understand?"

"Yes, please," they whispered.

"Look at me when you speak. Don't you know how to respect your elders?"

They met Darko's glare only barely.

"If I catch you with Sly one more time," Darko said, sharpening his tone, "you'll regret the day you were born."

He took his ID out of his pocket and showed them his badge. "What is this? Read it. Nii Kwei, can you read?"

"Yes, please."

"Then read it."

The boy managed to get through it.

"Do you know what that means?" Darko said. "It means I can arrest you and put you in jail. In fact, I can take you to jail right now. You think I don't know what you do? You're *Sakawa* boys. Isn't that true?"

Nii Kwei was scared, but tried not to show it. "No, please," he murmured. "I beg you, sir."

"Go," Darko said. "Get out of here before I change my mind."

He shoved them away and watched them leave. Darko would remember them, and he had a feeling he hadn't seen the last of Nii Kwei and his pal.

Sly had turned away, his head bowed. Darko put his hand on the boy's shoulder, and Sly flinched.

"Come with me," Darko said, escorting him around the back of a stall, where they would be unobserved. "What's wrong, Sly, eh?"

Sly didn't answer. His bottom lip was quivering.

"Your mother and I are caring for you and Hosiah in the best way possible. We are not perfect, but we are trying, and we want something in return: good behavior. Do you understand?"

"Yes, Daddy."

"Only the day before yesterday, I warned you that hanging around these kinds of guys is bad behavior, and you promised me you would not. But here you are again. If you continue like this, your schoolwork is going to suffer, and you'll start to fail. You know you have to maintain a certain level to stay in St. Theresa, and once you fail, neither your mother nor I can save you. You realize that?"

"Yes, Daddy. I'm sorry."

"You said that the last time. What is it you like about these boys? Their clothes?"

Sly shrugged.

That meant, yes in Darko's estimation. "How and when did you meet them?"

"One day when I came here to buy *Kofi Broke Man*, they were also buying some, and they started to talk to me. They asked me if I was good at computers, and I said yes. They told me I could learn more, and they could teach me how to make money from them."

Darko had feared as much. The boys' clothes and possessions were an easy giveaway. They were Internet scammers popularly known as *Sakawa* boys, in reference to their use of so-called magical powers to render their bilking schemes successful.

"Do you know how they make money from computers, Sly?"

"No, Daddy."

"They get online and send emails to people in Europe, the US, and Canada pretending to be someone they're not. Sometimes they'll pretend to be an American who can't get out of Ghana because they've lost their money or passport, and need help. Other times they say they have some land or gold to invest in. All kinds of schemes. And people send money to them. That's how they can buy all those clothes and jewelry. You see what I mean?"

Sly nodded.

"But what they're doing is illegal," Darko continued. "We have a Cybercrime Unit at my office now, and CID has started to go after these people. When we catch them, they can go to prison for a long time."

Sly's expression took on some panic.

"Now, do you want to use computers for the right things, or do you want to join those guys in prison? Because if I or anyone else catches you engaged in cybercrime, you're going straight to jail. And if the judge sentences you to twenty years, I'll ask for fifty. Mama and Hosiah and I will visit you in prison once a month and bring you a little food if they allow it. Okay?"

"Yes," Sly stammered, his eyes wide. "I mean, *no*!"

"Now, we are going to talk to Sister Aboagye about this."

Sly looked as if he might die. The strict, upstanding headmistress of his school was the last person on earth he wanted to see right now.

AN HOUR LATER, Darko left the office of Sister Aboagye with a chastened Sly. The arrangement for the next three months was he would stay after school for about an hour doing his homework outside the staff office until either Darko or Christine arrived to take him home. Teachers and administrators went in and out of the office all the time and would be able to watch over him. Darko felt he had nipped his son's potential pitfall in the bud, but he knew he would face many more challenges in the course of bringing up his two boys in a world gone mad.

CHAPTER TWENTY-FOUR

THAT EVENING, DARKO MADE Sly recount to his mother what had happened earlier in the day with the *Sakawa* boys. Darko interjected here and there to fill in details Sly left out. Christine listened neutrally, but when her son had finished the narrative, she asked him what five lessons he had learned from the events of the day. Sly did extraordinarily well and came up with three. Frankly, Darko wasn't sure he could have come up with all five, but then his wife was a primary school teacher.

In Darko's estimation, the mental rite of passage Sly was enduring was far more effective than a beating. When Darko was a boy, the pain of his father's whippings obfuscated the original rebuke.

"Now, go take your shower and get to bed," Christine told her son curtly. He left looking dejected. Darko and Christine looked at each other.

"You think we've cured him?" he said.

"I'm ninety-five percent sure," Christine responded. "The remaining five will come over the next three months as we watch him carefully, and he stops hanging out with the delinquents. What made you go to check up on him?"

"I just had a feeling something might be up."

"Your intuition still works, I see."

"Thanks." He grinned. "Sometimes."

The lights went off as they had been expecting, more or less, since they had just enjoyed about twelve uninterrupted hours of power. Darko and Christine continued with the conversation as if nothing out of the ordinary had happened—which, in fact, was the case.

"I need to ask you something," Darko said. "Is it possible Katherine was having an affair with Peter Amalba?"

He couldn't see her surprise, but he could sense it.

"*No*," she said emphatically. "That's ridiculous. Where is this coming from?"

"Peter Amalba claims he and Kate were in love and planned to get married."

"What!" She sucked her teeth dismissively. "That is a bald-faced lie. It's not even conceivable. Kate went to work every day, getting out at what, five or six? And then she went home to make dinner. She was home by the time Solomon arrived. Where is the time to have an affair with this madman Amalba? I'm surprised you're even suggesting that."

"I'm not."

"Okay, good," she said huffily.

An awkward silence hung briefly.

Darko cleared his throat. "Amalba said he had gone to 'watch over' Kate the morning she died, and he saw Bishop Howard-Mills in the area around her home."

Darko told Christine about his meeting with Michael. "He thinks Peter is mentally unbalanced."

"All the more reason why he might have killed Kate," Christine said. "He had delusions about her being in love with him, and when she rejected him, Amalba butchered her to death. That's all. It's not complicated."

"But Michael said Peter was in bed all night Friday until at least five-thirty."

"He could be covering for his brother," Christine said.

"Yes, he could," Darko agreed. "By the way, do you still have a savings account at the Ring Road Central StanChart?"

"Yes, why?"

"The name 'Michael Amalba' doesn't ring a bell? Maybe you've dealt with him as one of the branch managers?"

"I'm pretty sure I haven't. I only go to that bank occasionally to deposit a little bit of money, so I don't deal with upper management there. I know one of the female account managers, though. A Mary something. I can check if I still have her number in my contacts. Anything special I should ask her?"

"Find out if Michael has a close friend at work," Darko said. "Someone who might be able to confirm Michael was at home Friday night and Saturday morning. Not very likely, but worth a try."

"Sure," Christine said. "I'll look into it." She sounded happy to take on a little bit of investigation of her own.

"Oh, I forgot to tell you," Darko said. "I started training a new detective today."

"Is he from HQ or one of the districts?"

"It's a she, not a he."

"Really!" she said, surprised.

"Yes. Lance Corporal Mabel Safo. She transferred from Kumasi."

"It's good to hear there's a female detective for a change. Is she promising?"

"Too early to say. She's very young and will need to toughen up a bit."

Darko related to Christine how fragile Safo had appeared. "And she called me 'Daddy' once," he added. "Instead of 'boss' or 'sir.' I found that strange."

"But Ghanaians do that all the time." Christine pointed out.

"Not in a formal police setting," Darko disagreed. "I've never heard a junior officer address a senior one that way. She picked the wrong authority figure—it seemed like a slip of the tongue."

"Maybe." Christine giggled. "Or you could just be getting old."

"Oh, I see how it is. Getting old? Is that what you said?"

In the gloom, she saw him get up and come toward her. She squealed as she tried to get away, but it was too late. He piled on top of her and began to nuzzle her neck, one of her ticklish spots. She shrieked with uncontrollable laughter as she begged him to stop.

"Not until you apologize for calling me old."

Unable to speak and practically wheezing for breath, she shook her head in refusal.

"Okay, then," he said, beginning to tickle her in the ribs as well. "More torture for you."

"Stop, *stop*!" she gasped. "I apologize."

"That's better." He had become aroused, and she could feel it.

"Not now, Darko," she said. "I'm dirty and sweaty from today. I'm going for my shower, and then you go for yours."

"And after that?"

"Maybe."

IN THE MORNING before he left for work, Darko got a call from Sergeant Mustapha in the charge office.

"What's going on?" Darko asked.

"Please, sir," Mustapha said, "suspect Peter Amalba has attacked a fellow prisoner."

SAFO WAS ALREADY at CID by the time Darko arrived, which impressed him. She and a group of other officers crowded into the charge office to gawk at the spectacle. Darko weaved his way to the front counter, where Oppong was questioning a frazzled Sergeant Mustapha.

"How could you allow this to happen?" Oppong demanded.

"*Mepa wo kyew*," Mustapha pleaded, "I'm sorry, sir. I didn't see anything, sir. He must have gotten the ballpoint pen while we were booking him."

"What happened?" Darko asked, lifting the barrier to cross to the inside of the counter.

Oppong gestured to a cluster of people kneeling on the floor around a man who was lying on his back. "Amalba attacked an inmate and stabbed him in the neck with a ballpoint pen."

Darko's eyebrows shot up. "Seriously, sir?"

"Seriously."

The victim, whose name was Chinery, was a small man of about twenty-two. Lying motionless in his underpants, he stared up at the ceiling with an expression Darko had seen before: the fear of impending death. Projecting from Chinery's neck was a quarter of the deeply embedded ballpoint pen, which flicked rhythmically with his heartbeat like a stuck lever. Blood was seeping from the wound into a towel someone was holding to the inmate's neck.

A female officer with nursing experience had arrived just in time to stop someone from pulling out the pen. She crouched beside Chinery, speaking Ga in a soothing tone to assure him that help was on its way. Darko thought it should have been there already. The brand new police hospital was only two minutes away. For now, the ballpoint was acting as a temporary plug in whatever artery it had penetrated, but the inmate could die at any instant if a vessel in him blew open.

The jail area was in the rear of the charge office. Two cells existed, Number One being the larger. Like practically all jails in Ghana, this one was overcrowded and rusted with age. The time it took to transfer suspects over to the custody of the prisons, which were also filled beyond capacity, was excessive. Inmates languished for ages before they ever saw the inside of a courtroom.

From where Darko stood, he could see the faces of prisoners pressed against the bars as they watched the spectacle and provided a running commentary for the benefit of their fellow jailbirds in the rear. When the incident had occurred, Mustapha and an armed guard had removed Amalba and handcuffed him prone to the leg of a substantial table at the far end of the room.

"Let's talk to Amalba now," Oppong said to Darko.

From the depth of one of the cells, an inmate shouted out in Twi what roughly meant, "When you pack us like sardines, we turn rotten."

The other prisoners cheered and hooted in accord.

"*Heh!*" Mustapha yelled, already stressed. "Shut up! *Kwaseasem.*"

The prisoners guffawed but quieted down.

Darko beckoned to Safo to join him and Oppong. Darko

wanted her to experience the episode in full. They looked down at Amalba.

"Why did you stab Chinery?" Oppong asked him.

"He is evil," Amalba said craning his neck upward. "He molested a child."

"Who told you he molested a child?"

"He did," Amalba said, gazing steadily at Oppong. "He confessed it to me last night."

"What do you mean, he confessed it to you?"

"I preached to him, and he came to repent of his sins. '*Repent and be baptized, every one of you, in the name of Jesus Christ for the forgiveness of your sins. And you will receive the gift of the Holy Spirit.*' The words of the apostle Peter, my namesake."

"Who gave you the authority to preach?" Oppong demanded.

"It comes naturally to me."

"You convinced him of what you were saying, and then you stabbed him?" Oppong said in disbelief. "What kind of evil man are you?"

"I obeyed what the Lord told me."

"You're saying God talks to you?"

Amalba nodded, a smile hovering on his lips. "Yes, please."

Darko studied him, trying to discern perhaps a wild look in Amalba's eyes—anything to substantiate that he was crazy, but Darko found nothing except a calmness—even a confidence—in the prisoner's demeanor.

Darko, Oppong, and Safo withdrew to another corner of the room.

"He's a madman," Oppong said.

Darko was doubtful. "I'm not sure, sir. I believe he's pretending to be."

"I think it's difficult to feign madness," Oppong disagreed. "In any case, the point is moot. In the end, it's not for us to decide. We'll ask the judge tomorrow at the arraignment if we can admit Amalba to the psychiatric unit at the police hospital under armed guard for an evaluation."

The ambulance finally arrived with two technicians and a stretcher between them. They seemed unfazed by Chinery's condition, and in fact it seemed to Darko that they were taking their time over something that required due haste. At last they were gone, carting the suspect away with an armed officer. The spectators dissipated in turn.

"What about Amalba and his whereabouts Friday night?" Oppong asked Darko.

"His brother, Michael, says both of them slept at home overnight, in which case Peter could not have been at the murder scene before about six-thirty. But we still need to check the accuracy of Michael's statement. We're working on that."

"Come on, Dawson," Oppong urged. "Tie up these loose ends. Maybe someone is mixing up times, or Michael could be lying for his brother, and so on. Have you spoken to Bishop Howard-Mills yet?"

"No, sir," Darko said. "We're about to do that right now."

CHAPTER TWENTY-FIVE

By the time Darko and Safo got to Korle Bu Hospital, where Howard-Mills had been a patient on Sunday, the bishop had signed himself out. Darko and Safo proceeded to the bishop's church on Kotei Robertson Street in North Kaneshie.

The buildings comprising his Qedesh compound resembled three enormous immovable ships at port, all white and spotless in the scorching sun. The windows were circular with dark, robust latticework that invited one to peep in. Perhaps that's what Howard-Mills wanted.

Darko got directions to the bishop's office from a passerby, and he and Safo walked across a grassy area with burgundy bougainvillea bushes. Several people sat on benches underneath trees that provided welcome shade. It was the best approximation of a park Darko had seen, and Accra needed more like it.

They approached the smallest of the three buildings. It was open on all sides, unlike the other two. At earsplitting levels, a loudspeaker blasted as a pastor—not Howard-Mills—stood on the stage and chanted a prayer. The pews were less than half full; after all, it was a Tuesday afternoon. In the evening, and even more so that weekend, the space would be packed.

"*Jee*-sus-uh," the pastor was growling with ponderous breath that made Darko's eardrums flutter, "Son of *God*-uh, teach us the *way*-uh, banish *Sa*-tan-uh, take away tempt-*ation*-uh—"

"Have you ever been to this church?" Darko asked Safo.

"Only once, sir."

"Have you met Bishop Howard-Mills?"

She shook her head. "I've seen him preach, but never met him. You can't go to him unless you can afford his consultation fees."

"How much is that roughly?"

"It can be up to eight hundred *cedis*."

Darko whistled. Pricey. He paused to take a good look inside the church. Shrubbery and vines festooned the top rafters, while a massive bouquet decorated the rear of the stage, where, behind the growling pastor stood a man in a dark robe speaking rapidly and quietly into another microphone. It sounded like gibberish.

"What is he saying?" Darko asked Safo.

"He's speaking in tongues," she explained.

In the pews, members of the congregation walked back and forth, talking rapidly and gesticulating to themselves as if conversing with unseen beings in some private world.

"Them too?" he asked.

"Yes, please," she said. "'And there appeared unto them cloven tongues like as of fire, and it sat upon each of them. And they were all filled with the Holy Ghost, and began to speak with other tongues, as the Spirit gave them utterance.' Acts two, verse three."

Darko was impressed. "You know your Bible. Can you also speak in tongues?"

"At times. When the Holy Spirit enables me to do so."

"I see," Darko said, studying Safo for a moment. Christine was a believer in God and Christ, but she wasn't in Safo's league—not even close.

They continued beyond the building and found the bishop's office behind it. Safo knocked on a door the same color as the latticework in the windows, and they entered. John Papafio was at the desk in the room and rose when he saw them.

"Inspector Dawson," he said with a broad smile. "You are welcome."

"Good afternoon, John," Darko said. "This is my partner, Detective Lance Corporal Safo."

"Afternoon, madam. You seem familiar. Have I seen you here before?"

"You might have," Safo said. "I've attended one of Bishop Howard-Mills's services before."

"That's great," John said. "Welcome to both of you."

"We went to the hospital looking for Bishop Howard-Mills," Darko said, "but we learned he had already left the hospital."

"Yes, sir," John said. "He has already returned to work, praise God."

"He's okay?" Darko asked, surprised at the rapid recovery.

"He is blessed, thank you, Inspector. Please have a seat. I'll check if he can see you now."

The office was compact and air-conditioned. John's small, busy desk sat against the wall. He opened the door next to a file cabinet and disappeared into the adjacent room.

Safo sat, but Darko remained on his feet to look up at the large, framed photographs of Bishop Howard-Mills looking down with a smile or in action preaching. In one picture, the bishop was shaking hands with the current president, and in another, he was presenting a giant check to a Christian charity.

John came back into the room. "Please, Bishop is available to speak with you now."

"Thank you," Darko said, beckoning to Safo, who rose and followed him. John held the door open for them and left discreetly.

Howard-Mills's office was even colder than the anteroom. His polished desk was broad and long. He had more large photos hanging on the wall, and Darko was startled to see one of him shaking hands with Barack Obama when the American president had visited Ghana. Apparently, Howard-Mills had been one of a long line of dignitaries who had met him. It indicated the bishop's political connections.

Howard-Mills got up from his chair behind the desk with a wince as he did so. He had a large bandage on the left side of his neck.

"Bishop?" Darko said, meeting him halfway to shake hands. "Are you okay?"

"I'm well, Chief Inspector," he said with a smile, albeit anemic. "Thank you for asking."

Darko introduced Safo and was certain he saw her curtsey slightly. Howard-Mills offered them two comfortable chairs to the side of the room and pulled up a third.

"I'm surprised you're back at work so soon, Bishop," Darko said.

"The doctors wanted to keep me longer," Howard-Mills said, "but I have a flock of congregants to attend. God has called me to do this work, and I cannot shirk it just because of an unfortunate incident."

Darko smiled. "If you don't mind my saying, sir, I think it was more than an unfortunate incident. Anyway, I'm happy to see you are recovering."

"Physically," the bishop said. "Emotionally I'm still feeling the pain of dear Katherine's death."

"Understandably," Darko said.

"And Mr. Amalba?" Howard-Mills asked. "How is he?"

"We questioned him today," Darko said. "I'm not sure how sane he is." He didn't go on to mention the attack at the police station Amalba had unleashed.

"I have been praying for him," the bishop said. "May God have mercy upon him. I forgive him for what he did."

"Did you know him before the attack, Bishop?"

"Never met him in my life," Howard-Mills said, shaking his head decisively.

"He claims to have seen you on the morning of Kate's murder."

"Where? When?"

"Around three in the morning, coming from the direction of Kate's house."

Howard-Mills at first appeared startled, and then grave. "I'm sorry, but he's mistaken. If he saw someone, it wasn't me. At that time, I had finished my all-night prayer vigil at Baden Powell Memorial Hall on High Street." He got up and went to his desk, returning with a glossy pamphlet, which he handed to Darko. "Here's the evidence."

Next to a dramatic photograph of Howard-Mills was wording in bright red:

A NIGHT OF PROPHECY, PRAYER & PRAISE
Friday 28 April
At the Baden Powell Memorial Hall, High Street

The Night GOD declares "NO" To The Enemy
BANISH INIQUITY
BANISH WICKEDNESS
BANISH SORCERY

"I think you will have more than enough witnesses to say I was there the whole night long," the bishop.

"May I keep this?" Darko asked.

"By all means, Inspector."

"And I will need one or two names of people who can confirm your presence at the vigil all night."

"But of course. You can even start with John, my assistant—he always accompanies me to the events. You can also ask Reverend Patrick Atiemo, the one you saw preaching as you were coming. He was with the salvation team as well."

"What happens exactly during an all-night vigil?" Darko asked.

Howard-Mills laced his fingers. "It depends. If it is a prayer vigil, then it's all about salvation and coming to know the Lord. If you already know Him, then you will be brought closer. If it is a *deliverance* vigil, we concentrate on casting out evil spirits and demons from members who come forward."

"Who is 'we'?"

"I usually work with two or three pastors," Howard-Mills explained. "Reverend Atiemo, for instance. We take turns in leading the congregation through the vigil. It's exhausting, so one person cannot take the whole night—at least, I certainly can't. I normally take a break between about one and three, and then we finish up at around four, four-fifteen."

"You still have a congregation at that hour?"

"Yes. Surprising, isn't it? But they come. God has no time limit for redemption."

"I suppose not," Darko said. "Where do you take your break, Bishop?"

"The hosting venue typically provides us with a room or lounge where we can relax, have something to eat or drink, and so on," Howard-Mills explained. "Especially Baden Powell Hall, where we were Friday night. They are very accommodating. I will be holding another vigil tomorrow night at Independence Square. Would you like to come?"

Darko had seen videos of priests "casting out demons," but never witnessed it in person. It should be interesting. "I would, yes," he said.

"I believe John has one last pass to the VIP area near the stage."

"Thank you very much, Bishop. I appreciate that."

"Always welcome."

"Bishop, what time did Gifty call you on Saturday morning, please?"

Howard-Mills smiled slightly. "She has revealed herself as the mystery caller?"

"You could say that."

"Gifty is one of my most active congregants and a lovely lady. She called me at around eight or so. I said I would go to Kate's house immediately."

In the periphery of his vision, Darko saw Safo's head slightly bowed as she unconsciously rubbed the palm of her left hand with the thumb of her right. He would prefer she watch a witness or suspect closely, but he suspected she felt awed by the bishop.

"I've known Kate's family for many years," Howard-Mills continued. "I felt a special connection to her."

"I understand she and her husband, Solomon, sought your counseling during their marital turmoil."

Howard-Mills put his palms flat on his thighs. "That's true, but more Kate than her husband. He was not as comfortable sharing his feelings as Kate was. After a while, he stopped coming for the sessions, and Kate made appointments with me on her own."

"Several times a week, a month?"

"Probably no more than twice in a month," Howard-Mills said, getting up again to his desk. "I can tell you exactly how often." He looked at his laptop screen, which was the latest MacBook. Darko would have liked to have owned one himself, but the price of Apple products in Ghana was far beyond his reach.

"In April, I saw her twice," the bishop said. In March, three times. February, twice; January, just once." He returned to sit with the two detectives.

"And you always saw her here in your office?" Darko asked.

"Yes—or in the church itself sometimes if there wasn't a service or other activity."

"Which could not have been very often," Darko observed. "You have a packed schedule of services."

"You're right, Inspector."

"But you never met with Kate outside of the church setting?"

The bishop shook his head. "No, not at all."

"This is in confidence, of course, Bishop," Darko said, leaning forward, "but since you knew the couple well, is it possible Solomon might have—"

"Murdered Katherine?" Howard-Mills finished. "It's okay; I'm not afraid of the question, Inspector. Anything is possible, but honestly, Inspector, as bad as things became between Kate and Solomon, I can't see it in his heart to commit such an act. He was stressed, but not murderous."

"Anyone else come to mind?"

"Not as such, Mr. Dawson."

Darko stood up. "Thank you, Bishop."

"You're very welcome, Inspector," Howard-Mills said. He looked at Safo with a sparkle in his eyes. "Miss Safo, you are as quiet as a little mouse!"

She smiled, twisting and squirming like a fondled puppy.

Howard-Mills switched to Twi, joking with Safo as he told her she was attractive, but now it was time to get tough as a policewoman. Darko noted the bishop's effect on Safo, who giggled shyly.

"You look somehow familiar," Howard-Mills continued with her. "Have you attended my church?"

"Yes, please," she said.

"Aha—I thought so! Are you happy with it?"

"I am," she said, beaming.

"Well," Howard-Mills said to Darko, "let's go outside and I'll ask John to give you an invite."

He held open the door, and Darko didn't miss the bishop touching the small of Safo's back lightly as she followed Darko through the doorway. He loves women and women want *him*, Darko thought with sudden clarity. Had Kate fallen in love with the bishop? Where had they been seeing each other, and when had it started?

Darko and Safo hadn't gotten very far out of the bishop's office when he stopped. "Wait here one second," he said to her.

Darko trotted back, knocked on John's door and went in. Howard-Mills had returned to his quarters.

"Yes, sir?" John said.

"I forgot to ask you," Darko said, "when Mrs. Vanderpuye used to come to counseling with the bishop, did he shut the door or leave it open?"

"Yes, please."

"Which one—open or closed?"

"Sorry, Inspector," John said in some embarrassment. "Closed. The sessions are always private. They are none of my business, so unless I am not here, Bishop Howard-Mills keeps the door closed."

If what John was telling him was true, anything could have been going on in the bishop's office behind the closed door.

"Did you ever accidentally overhear any of their conversations?" Darko asked John bluntly.

"Oh, no—not at all," John said with a reassuring smile.

A fine vibration, like an electrical thrill, spread over Darko's left palm. John was lying, but it wasn't particularly surprising. Why would he reveal anything confidential from within this office? Still, the lie pushed him up one rung on the ladder of suspicion.

"Did you attend the vigil at the Baden Powell Hall?" Darko asked.

"Yes, please. Always."

"And you were there all night, John?"

He seemed puzzled. "Of course, Inspector. Me, Bishop Howard-Mills, Reverend Atiemo—we were all there."

"No one left the venue at any time?" Darko persisted.

"No, sir," John said, appearing uncomfortable. "How can any of us be absent during the vigil?"

"The bishop took a rest between one and three in the morning, isn't that so?"

"Yes, but he was there all the time," John asserted. "He normally stays in the lounge area and has some refreshments. He likes coffee."

Coffee, Darko thought. The latest craze among rich Ghanaians. "Thank you, John," he said. "You have been very helpful. Have a nice day."

DARKO AND SAFO waited about forty-five minutes for Reverend Atiemo's service to end, then watched as the reverend went up to the stage, took off his jacket, and chatted with the choir, shaking hands and hugging a few of the female members.

"Let's go," Darko said to Safo.

They mounted the stage and Atiemo turned to them. "Can I help you?" He was quite young, athletic, and lean with dark skin, lively eyes and an artfully trimmed beard. His clerical shirt was still wet with perspiration from his energetic sermon.

"Reverend Atiemo?" Darko said. "I'm Detective Chief Inspector Dawson. My partner, Lance Corporal Safo. We're investigating the death of Katherine Vanderpuye."

Atiemo's expression saddened at once. "What a terrible crime," he said, shaking his head. "Impossible to fathom."

"Can we talk with you about it for a moment?" Darko asked.

"Let's have a seat over there," Atiemo said, gesturing to the now empty choir chairs. He pulled three of them out to form a triangle.

"We believe Katherine was murdered sometime between eleven last Friday night and five Saturday morning," Darko said.

"I see," Atiemo said, his brow furrowed. "And the watchman as well, I understand?"

Darko nodded. "Yes. Katherine hosted a *bussell* last Wednesday night, correct?"

"Yes, sir."

"That was the last time you saw her?"

"Yes. She was obviously still carrying the burden stemming from her discord with her husband, but I sensed she was healing, leaving some of the pain behind."

"You felt deeply for her," Darko said.

"We all did," the reverend said.

"Any idea who might have wanted her dead?"

Atiemo sighed. "I can't even imagine that, Inspector."

"Can you try, please?" Darko pressed him. "Someone who might have hated her enough to kill her?"

The reverend shook his head. "Only the Lord knows who has committed this heinous act. I pray that He leads you to the culprit."

Convenient answer, Darko thought. "What about anyone in the congregation, Reverend? Did you ever witness a negative interaction between Katherine and a fellow church attendee?"

"Never," Atiemo said firmly. "Not Madam Katherine. She was a goodhearted Christian woman. Always kind to others."

"Peter Amalba, the man who attacked the bishop—have you ever met him or seen him in the congregation, Reverend?"

"Not that I recall, sir. I have a good memory for faces, so I think I would remember."

"Thank you, Reverend." Darko stood up to leave. "Oh, one other thing. Did you attend the vigil last Friday at the Baden Powell Hall?"

"Yes, please. I always accompany the bishop. I took over from him at one A.M. for about three hours, and then we finished up together."

"In that three-hour interval, then," Darko said, "you didn't see either Mr. Howard-Mills or Mr. Papafio?"

Atiemo shrugged. "No, sir, but they are always there backstage—they may be resting, but they are vigilant. Why do you ask, please?"

"Just routine inquiries, Reverend. Thank you for your time."

"WHAT DO YOU think?" Darko asked Safo once they were out of earshot and on the way back to the car park.

"Seems like they all have an alibi," she said.

"But it's a shared alibi," Darko said. "If it's good for one, it's good for all. Remember the bishop, John Papafio, and Reverend Atiemo are in a way a family, and family members stick up for each other. They will lie to your face as easily as breathing oxygen. What I've learned in this business, Safo, is that it's best to assume everyone is lying until proven otherwise. John Papafio has already lied to me at least once."

Safo raised her eyebrows. "Please, how do you know? What did he say?"

Darko related his conversation with John, but didn't elaborate on how exactly he had detected John's lie. Except with close family, Darko did not talk about his synesthesia. No would understand, anyway.

"So," Darko continued, "we have to find someone neutral to all parties who can confirm their whereabouts."

"Yes, sir." Safo hesitated. "But maybe none of them killed Katherine, sir."

"That is true," Darko agreed. "That's why we have to talk the person closest to Katherine. Her husband."

CHAPTER TWENTY-SIX

AFTER THE BOYS WERE in bed, Darko and Christine shared a large bowl of *banku* and steaming *okro* stew.

"How is the investigation going?" she asked.

"Mr. Amalba stabbed a fellow prisoner this morning," Darko said.

"*Awurade*," Christine said.

"Oppong thinks Amalba is crazy. I'm not so sure."

"What difference does it make if he's a murderer?" she said.

Darko grunted. "It might at trial." He pinched off a chunk of *banku* and dipped it in stew. "Let me ask you something. Solomon's parents opposed his marriage to Kate, right?"

"His father, Ezekiel, was in favor of it, but Maude and her daughter, Georgina, did not like Kate one bit. They felt she wasn't good enough for Solo."

"Why?"

"On the face of it, it was social class and ethnic group. You know, Kate's family didn't have the social status of the Vanderpuyes. Kate didn't go to a prestigious boarding school the way Solomon did, and so on. And then Kate wasn't a Ga like Solomon, and Maude appears to think the only people that matter in this world are the Ga. Those are the outward, conscious rationalizations, but I believe that *inside* the small minds of the likes of Maude and Georgina, the issue boiled down to cheap, gutter jealousy."

"Really? Jealous of Kate's looks?"

"Her looks, her charm. Kate was the evil, beguiling woman who stole Solomon from his mother."

Darko was slurping stew off his fingers with relish. "So," he said, in between smacking his lips, "could Maude and Georgina have killed Kate? Or had her killed?"

Christine, who had finished, was rinsing off her hands in a bowl of clean water on the table. "No," she said, shaking her head. "You see, rather than kill Kate physically, Maude and her disciple child, Georgina, would have much preferred to steadily destroy Kate's soul and watch her slowly die emotionally." Christine smiled grimly. "It's the Ghanaian woman's way."

Darko considered that for a moment. Could be, he supposed. "I went to see Bishop Howard-Mills today at the Qedesh," he said, devouring what his wife had left in the bowl. She had about one-quarter his appetite. "He's out of the hospital."

"Praise God," Christine said. "How is the bishop doing?"

"He seemed a little weak, but I would expect that."

"What did you discuss with him?"

"His alibi. And John's and Reverend Atiemo's too."

"And what conclusion did you reach?"

"Too early to reach a conclusion."

"I don't think the solution lies with those three," Christine said.

"Because they are so-called men of God?"

"No, Darko. Because there's Peter Amalba. That's where you should be focusing your attention—certainly not on Bishop Howard-Mills. What motive could he possibly have?"

"Howard-Mills was seeing Kate over several weeks for so-called counseling, most of that time alone with her in his office. I can see him making indecent proposals to her and getting turned down. That might have lead to rage and murder."

Christine frowned and sat back. "Why do you have such a poor impression of the bishop?"

"It has nothing to do with impressions," Darko said, shaking his head and wiping his mouth with a napkin. "We look at those who were close or became close to the victim. The bishop must have shared some intimate moments with Katherine. He could easily have fallen in love with her. A man who is used to getting what he wants through power and wealth can turn bitter when a woman rejects his advances."

"You don't know him that well," Christine said. "He's not that kind of man. I've known him a long time. He's a caring person and a friend."

"But you don't go to his church usually, do you?"

"Rarely. I prefer Ascendancy Gospel. Smaller and more personal."

"So how do you know the bishop so well, then?"

Christine hesitated. "Okay," she said. "I'll tell you the truth. Maybe I should have a long time ago. You remember when Mama took Hosiah to the traditional healer and Hosiah slipped in the wash pan and cut his scalp?"

"How could I forget?"

"Well, you had an issue with Mama over it, and she and I started to bear our grudges against each other as well. We had some quarrels. I was getting depressed. You were working on the Ketanu murder, so I couldn't really talk it over with you, and in any case I thought it might just complicate things even more. So Kate suggested Mama and I get some counseling from Bishop Howard-Mills. Kate had been to him before over some problems, and he had been very helpful. I took her advice."

This was all news to Darko. "You and Mama actually went for counseling from the bishop?" he asked in surprise.

"Not exactly counseling. It's hard to explain. He prays with you and advises love and understanding. And forgiveness."

"And the sessions helped you?"

"Very much so. It was like therapy."

Darko suddenly felt excluded, which was unusual between him and his wife. "Why didn't you tell me?"

"I was going to," Christine said. "But . . . I don't know. I'm sorry. The more time passed, the less important it seemed. All that mattered to me was that I felt better and had more energy and love for you and Hosiah."

Darko felt both hot and cold around his neck. "These sessions with him—you never went to him by yourself, did you?"

"Of course not. Come on."

"Okay, forget it," Darko said abruptly, feeling peeved and oddly unbalanced. "Let's turn to Solo now. If he thought—or knew—Kate was having an affair, could he have taken revenge and murdered her?"

"You're back to the affair idea again?" Christine said irritably. "It didn't even have to be that scenario. Solo was crazed over her inability to bear a child, and then he began accusing her of being a witch and bringing evil to the home. In fact, Kate began receiving anonymous calls to that effect. I don't know if it was Solo making the calls, but the point is, people sometimes kill what they fear."

"True," Darko agreed. "What other possible motives?"

"Kate was filing a lawsuit against him."

"So he might have wanted to stop her. Filing for divorce?"

"No, it was over the house in Dzorwulu. Both their names had been on the loan document, but the arrangement was Kate paid Solo her share in cash, and then he paid a check to the bank for the full mortgage amount. At some point when the marriage was going down the drain, Solo went to the bank and somehow got a new loan, this time with his name and his mother's instead of Kate's."

Darko frowned. "Really? Was that legal?"

"I don't know," Christine said. "I'm no real estate attorney, but it sounds shady to me. You know, Solo has connections. He can swing anything the way he wants to."

"Who was Christine's lawyer?"

"James Bentsi-Enchill."

"Ah, I know him," Darko said. "I see him at the courthouse from time to time. Big shot in town. He must have been costing Kate a pretty penny."

"She and James were family friends." After a brief pause she added, "To be more precise, James and Kate had a thing going in senior high."

"Is that so?" Darko said with interest. "Could there be something in that? Like a rekindling of an old flame between them that made Solomon jealous?"

"It's possible."

"I'll need to talk to Bentsi-Enchill in any case. Thank you for the information. What about your bank manager friend? Did you reach her?"

"Sorry," Christine said. "Not yet, but I'll keep trying. Her number could have changed."

Darko remembered something. "Bishop Howard-Mills has invited me to a vigil tomorrow night, and I've accepted. I won't be staying all night, but I wanted to see what goes on."

"Do you get a ringside seat?"

"Apparently so."

"Impressive," Christine said. "I've never seen him in action. Are you taking your trainee with you?"

"The bishop provided me with only one pass."

"I would have loved to go."

"Next time."

"Right," she said. "You know very well this will probably the first and last time you ever go to a prayer vigil."

He winked at her. "You never know. I might be born again and turn to the ministry."

She laughed. "That will be the day."

CHAPTER TWENTY-SEVEN

SOLOMON VANDERPUYE WAS STAYING at his parents' residence, a sprawling olive-green house on walled-off, spacious surroundings in the posh neighborhood of Roman Ridge. Darko and Safo waited in the sitting room while the houseboy went to fetch Solomon from somewhere inside. Darko checked his phone for calls.

Safo was gazing around at the leather furniture, glass center table, fancy floor lamps, LED lights on the ceiling, expensive rugs on the floor, African paintings and masks on the wall. Darko counted six framed photographs of Solomon, his parents Maude and Ezekiel, and his sister Georgina in different permutations.

"Nice place," Safo whispered.

"It is," Darko agreed.

The houseboy came back. "Please, Mr. Vanderpuye is coming."

Solomon came out dressed in black shorts and a collarless indigo shirt embroidered with a Ghanaian pattern. Darko had met him at the wedding, and he remembered him as a smallish man—certainly shorter than Kate. But he had put on weight and grown a beard since. Most of all, Solomon's eyes had lost the life and vibrancy they had had on that occasion.

"Good morning, Solomon," Darko said, standing up to shake hands. "I don't know if you remember me. I met you at your wedding—"

Solomon lifted a finger at him. "Christine Dawson's husband, right?"

"Yes, my name is Darko. I'm a chief inspector with CID."

"I remember now, yes. Welcome."

"Thank you. This is Lance Corporal Safo."

"Please have a seat."

"My condolences for your loss," Darko said. "How are you doing?"

"Well, I'm managing through God's mercy," Solomon said, turning the corners of his lips down. "Is that why you're here? About Kate's murder?"

"Yes, I'm in charge of the investigation."

"I see," Solomon said. "This morning, Nana and Ransford came here creating a ruckus, accusing me of killing Kate. It was horrible."

"Any reason to accuse you?"

Solomon scowled. "None except they need a scapegoat and I'm the easiest target. It's true Kate and I separated in duress, but it doesn't mean I would butcher her with a machete like it said in the papers."

"We can't say for sure whether it was a machete," Darko commented. "The weapon wasn't recovered at the site."

"Could it have been a burglar who turned on Kate when she caught him?"

"I doubt it," Darko said. "It looks like she opened the door to someone she knew."

"Someone she knew," Solomon repeated. "Well, ask me anything you want." He raised his tired eyes to the detectives. "Maybe everyone thinks I killed Kate, but I'm innocent, that much I can tell you."

"Where were you late Friday night to Saturday morning?"

"I was here at home."

"Can anyone confirm that?"

"Well, up to around ten, when my father and mother go to bed. But not later than that."

"What about a watchman who can verify you didn't leave home at some point overnight."

"We had one," Solomon said, "but we sacked him last week after we found him sleeping on the job. We're looking for a new one."

"Before her death, Kate alleged she was receiving phone calls accusing her of being a witch. What do you know about that?"

"I seriously doubt that story. More likely, Kate made it up. Over the two months leading up to her death, she became increasingly paranoid."

"Did *you* ever call her a witch? Either to her face or behind her back?"

"No, of course I didn't, Inspector."

Darko's palm stung like the bite of a fire ant. Another liar, he thought. "You were aware Kate was going to sue you for ownership of the house?"

"Yes, I know."

"How did you feel about that?"

Solomon sucked his teeth in dismissal. "It made no difference to me whatsoever."

"Why wouldn't it?" Darko asked. "Kate was threatening the legality of your replacing her name with your mother's."

"Perfectly legal," Solomon said bluntly. "James Bentsi-Enchill took the case out of revenge. This man wanted Kate as far back as when we were all in secondary school. He tried to woo her and failed. Then I came along and swept Kate off her feet. And so, to spite me, she turns to him." Solomon's lip curled as if he had just tasted bitter sap.

"You hated that," Darko said. "And you still do."

Solomon shook it off like a dog ridding itself of fleas. "I didn't care that much."

"Your expression says otherwise," Darko said. "I'll put it to you that you became bitter and angry. Perhaps enough to kill Kate."

Solomon shook his head, closed his eyes and rubbed his brow. "Please, Inspector. I'm very tired. I don't want this kind of stress, especially after the Yeboahs this morning. I've been hospitable to you because of our connection through Christine, but you have now become hostile. With all due respect, please leave."

"As you wish, sir." Darko stood up. "We'll talk again soon."

Solomon looked away in annoyance.

"Just one more thing," Darko said, as he and Safo started to leave. "To which bank do you pay your mortgage?"

"Standard Chartered Bank," Solomon replied. "Central Branch."

"And the name of the loan officer, please?"

"Michael Amalba."

Darko started. "Michael Amalba?"

"Yes. Why do you seem so surprised?"

"Because," Darko said, "it changes the entire picture."

CHAPTER TWENTY-EIGHT

MICHAEL WASN'T AT THE bank—off until the next day, the receptionist said.

"Can I help you with something?" she offered.

"No, it's fine," Darko said. "Thank you."

He and Safo left the bank and went outside into the vicious heat.

"I'm hungry," he said. "Let's go to Aunty Jane's, and we can talk about the case."

Aunty Jane welcomed them, happy to see Darko again. He wanted *red-red,* but Safo said she wasn't hungry.

Jane brought them two bottled waters on the house, and Darko guzzled down half of his in one shot. Safo sipped hers.

"So," he said, "what do you think so far?"

"About Michael Amalba?" she asked tentatively.

"About everything. Start from what we know."

"We know someone killed Katherine Vanderpuye last Friday night," she said.

"Speak up a little, please," Darko said. "I can't hear you because of the traffic."

She repeated herself, louder, this time.

"Yes," Darko agreed. "What time do we know this murder to have taken place?"

"Maybe about one in the morning," she suggested. "Or two."

"We don't know that. You're speculating. If you were on the

witness stand, you would already be in trouble. Between what time and what time are we *certain* the killing occurred?"

"Between the time your wife and Katherine's mother left her on Friday night at around eleven o'clock and Saturday morning around five, when Esi came to work."

"Good. What do we know about how the murderer gained access to the home?"

"No forced entry."

"Which means what?"

"She might have known the murderer."

"Or if she didn't, perhaps he pushed his way in as soon as she opened the door a bit. What do we know about the cause of death?"

"She was mortally wounded by a sharp instrument like a large knife or machete."

"Probably so. But also consider for example if the assailant strangled her to death first and then used the weapon? So we have to wait for the autopsy results to get a better idea. That will take some time, though."

Darko's *red-red* arrived, and he asked for an extra plate, which he slid in front of Safo. He spooned half of his plate onto hers. "Eat," he commanded. "You can't solve murders if your brain is not working, and your brain can't work without fuel."

"Honestly, I wasn't hungry, sir."

"You're lying," he said, rinsing his hands off in the bowl of water one of the servers had brought. "You have to learn to lie better."

"How do you know I'm lying?" she asked, her face lighting up with curiosity.

"Don't ask me to explain. Eat."

"Yes, sir. Thank you very much, sir."

Darko closed his eyes for a moment and savored the succulence of the soft, juicy fried plantain dripping with creamy palm oil that exploded in his mouth. He got up and helped himself to Malta Guinness from the assortment of drinks in the glass-fronted refrigerator. The attendants would add it to the bill.

Darko took a healthy swig of the sweet, non-alcoholic drink that had been his favorite since childhood. "Solomon had a motive for murdering his wife," he said to Safo. "In fact, he has more than one. Give me one."

She looked like a student called on by the teacher. "Em, I think . . . well, Solomon hated her for not giving him a child, sir."

"Yes, and another possibility: Solomon could have become jealous when she turned to his old rival James Bentsi-Enchill."

"That's true," Safo said, scooping up more beans with her plantain. "Add to that her suing him over the house."

Darko agreed. "That's where Michael Amalba might come in because he could be complicit in helping Solomon remove his mother's name."

"So maybe the two men conspired to kill her?"

"Yes. That's the importance of what Solomon has just told us."

They ate in silence for a while.

"Arc your parents alive?" Darko asked.

"My mother is." Safo's eyes saddened. "My father is dead."

"My condolences," Darko said. "What happened?"

"Stomach ulcer. It was about eight years ago. He was having severe abdominal pains. We took him to the hospital, where we waited more than fourteen hours for them to admit him, and all that time he was complaining the pain was getting worse." Safo winced. "All of a sudden he doubled over and started throwing up blood, and then he collapsed and died right there."

"I'm sorry," Darko said. "What did he do for a living?"

"Police officer. Superintendent."

"Oh!" Darko exclaimed. "I didn't know."

She nodded, the pain clearing from her face now. "When I was a little girl, he always took my brother and me to his office on the weekends and we played around while he was doing his work. All the officers there knew us."

"So, it was your father who inspired you to become a police officer."

"Yes, please." She smiled. "I have a picture of my father."

Safo scrolled through her phone, found it, and showed it to Darko. She must have been about fifteen or sixteen then, standing outside a police station next to her father, who appeared to be fiftyish. He was solemn and a little stiff, angular and lean.

"Was he strict?" Darko asked.

"Yes, please. Very."

He noticed a change in her voice. It had always been soft, but now it took on a girlish quality. Darko became uncomfortable.

His phone rang. Cairo was on the line. "Daddy's room is ready. I wanted to start moving his things today and then bring him to the house on Saturday. Are you free tonight?"

Darko was about to answer yes, but then he remembered the vigil. "Sorry, no, Cairo," he said. "But I can help on Saturday. Will you be okay?"

"Sure, I can manage with Audrey and Franklin. We'll leave the heavy stuff for the weekend."

Darko checked his messages, one from Christine asking him to call her.

"What's up?" he asked when she answered.

"I reached Mary—the manager I said I knew at StanChart."

"Yes?"

"She's still there, but she's leaving because she's just had an offer from Zenith Bank she can't refuse. Besides, she and Michael Amalba don't get along. Apparently, Michael created a cushy position for one of the tellers he's seeing, and Mary didn't like that."

"Okay. So?"

"I got Mary gossiping," Christine continued, "and she told me Michael went for a training course in Takoradi this last weekend on Friday *and* Saturday."

Darko frowned. "Wait, Michael said he was here in Accra with Peter in their apartment Friday night through to Saturday. Maybe he didn't go to Takoradi after all?"

"Oh, yes he did," Christine said. "He has pictures of the party

Saturday night in Takoradi right there on his Facebook page. I'll show it to you when I get home. So you see, Michael was deliberately giving his brother a false alibi. I'm convinced Michael knows Peter murdered Kate."

CHAPTER TWENTY-NINE

EARLY WEDNESDAY EVENING, CHRISTINE and Darko paid respects to the Yeboahs at home. Ransford was dressed plainly in comparison to Nana, who was magnificent in a deep red and black outfit of mourning. She looked lovely but sad. Friends and extended family came in and out and had a little to eat and drink. Funerals in Ghana could be financially ruinous, so Darko and Christine gave what they felt was a generous donation.

Uncommonly subdued, Gifty sat next to her brother. By about 8 P.M., the atmosphere was more relaxed, with pockets of conversation between and among guests.

Darko was due at the prayer vigil in another hour, so he shared his final condolences with the bereaved parents as he prepared to depart.

"Do you have a minute?" Nana asked him. "I wanted to share something with you in private."

"Sure," Darko said.

He accompanied her out to the mosquito-netted veranda and the two sat down.

"It will be a long time before I go back to Katherine's house, if ever," Nana said, her voice wavering. "Ransford and I have been wondering if you've come across anything she left behind in the home like a diary or journal."

"How do you mean, Aunty?"

"When she was going through all her troubles," Nana explained,

"I suggested she keep a journal of everything that was happening. I felt if she did it even once, twice, three times a week, she would be able to work through some of her stress, her sadness, her pain. She was suffering." Nana's eyes welled up. "When I was a girl, I enjoyed having a journal. I didn't always write anything earth-shaking. Sometimes I just drew flowers, but I always felt better, regardless."

"Did she begin the journal or diary to your knowledge?"

"That's what we don't know," Nana replied. "The reason I'm telling you is if she did, she might have written down sensitive information, like maybe she was afraid of Solomon, or that he had threatened her—anything like that. Maybe you can get some clues."

"Thank you for letting me know, Aunty Nana," Darko said. "Her boxes are in the evidence room now, so I'll have my partner go through them one more time. Do I have your permission to read her diary if there is one?"

She smiled and pinched his cheek. "Of course. It means so much to us that you're investigating the case. God bless you in all your efforts."

"Thank you very much, Aunty."

ONE CHARTERED BUS after another other pulled up to park and unload passengers at the perimeter of Independence Square. In this vast asphalt-paved space where military parades were held, the faithful were gathering for A Night of Redemption and Deliverance with Bishop Howard-Mills and the Power Ministry of God.

Powerful, generator-run floodlights shone through the swirling dust and smoke. The air was sticky with the salty breeze off the Atlantic a quarter mile behind the Independence Arch at the far end of the square. Darko could feel the excitement and anticipation in the milling crowd, which he skirted to the southernmost side where the stage stood. Two jumbo screens faced the gathering mass so even those who were far back could see the bishop preach and perform miracles. At the moment, a woman on the stage with a choir and band behind her was singing praises to Jesus. She was off key, and the sound over the stacks of giant speakers was distorted, but no one seemed concerned.

Darko got to the VIP entrance, which was overrun by people trying to get in. Some were dressed to kill while others appeared shabby. Tropical sweat could defeat even the best deodorant, so there was plenty of body odor to go around.

Darko noticed a secured area about two hundred meters away to the left where gleaming BMW and Mercedes vehicles were parked next to three Toyotas with Power of God Ministry decals.

Darko began forcing his way to the front, firmly moving people out of the way. At the head of the line, policemen and chaperones in orange reflective jackets checked the credentials of guests, rejecting the posers and yelling at hustlers. Everyone knew a friend of a friend of the bishop, or variations thereof. One of the largest policemen Darko had ever seen examined his ticket.

"Who gave you these?" the policeman demanded.

"John Papafio," Darko replied, leaning in so hc could be heard above the din.

"You know him?" the officer snapped.

Of course, I know him, Darko thought. "Yes," he said, prepared to pull rank if the giant gave him any problems. The officer nodded and waved Darko through to the other side of the cordon where the chaff had been weeded out. Around a large, white tent from which loud hip-life blasted, scores of well-turned-out people hung around chatting and drinking. Darko realized he was underdressed.

He peeped into the tent to find it full of people eating, drinking, and laughing. Apart from the bar and a DJ, there was a full buffet. Darko stepped back to give way to guests moving in and out.

"Inspector!"

Darko looked right and left before spotting John Papafio in a dark suit and a black-and-white *kente* vest.

"Welcome, welcome!" he said, laughing and pumping Darko's hand. "Come in, come in! You don't have to stand there. Please, help yourself to food and drink. If you can excuse me for one moment—I have to check on something outside. Enjoy!"

John left as quickly as he had appeared. Looking around, Darko recognized a couple of ministers of parliament, some military brass, and then with a jolt, the Inspector General of Police—the highest police officer in the land, appointed by the president. What was *he* doing here? Darko had crossed from one reality—his ordinary life—to another to which he didn't belong. The way he had imagined this so-called vigil as a sincere and prayerful gathering had been far off the mark. He had forgotten that charismatic evangelists like Bishop Howard-Mills espoused material wealth as bestowed by God. Praying for riches was quite all right.

Darko's attention was drawn to a tall woman wearing a stunning teal headdress. She was chatting with a group of guests. She had a gap in her front teeth when she smiled. Not beautiful in any conventional way, but her carriage, physical presence, and authoritative air fixed Darko's gaze. Thinking back to a photograph he'd seen in the papers or online, he was sure the woman was Mrs. Howard-Mills.

He scanned the crowded space under the tent further. Bodies shifted and moved around like a fast-forwarded video. In a space that opened up for a few seconds, Darko spotted the face of the man he and Safo had sought earlier that day: Michael Amalba.

Darko made his way through the tent's dense crowd. The music was loud, the drink plentiful, and everyone was happy. The tent was air-conditioned under the power of the mega-generators outside. The women inside were beautiful, perfumed, festooned with jewelry, and impeccably coiffed.

Michael had clearly had quite a bit to drink. His face lit up. "*Ei*, Inspector!" he slurred as Darko got to him. "What a surprise! How are you?"

He was dressed in a navy suit with a pink shirt, the top two undone buttons revealing a few strands of hair on his chest. Darko sidled up close to him and smiled frostily down at his outstretched hand. "Let's go outside," he said into Michael's ear. "Take the lead; I'm right behind you."

They emerged from the tent. "This way," Darko said, guiding him around the corner to the rear, where it was relatively secluded.

Michael was sweating and nervous. "Is something wrong, Inspector?"

"Let's start with why you lied to my partner and me," Darko said. "You said you were with your brother all night Friday, but we know you were in Takoradi at that time. I've seen your Facebook photos. Why did you say you were with your brother here in Accra?"

Michael's brow knotted up. "I'm very sorry, Inspector. I shouldn't have done that. Forgive me."

"Whether I forgive you is neither here nor there. Answer the question. Why did you do it?"

"I was trying to protect him," he said.

"Because you know he killed Katherine Vanderpuye?"

"No, please," Michael stammered. "Inspector Dawson, I beg you for your understanding. Please, let me explain."

"I'm listening."

"I've been struggling with Peter ever since he moved in with me," Michael began. "He has been getting worse with delusions, paranoia, and erratic behavior. I can barely persuade him to go for treatment at the psychiatric hospital, and I can't blame him because over there, you sit and wait and wait for hours. It's as if your turn will never come.

"I didn't know what to do, but since I'm a man of faith, I turned to God in prayer, and He let me know that I must bring Peter to accept the Lord as his personal savior. If only Peter could do that, all would be well. I attend Bishop Howard-Mills's church regularly, so I began to take Peter with me to the Qedesh every Sunday for worship."

"When was that?"

"Just after the new year. Three months ago or so."

"Go on."

"For a while, Peter seemed to be getting better and better. He even began to go to the Qedesh on Tuesdays. Then, one evening he came home looking as if he had been to the moon and back. He told me he had met a beautiful woman and had fallen in love. I asked him who it was, but he said he wanted to keep it a secret until he was ready to reveal her. When Peter finally showed me the picture of her on his phone, I thought he was joking. It was a photograph of Katherine Vanderpuye coming out of a Qedesh prayer meeting.

"I said, 'Peter, don't you know who that is? That's Solomon Vanderpuye's wife.' I was laughing, but the way he looked at me made me stop at once. He said, 'She is leaving Solomon to marry me.' I was baffled, but because he didn't say anything more about it in the next few days, I decided it was only Peter being himself—you know, his fabrications."

More comfortable now, Michael leaned back against the tree, his arms folded. "But as time went on, his mood changed again, this time for the worse. He stopped talking and became depressed. After asking him over and over again what was wrong, he told me he thought Katherine had been unfaithful to him by fornicating with Bishop Howard-Mills. That alarmed me because I knew he was getting delusional again. We had some medicines left over from the last time he had seen a psychiatrist, but he refused to take them."

Michael's shoulders slumped, and his hands dropped. Darko could feel his profound defeat.

"Honestly, I was at a loss," Michael continued. "Last Friday, I was supposed to go to the training in Takoradi. I tried to cancel it because I was worried about Peter, but it was too late. StanChart's regional director said I had to go. When I returned Sunday, Peter was gone. I called everyone in the family including my parents, but no one knew where Peter was.

"Monday morning, I learned about Katherine's death and then when you told me Peter had attacked the bishop, I became worried."

"So you were willing to protect a suspected murderer?" Darko demanded.

Michael hung his head. "He's my brother, Inspector. He's family. My mother always told me to watch over him, and I've become so accustomed to covering for him." He shrugged. "But I'm not proud of lying to you about him, and I'm ashamed of what he did to the bishop."

"Yet here you are at this party drinking beer," Darko pointed out.

With a rueful smile, Michael looked away toward the distant sound of the ocean. "I knew you were going to ask me about that."

"And what is your response?"

"Yesterday evening, I went to see Bishop Howard-Mills at his office to apologize to him on Peter's behalf, but he wasn't in. He was resting at home. John said I could meet with the bishop for a few minutes this evening before the vigil, so I came early to talk to him. He prayed for me, and we prayed for Peter too. When I was about to leave, the bishop asked me why not stay and have some food and drink, so I did. That's how you came to find me here. It's true, I have drunk too much beer, but not necessarily because I'm feeling happy."

"Where is the bishop now?"

"Please, I don't know. People say he doesn't attend these parties. His wife always represents him. He comes to check everything is okay early in the day, and then he leaves and returns at around ten."

"I see." Darko observed him awhile. "Mr. Amalba, you certainly know how to flirt with danger."

Michael squirmed under Darko's gaze.

"How, and why," Darko said, "did you and Solomon remove Katherine's name from the house deed and replace it with Maude Vanderpuye's?"

"I didn't do it without misgivings," Michael said, "but Solomon is a good friend and well, he's persuasive. You know, in Ghana, we do things for our friends. Solo has done favors for me as well."

"Was what you did legal?"

"Please, the fact is that Katherine was giving her share of the mortgage to Solo in cash, but the funds were directly from Solomon's individual account. So, unfortunately for her, as far as the bank is concerned, she's invisible."

"Still, her name is legally in the original document," Darko pointed out. "How could you just pull the property from under her like that?"

Michael fidgeted. "I told Solo to have Kate sign a letter permitting a transfer of ownership to his mother."

Darko frowned. "She came into the bank to sign the letter in person?"

Michael cleared his throat. "No, he persuaded me to allow her to sign it at home and then he returned with it."

Darko shook his head. "What a joke, Mr. Amalba. Solomon forged the signature, and you know it. The letter might appear legal, but the transfer is still fraudulent. You didn't have permission to execute it."

Michael bowed his head again, one leg twitching back and forth.

"Did you get cash back from the transaction?" Darko asked.

"No, please," Michael whispered.

"Were you aware that Katherine was taking Solo to court over this issue?"

Michael looked up. "Inspector, she wasn't only suing Solo; she also named me and the entire StanChart branch in the suit."

Interesting, Darko thought. That potentially gave Michael a motive to kill Katherine. "Did Solo ever tell you he was going to kill his wife?" Darko asked.

Michael groaned and looked up at the sky. No stars were out tonight. "*Awurade*. I beg you, Inspector. Can I decline to answer?"

"You are free to refuse, but then I will bring both you and Solo in as accessories to murder."

Michael panicked. "Please, are you serious?"

"Do I look like I'm joking?"

"Okay, okay. Solomon never said he wanted to kill Katherine, but he did say he hated her and that he thought maybe what Maude said—that Kate was a witch—might be true."

"Did he ever ask you to help kill her?"

"No, no," Michael said, shaking his head repeatedly. "I'm telling you the truth, Mr. Dawson."

Darko grunted in disgust. At this point, he believed no one. "What about your brother?" he demanded. "Answer me honestly. Did he kill Katherine?"

Michael chewed on his bottom lip. "Honestly, I don't know."

"But it's possible?"

"*Awurade*, forgive me." Michael wiped his face with his palm. "I don't believe I'm saying this about my own kin, but yes, Inspector. It's possible."

CHAPTER THIRTY

BISHOP HOWARD-MILLS CUT A commanding figure in a tailored, vanilla suit with a bronze stripe down the length of the thigh-length tunic. Darko and the other guests occupied a bank of seats closest to the stage and accessed via the tent. The choir stood behind the Bishop in a crescent configuration with the band in the center and began a performance of gospel hip-life. The crowd danced and sang as they waved white handkerchiefs. On the jumbo screens, it looked like a giant flock of seagulls. When Howard-Mills joined in the performance with a few dance moves of his own, his audience went wild.

Afterward, the choir members took their seats and the bishop, breathing a little heavily, got his followers to settle down. For over an hour, he delivered a sermon on how spitefulness ruins the life of the individual, the family, and the nation. Sometimes Howard-Mills mixed in Twi with English, which Darko called *Twinglish*. When he quoted from the Bible, the jumbo screens captioned the passages.

> *1 Peter 2:1-25*
> So put away all malice and all deceit and hypocrisy and envy and all slander.

> *Ephesians 4:31*
> Let all bitterness and wrath and anger and clamor and slander be put away from you, along with all malice.

Psalm 140:3
They sharpen their tongues as a serpent; poison of a viper is under their lips.

1 Corinthians 5:8
Therefore let us celebrate the feast, not with old leaven, nor with the leaven of malice and wickedness, but with the unleavened bread of sincerity and truth.

"Are you troubled by spitefulness?" Howard-Mills asked, pacing the stage and dropping his voice almost to a whisper into his microphone. "Is your soul bound by malice or overwhelmed by demons and evil? If you know this in your heart, and you are ready to be healed *now*, then come to me. God has invested power in me to cast out the iniquity and wickedness from you."

Flanked by bodyguards—no one wanted history to repeat—the bishop came off the stage to ground level. Some of the chaperones, wearing reflective orange jackets marked STAFF shepherded congregants to form two long lines approaching the bishop at right angles to each other. Other members of the staff, the "catchers," took their positions along the sides of the congregation and in the breaks between the rows of chairs.

But any semblance of orderliness didn't last long. Within minutes, two chaperones half carried, half dragged a screaming, writhing woman to the bishop's feet. She had clumped, matted hair, and her clothes were ragged. Every so often, one of the chaperones had to pull down her skirt as it rose indecorously above her thighs with her thrashing about. The crowd stood and craned forward to see, or else watched the screens.

Howard-Mills came closer and kneeled down. John, who seemed to have appeared from nowhere, held a microphone to pick up both the bishop and the stricken woman.

"*Awura*," Howard-Mills said in Twi, "*ye fre wo sen?*"

"*Ye fre me* Abena," she moaned. "Please, Bishop Howard-Mills, help me."

"What troubles you so much?"

Abena twisted and turned. "It's my sister!" she cried out.

"What has she done?"

"She won't leave me alone. She torments me day and night."

"What is her name?"

"Grace."

"Where does she live?"

"Brong-Ahafo Region."

"Is it her spirit that comes to disturb you?" the bishop asked.

"Yes, please."

"Why does she come?"

"She says I am the one preventing her from giving birth to a child."

"Is that the truth?"

"Oh, no please, Bishop!"

"Then let's pray to cast out Grace's spirit." To the chaperones, Howard-Mills said, "Help Abena stand up."

The chaperones held Abena up on either side, which was difficult because she was dead weight. Howard-Mills began to pray, his voice rising and falling. Abena let out a shriek that distorted the loudspeakers. She began to flail so wildly the chaperones had to block her hands and let her back down to the ground for fear of her striking them.

"She's hurting me!" she screamed, holding her head, then clutching at her back, abdomen, and finally her legs, as if her sister was moving down Abena's body. "She's trying to kill me!"

"Let me speak to her!" the bishop shouted. "Let me talk to her, *now*!"

Strangely, a different, much deeper voice emerged from Abena. "I am Grace. You can't cast me out, Bishop!"

"Are you sure?" Howard-Mills challenged. "Do you know the power of God?"

The audience jumped up and down, screaming their approval, raising their hands and waving handkerchiefs.

Howard-Mills knelt and pressed his hand on Abena's forehead

as she bucked and kicked. "Come out, Grace!" he yelled. "The Lord Jesus is here! You have no power over Him, for He rules over all dominions. I say, be *gone, Grace!*"

She bellowed, and Howard-Mills shouted back at her. They went back and forth like this for at least several cycles until the bishop stood up and raised his hand. "Abena!" he cried out, "she is leaving!"

The audience yelled, cheering Abena on as she went through the last throes of her battle.

"Help her up," the bishop said to the chaperones.

Abena stood, this time mostly on her own. She was drenched with sweat and clearly exhausted, but her expression was one of relief, almost elation.

"See the wondrous power of the Lord, Abena," the bishop said. "Now go in peace. May God be with you."

Pandemonium broke loose as people shouted and danced in the aisles. The catchers began to rush back and forth to keep people from harm as they collapsed. Darko asked the gentleman beside him what the falling meant.

"They are slain in the spirit," the man shouted, his eyes wide with excitement and the thrill of the spectacle.

As the cheering died down, more people came forward—a man bent over with age received power from the bishop and was able to throw away his cane and leave walking ramrod straight without assistance. A woman's baby who suffered from evil spirits in the form of convulsions was cured by Howard-Mills's touch. Gradually, the space in front of the stage filled up with people rolling around, quivering, speaking in tongues, pacing up and down, and self-flagellating. And still, the catchers scurried around to secure those who were falling as they were "slain in the spirit." When they stood up again, they were renewed in the spirit or converted by it.

The bishop kept this up for an astounding two hours at least. To Darko, it was an exhausting display, but he had brief moments of feeling swept up by the emotion and euphoria of the crowd, the way he might feel in a soccer stadium full of exuberant fans.

Past midnight, Darko felt chilly and exceptionally weary. As Howard-Mills joined the choir in another performance and the audience sang along while swaying and waving their hands in the air, people came up and deposited their small and large church donations into shoulder-high barrels, which would be full to capacity at the end of the night. How did the bank count all that? Darko wondered. And what cut did the Bishop take?

On that thought, he decided he had had enough. He got up, went back through the tent, which had very few people in it now, and continued to the entrance. The huge policeman sitting in a chair at the entrance was still watchful but considerably more relaxed than before. Darko nodded and smiled at him, and just as he was about to leave, the big guy beckoned to him. "Come over," he said.

Darko went. "Yes, my friend?"

They shook hands and snapped fingers.

"Are you leaving now?" the policeman asked. His ID badge read CPL. BLANKSON.

"Yes, I have to work tomorrow," Darko said.

Blankson made a face. "Me too."

"Is this what you do on the side for extra cash?"

"Man has to survive," Blankson said with resignation. "I have worked four or five of Bishop Howard-Mills's prayer vigils. Is this your first time attending?"

"Yes, sir."

"How did you find it?"

"Fascinating. How does the bishop perform all night long?"

"Not all night, though," Blankson said. "Usually one of his junior bishops will take over between about one and three in the morning, and then the bishop will return to the stage to finish the vigil."

That corroborated what both Bishop Howard-Mills and Reverend Atiemo had told Darko and Safo. "During the break, what does Bishop Howard-Mills do?"

Blankson shrugged. "Sometimes he will just come and rest in

the tent or read the scriptures, other times he will get in his car and go somewhere for a while."

"Ah, okay," Darko said, keeping his manner offhand. "To where?"

"Eh? I don't know."

"The bishop had a vigil at Baden Powell Hall last Friday," Darko said. "Did you work that one too?"

Blankson nodded. "Yes."

"Do you know or remember if Mr. Howard-Mills was away between one and three?"

The corporal frowned. "My friend, why these questions?"

Darko decided it was time to come clean, but a few people were hanging around within earshot. "Can I talk to you in private for one moment, Corporal Blankson? Over there."

Looking both wary and curious, Blankson followed Darko a few meters.

"My name is Chief Inspector Dawson," Darko said, showing the corporal his ID under the beam of the floodlights.

Blankson looked at it and immediately braced, chest out and hands by his sides. "Yes, sir. Sorry, sir."

"Relax. I'm looking into the death of a certain woman. Maybe you can help me. Hold on one second." Darko got out his phone and scrolled to Katherine's picture. "Have you ever seen this woman at any of the bishop's prayer meetings?"

Blankson scrutinized it and then shook his head.

"And my question about Friday night at Baden Powell—did you see the bishop leave the premises?"

The corporal cleared his throat. "Please, I know he went to his vehicle, but I didn't notice when he came back."

"Do you know where the bishop's vehicle is parked at the moment?" Darko asked.

"Yes, sir. I can show you."

Darko walked with him to the secured parking area, where a watchman hung around looking at his phone but putting it away as the two policemen came up. They greeted him. Blankson pointed out the bishop's black Mercedes SUV.

"Thanks," Darko said. "What about Mrs. Howard-Mills? Is she still here at the event?"

"No, please," Blankson said. "Normally, she leaves after the party."

Convenient for the bishop, Darko thought. "And Reverend Atiemo?"

"For sure he was there through the whole night until morning," Blankson said. "I know because at one point even, I had to help remove somebody from around the reverend's neck." Blankson began to laugh. "He was blessing a certain woman after he cast out her demons. She said she loved him and wrapped herself around him like an octopus. It took me and three chaperones about four minutes to get her off."

Darko joined in the laughter. "Funny story, Corporal. And John Papafio?"

"Well, you know, boss, he is running around all night. Seems like he's everywhere at once."

"Was he involved in the altercation with the woman and the reverend?"

Blankson shook his head. "No. We security people handle that kind of problem, not John."

"Do you recall if you saw him after one A.M.?"

"Yes, please."

"Yes, please, what? You recall or you saw him?"

"Yeah, I'm sure I saw him, but to be honest, I can't tell you exactly when, sir. I wasn't paying that much attention."

"Would it be unusual if you didn't see John around for a couple of hours?"

"Not at all. Like I was saying, boss, he roams around, always checking if everything is running smoothly and never staying in one place for long."

Darko nodded. "Thank you, Blankson. I might need to get in touch with you later."

They traded phone numbers, Darko said good night and walked to his motorcycle. Scores of buses were still parked, but many had departed. Darko navigated out of the parking lot and turned right onto La Road, which encircled the Black Star Square Monument. Traffic was moderately heavy only because of the prayer vigil. Typically, this part of town was deserted late at night.

Darko passed the entrance to the VIP lot and pulled off onto the shoulder, bumping over dirt and patches of dry grass. He turned and stopped where he had a good view of the car park and Howard-Mills's Mercedes.

Darko sat there more than thirty minutes feeling sleepy and progressively weary—a heaviness and profound exhaustion he wasn't used to. He thought he might be having chills. He dozed slightly and started awake in time to see Bishop Howard-Mills's vehicle emerging from the VIP exit. Darko started up the motorcycle and pulled out. He had to step on the gas to make ground because the Mercedes had gone in the opposite direction around the Black Star Monument.

Darko followed the SUV to 37 Circle, where several thousand tree-dwelling bats left every evening at dusk and returned the following dawn. Then the SUV took Achimota Road toward the forest of the same name.

Traffic thinned out to almost nothing. Building was limited in this protected area, and the night was pitch black. Howard-Mills made a left onto a small unpaved road. Darko rode past to avoid raising suspicion, then made a U-turn a few meters on. He switched off the motorcycle and wheeled it onto the dirt road. Howard-Mills had parked next to a sprawling, low profile bungalow nestled among trees and enclosed by a high chain-link fence. Darko parked and moved forward, stopping at a safe distance. By a light on the outside of the house, Darko could see the bishop walk up to the door and knock. Another light went on, this time inside, and the door opened. The person behind it stepped out just enough for Darko to see it was a young woman of fair complexion. A romantic tryst? That was Darko's educated guess.

Most important, the bishop had just demonstrated he could leave the premises of one of his prayer vigils. As such, he did have an alibi for last Friday night, but it was only partial. Just as Howard-Mills was visiting this young woman, he could have visited Katherine Vanderpuye to murder her.

CHAPTER THIRTY-ONE

BY THE TIME DARKO got into bed around three in the morning, he was ill. His muscles and joints had begun to ache, his head was pounding, and intermittent chills shook his body like a *bola* truck juddering over a potholed street. He went into a troubled sleep but woke up soon afterward soaked in sweat. His throat felt like asphalt and tasted like an Agbogbloshie sewer. He got up, swaying for a moment like a drunkard. He changed his T-shirt and drank a glass of water. He could tell he had a raging fever. He took two paracetamol tablets and went back to bed, pulling the sheets over him. He felt as if he was freezing, even though he knew he was burning up. Beside him, Christine slept peacefully.

He sensed his temperature reducing, and he drifted to sleep once more. When he awoke again, he was shivering with a vengeance, and Christine was sitting at the bedside sponging his face and torso with a moist towel. It was intolerable.

"Stop, Christine," he muttered. "*Stop!* I'm cold."

"You *think* you're cold," she said. "We have to bring your fever down."

"Malaria," he tried to say between the clattering of his teeth. "It's been a long time since I've had an attack this bad."

"I know. Don't talk, just rest. You've been talking in your sleep enough as it is. Hallucinating too."

"Are you a hallucination?" he asked wryly, trying to laugh—until a red-hot shaft of pain blasted the space between his eyes.

She gave him ibuprofen with sips of water. "I'll go to the pharmacy for some antimalarial medicine in a little while. Mama is coming down to watch you while I'm gone."

Darko groaned but didn't have enough strength to object. Thirty minutes later, he was wet with perspiration again as the fever broke. He slept a little and then became aware of Christine talking to someone outside in the sitting room. Oh—Gifty, most likely.

His eyes closed and he thought he might be dozing off again until he woke with a start. Gifty's face was in view, but she appeared distorted and seemed to change shape every few seconds.

"Christine told me you went to Bishop Howard-Mills's prayer meeting last night," she said, mopping his forehead gently with a tepid washcloth. "I watched it on TV. It was beautiful."

Darko moaned. Gifty's voice made his headache worse.

"Did the words of the bishop reach you?" she murmured. "Did Jesus touch you?"

"Leave me alone." His lips were moving, but he wasn't sure he was producing any sound.

"Did you hear our great Bishop Howard-Mills?" she persisted. "He was telling us to accept the Lord and remove all spitefulness from our hearts. But you resisted the bishop's admonition, didn't you, Darko? I know you did. That's why, after you had left the rally, you fell ill. It's a sign from God. Repent, now. Erase the malice you hold in your heart against me, and God will guide your ship safely into port. Why do you continue to hold a grudge against me, hm?"

He opened his eyes and sat up with the little strength he had. The room was spinning. "Go away," he muttered. "Get away from me!" He gave her a shove, and she stumbled back.

"You are wicked even when you are sick, Darko Dawson," she whispered furiously. "Wicked!"

"Get out," he mouthed, falling back to his pillow with a groan. Sitting up had made the room spin. He turned, put his head over the side of the bed and threw up.

• • •

He became somewhat aware of Christine holding him up and giving him his anti-malarial medicine, forcing him to drink fluids. He had shaking chills and drenching sweats as he slept on and off. Sometimes he thought Sly and Hosiah came in to look at him and then leave. Or Darko might have dreamt it.

When he woke up fully again, soft light was coming from the window. Was it dawn or dusk?

Hosiah was at the bedside peering at him. "Daddy, are you better?"

Darko nodded. His body pains, headaches, and fever had left as if thunderclouds had gone and a crushing weight had been lifted off his body. He felt light and weak and better all at the same time. "Come," he said to Hosiah.

The boy clambered on the bed to hug his dad.

"How are you?" Darko asked him, holding him close. "I love you, little man."

"I'm fine, and I love you too, Daddy. Wait, I want to tell Mama you're awake."

He catapulted off the bed and ran outside yelling, "Mama! Daddy woke up."

Darko gingerly sat up at the side of the bed as Christine came in with the boys.

"Are you okay?" she asked.

"Yes," he said. "Just thirsty."

"Bring Daddy some water, Hosiah," Christine said.

Sly sat beside Darko and tucked his hand on the inside of his father's arm.

"Is it Thursday?" Darko asked.

Christine chuckled and stood in front of him, cradling his head against her body. "No, it's five forty-five on Friday evening."

"What!" he exclaimed, aghast.

"You've been sleeping off and on for more than twenty-four hours," she told him.

Darko shook his head in disbelief and sucked down the cold water Hosiah had brought him. Water had never tasted so good.

"Lance Corporal Safo has been checking up on you," Christine said.

Darko nodded. "Okay, I'll call her."

"Tomorrow, not tonight," Christine said sharply. "First you have to eat and get back your strength."

"No, first I have to shower," Darko said, sniffing an armpit and pulling a face. "I stink."

Sly and Hosiah looked at each other and began to giggle.

"Oh, funny, eh?" Darko said with mock indignation.

The boys laughed even harder.

"I can't believe you could laugh at your dear, sick father," Darko said, getting up to the bathroom.

"Daddy?" Sly said, grinning. "Do you need help taking your bath?"

"*No!*" he yelled back. "Don't disrespect, eh?"

Darko's sons fell on the floor in stitches.

"You boys are just silly," Christine commented, stepping over them. "When you're finished laughing, please set the table for dinner."

CHAPTER THIRTY-TWO

EARLY SATURDAY MORNING, DARKO called Cairo to say he would be able to help move their father's remaining belongings to Cairo's house.

"Are you sure?" Cairo said. "Shouldn't you rest?"

"I'm tired of resting," Darko said. "I've been doing that for two days. I feel fine. I'll see you at Papa's place in about an hour."

Next, Darko received a call from Chief Superintendent Oppong.

"I'm glad you're doing better," he said to Darko.

"Yes, thank you, sir. I'll be back at work on Monday."

Darko briefed his boss about what had happened Wednesday night. "Do you know who lives in that house in Achimota Forest, sir?" he asked.

"That's the home of Sandra Simpson. You know the guy who designed those three high-rise buildings near the Accra Mall?"

"Yes, sir."

Simpson had designed the million-dollar high-rise complexes in the colors of the Ghanaian flag: red, yellow, and green.

"That's his daughter," Oppong said.

"Is she married, sir?"

"Yes. Simpson is her married name. Her husband owns National Freight Incorporated, an import-export company. He's rich, and he travels a lot."

"Which gives her a chance to have an affair all alone in that secluded house."

"I don't see what else the bishop would be doing at Sandra's house at two in the morning," Oppong agreed.

"I think we should bring him in for questioning," Darko said. "He's just shown us that he could leave the premises of his prayer vigil."

"Talk to Simpson first. If she admits to Howard-Mills spending a couple hours with her on the night of Kate Vanderpuye's murder, then he has an alibi."

Good point, Darko thought. "Okay, sir."

"Just be careful with Howard-Mills," Oppong warned. "He's politically connected."

"I think I've been careful enough with him, sir."

Oppong was silent for a moment. "We'll discuss it more on Monday," he said in a clipped voice.

Next, Darko called Safo, who sounded relieved Darko was on the mend.

"Sir," she continued, "today I went through the texts and call logs in Madam Katherine's mobile phones."

Darko was pleased by this show of initiative. "Well done. What did you find?"

"She had three different sim cards. On the first one, I found that beginning February, about ninety percent of her texts were back and forth between Solomon and herself. Kind of like arguments. You said this, I said that, and so on. They became even more frequent from the beginning of April until her death."

"Did he ever threaten to hurt her?"

"Never."

"What about the other texts?"

"A few were to and from James Bentsi-Enchill, setting up appointments and so on, but in one, Mr. Bentsi-Enchill said, 'I can't wait to see you on Friday, my lovely flower.'"

Darko snorted mentally. How banal. "And her response?"

"She said, 'Let's keep it professional.'"

"So Bentsi-Enchill's prior passions for Katherine might have resurfaced. She turned to James as someone she knew and trusted, regardless of a failed romance in the past. But he might have taken advantage of her needs and demanded sex in return."

"So unethical, sir."

"I've seen worse," Darko said. "Did you find any other flirtations from him?"

"Not in his texts. But calls went back and forth between them, some up to twenty-five minutes long, and we don't know what was said."

"Right. James and Kate could have been discussing the case, or he might have been trying to romance her. Maybe she refused him multiple times and that enraged him. What else? Texts between the bishop and Katherine?"

"There are many, sir. Most of them are some kind of encouragement. For example, on twenty-third March, he wrote, 'Your heart is heavy these days, dear Katherine. Read your Bible and take strength from it. Psalm 28:7 says, 'The LORD is my strength and my shield; in him my heart trusts, and I am helped; my heart exults, and with my song I give thanks to him.'

"The following day, Katherine asks if she can meet him later on, and he tells her, 'You can come to me, or I can come to you. Let us know each other.'"

Darko frowned. "Odd, the use of the word 'know.' Somewhere in Genesis—I don't remember where—it says something about Adam knowing his wife."

Safo said nothing. For a moment, Darko thought he had lost the connection. "Safo?"

"Yes, sir. Genesis four: 'Now Adam knew Eve his wife, and she conceived and bore Cain.' Please, I don't think that's what the bishop meant."

"Maybe not," Darko said, moving on. "What about the other two sims? Did you check them as well?"

"Yes, sir. One has almost nothing, but the other has texts and calls to and from Kate's mother, and, please, also your wife, just asking how she's doing and is everything okay."

"Did Kate communicate with her mother or my wife that she felt her life was in danger or someone was threatening her?"

"No, sir. Everything is positive."

"Anything else? What about texts to or from Peter or Michael Amalba—or calls?"

"Not that I can find, sir."

"Okay, then. Nice job, Safo. I will see you on Monday."

As Darko put his phone down at the bedside, he had a flashback from his illness.

"Christine?" he called out.

She was cleaning the bathroom and came out to find him sitting on the bed in contemplation. "What's up?"

"Your mother was here while I was sick, right?"

She hesitated. "Yes, why?"

"I don't know if I dreamt it, but I seem to recall her telling me something about how she had watched Wednesday night's prayer vigil on TV."

Christine leaned the mop against the wall. "Yeah, we have to talk about that. She said you got violent and shoved her away."

"*What?*" he said, trying to recall. "I might have pushed her, but I wasn't violent."

"Em, I think pushing is kind of violent," Christine observed.

"You know what she was doing while supposedly watching over me?" Darko said indignantly. "She was talking about redemption and my accepting Jesus blah, blah, and getting rid of my grudges and malice against her and I don't know what else."

Christine was doubtful. "Are you sure she was saying those things? You were quite delirious, you know."

"Delirious or not, I remember that specifically."

"I don't think she meant any harm, Dark," Christine said, looking pained.

"Preaching to me while I'm burning up with fever?" Darko said. "What person in his or her right mind would do that? Would Jesus do that? I don't think so. Talk about malicious."

"But Dark," Christine protested, "you can't push an old lady like that. It's grossly disrespectful. And very un-Ghanaian, by the way."

"I wouldn't have done it if I weren't ill," Darko said. "There I am prostrate and dying, and she's giving me a self-righteous tongue-lashing."

"Ah!" Christine exclaimed with a dry laugh. "You weren't dying."

"Yes, I was," he insisted. "I was on death's bed."

Christine snorted. "But seriously," she said, "you have to apologize to her."

Darko groaned and dropped his forehead into his palm. "You're killing me, oh."

"You have to, Dark."

"Okay, okay. I'll go to her place this evening after I help Cairo with Papa. Do you want to come with me?"

"Actually, I was going to pick her up tonight to come to dinner. Why don't you go instead so you can sit down with her and talk beforehand?"

Darko couldn't think of anything more awkward. "If you say so," he said with a heavy sigh. "But I'm doing it only because I like you, not because I want to."

"*Like!*" she exclaimed, looking insulted. "Just '*like*?' After my bringing you back from the brink of death?"

"Come, on," he said, getting up to grab her around the waist. "You know what I mean." He kissed her full on the mouth. "Bye. I'm going to Papa's house."

WHEN DARKO ARRIVED, Cairo and Franklin were packing up Jacob's things in the bedroom. The old man stood in the doorway protesting. "What are you doing with my clothes? Where are you taking them?"

"You're coming to live with me, Papa," Cairo said. He looked at Darko. "Must be I've answered that question thirty or forty times this morning. Maybe you can try."

Franklin was emptying drawers and the wardrobe of clothes, which he put on the bed for Cairo in his wheelchair to fold and drop in boxes at the bedside.

"Papa," Darko said, "how are you doing?"

"Who are you?" Jacob demanded.

"Darko. Your son."

Jacob gazed at him, a glimmer coming to his eyes and a smile creeping across his face as he seemed to retrieve the memory.

"Who are you?" he asked again.

"He's bad today," Cairo said. "Doesn't remember anyone."

Darko looked around. The place was at the messy, half-packed stage. "How can I help?" he asked.

"We have quite a few boxes packed up already," Cairo said. "You and Franklin can take those out to the car."

As they began, Jacob made his way slowly over to them yelling. "Hey! Thieves! What are you doing? *Hey!*"

Darko put down his load, signaling Franklin to keep going. "Papa, come and sit down. This way. Come. No, don't worry about that box. Just come and have a seat here."

He guided his father to the only chair that hadn't yet been moved to Cairo's house during the week.

"There's some Sprite in the kitchen," Cairo said. "See if that will distract him."

Darko poured it into a plastic cup and handed it to his father, who took a few sips.

"Good?" Darko asked. "You like Sprite. You always did."

"But you like Malta," Jacob said.

Darko was startled. How, if his father hadn't even recognized him, had he remembered that Darko liked Malta? It was lightning from the blue. "Yes, Papa. You're right. I do."

Jacob gave the cup back.

"Had enough?" Darko asked.

Jacob nodded.

Darko knelt down by his father. "Listen, Papa. We just want you to be closer to us, so we can take care of you, okay? That's why we're moving you to Cairo's house. He has more space than I do. You'll like it there."

Jacob was staring at him, as if trying to decipher what Darko was saying. "But why are those men taking all my things away?"

"They're not," Darko said. "Well, they are, but they're taking them to Cairo's place, so they'll be with you."

"Who's that man?" Jacob asked, looking at his older son.

"His name is Cairo."

Cairo had turned his wheelchair to watch Jacob, and Darko saw his brother's eyes moisten. It was harder for him, maybe because Jacob had always favored Cairo over his younger brother. Darko felt the tragedy of his father's awful decline but not so much the pain. Maybe *he* should have been the one to take care of their father, but Cairo wanted to do it, and Darko couldn't take that away from him.

Cairo turned back to boxing up the clothes in silence, and Darko put a hand on his shoulder. "Are you okay, big brah?"

He smiled up at Darko. "I'm good, little brah."

Three hours later, most everything was packed up and either transferred to Cairo's car or set aside to be picked up later. Thankfully, Jacob had fallen asleep on the bed, allowing them to get through without interruption. But now it was time to get him up.

"Papa," Darko said, shaking him gently, "time to go."

Jacob lifted his head. "Where?"

"To Cairo's house."

Jacob frowned. "No."

"Come on. Sit up and let me put your shoes on."

Cairo was marking the last of the boxes and Franklin was outside moving the car so it would be easier for Jacob to access.

"All right," Darko said after getting his father's shoes on. "We're set to go. Ready?"

As Darko led him slowly out of the house in which he had lived most of his adult life, Jacob appeared more and more confused. Once they had left the front porch, he began to resist until Darko could coax him no longer.

"Come, Papa," Darko said. "Let's go. It's okay. Nothing bad is going to happen."

"No, no, no," Jacob said, pulling away. "No, I don't want to go."

"Papa—"

A stalemate was in effect. Jacob was pointed in one direction and Darko, who didn't want this to become a dragging match that might injure his father, in the opposite. There was only one thing to do. He dipped down under his father's arm, gripped him around the torso and swept him off his feet like he was carrying a bride across the threshold.

Jacob began to wail that he was falling.

"No, you're not, Papa," Darko said, carrying him to the car. "I've got you safe and sound."

Franklin opened the back door and Darko gingerly lowered his old man into the rear seat. "You can let go of my neck now, Papa. Papa, *let go*."

Darko managed to untangle himself and stepped away perspiring heavily. "My God," he muttered, wiping his face. "This man will be the death of me."

Franklin went around to the driver's side. Cairo transferred from his wheelchair into the front passenger seat, and Darko folded up his wheelchair to take back inside. Cairo had one at home and could always collect this one on the return trip.

"I'll meet you there," Darko said, raising his voice to be heard over his father's cries. As they drove away, Darko bent forward and rested his hands on his knees for an exhausted moment, admitting to himself the illness had taken quite a bite out of him. It would take a couple of meals of *kenkey* and two or three of *banku* to get back to normal.

CHAPTER THIRTY-THREE

ON SUNDAY WHEN DARKO woke up, Christine was at church with Hosiah, and only Sly was home. He was in the sitting room working in pencil on large sheets of paper.

"Good morning, Daddy," he said, looking up as Darko came in.

"How are you, Sly?" he said, standing next to his son with his arm around his shoulders. "What are you drawing?"

"A street scene," Sly explained. "Here are some truck pushers, market sellers over here, *tro-tro*, Mercedes Benzes, and some other cars."

"Okay, yeah," Darko said, admiring the detail. "Well done."

"Thanks, Daddy."

There wasn't any doubt Sly was talented, and Darko had encouraged him to keep all his drawings, even the ones he didn't like.

"Have you eaten?" he asked Sly.

"Yes, Daddy. Mama says there's *fufu* and light soup for you."

Darko rubbed his hands together in anticipation.

"Artificial *fufu*," Sly added.

"Artificial!" Darko exclaimed in dismay.

"From the box. You mix it with water and stir." Sly laughed. "Mama said, 'if Daddy thinks I'm going to spend hours pounding *fufu*, he's mistaken.'"

Darko went to the kitchen muttering, "Artificial *fufu*. What is the world coming to?"

• • •

AFTER CHRISTINE AND Hosiah had returned from church, Darko got on his motorcycle and rode to the Qedesh, where he found Howard-Mills preaching to a packed house in the largest of the auditoriums. Darko went around to the back of the building, where two dark, solid wood doors faced him. One was locked, but the other opened into a small office with a couple of steel-frame chairs and a gunmetal desk, the drawers of which were locked as well. So was an interior door in the room. Darko didn't know what he was looking for, and he probably shouldn't have been in there without permission in the first place.

He turned as a key jiggled on the other side of the interior door. It opened to reveal John, who jumped, startled to find Darko there.

"Oh!" he said in surprise.

"Good morning, John," Darko said. "Sorry; I was looking for you. I knocked."

"Okay, Inspector," he said, with a smile. "It's no problem at all. I went to get the bishop's clothes from the laundry." He put a pile of pressed, folded garments on the desk. "Please have a seat."

"Thanks. I won't take too much of your time. I know you're busy."

"Sure," John said, taking the other chair.

"I have one or two questions," Darko said. "Did Peter Amalba ever tell you he was in love with Katherine Vanderpuye?"

John rubbed his chin reflectively. "He never *told* me that, sir, but I know he was infatuated with her. On one occasion last year, he came to a *bussell* at Katherine's home without an invitation."

"I didn't know about that," Darko said.

"He showed up with one of the other church members," John said. "I told him it was okay that one time, but I didn't allow it to happen again. He sat staring at Kate for the whole session. It was troubling. I feel sorry for him in a way, and although we forgive him for what he did to the bishop, we should also realize that he was and still is a disturbed person."

"Is he so disturbed that he might harm Kate?"

John seemed discomfited. "I'm not qualified to say, Inspector."

"Perhaps that wasn't a fair question."

"It's no problem. Please, is there something else?"

"About the bishop," Darko said. "Were you aware he left the premises of the Independence Square vigil?"

"Yes, I was."

The truth for a change, Darko thought. "Do you know where he went?"

John shook his head. "No. It's none of my business."

"But you have your suspicions."

John smiled uncomfortably, but he didn't respond.

"I've asked you about Baden Powell Hall before, but I'm asking you again. Did the bishop leave the premises after Reverend Atiemo took over from him?"

This time, John did not deny it with the same certainty. "I'm not sure," he stammered. "He could have. I wasn't with him around that time."

So, Darko thought, a change of story. "I understand you want to protect your boss," he said. "What you tell me is in confidence. Was the bishop involved romantically with Kate?"

John was apparently wrestling with his loyalties. "Please, Inspector, the bishop can't know I'm telling you this."

"You have my word."

John lowered his head and covered his eyes. "It happened two Mondays ago in this room," he whispered. "I was next door and heard them. He wanted sex; she didn't. There was a struggle. She ran out of the room crying."

A shattering new piece of information, Darko thought. If it was true.

He and John were silent for a while. "Do you believe he raped her?" Darko asked.

"Oh, no, sir," John said, demonstrably alarmed. "Not that. But an attempt. That's why when the reverend and I attended the *bussell* on the following Wednesday, Kate was so sad. I felt bad for her. And I'm ashamed."

"Of the bishop?"

"Yes. And myself."

"Why?"

John looked up. "I should have tried to help Kate, but I didn't. I was a coward."

Darko nodded. "Sometimes these things happen so quickly, and they're over before you have a chance to act." He stood up. "Thank you."

"You're welcome, sir."

At the door, Darko turned. "I need to tie up any remaining loose ends. Can you please put me in touch with one or more people who can vouch for your presence at the Hall on Friday night starting around eleven P.M?"

"Of course, Inspector."

John scrolled through his phone list and gave Darko three names. One was Blankson, with whom Darko had already spoken, and the other two were members of the cleanup crew.

CHAPTER THIRTY-FOUR

ON MONDAY, DARKO AND Safo made a trek to Prampram, a beach resort where tourists and rich Ghanaians came to play and Maude Vanderpuye owned a restaurant.

"Inspector," she said, "I did not hate my daughter-in-law, nor did I have her killed if that's what you are implying."

She faced Darko and Safo on the restaurant patio, which provided an unobstructed, sweeping view of the blue-green sea. The tide was low. White foamy waves broke gently on the tawny sand. In the distance, fishing canoes bobbed up and down with the ocean's rhythm.

Maude looked like she was straight out of a beauty magazine with her long chestnut hair parted in the middle, manicured nails, immaculate makeup, long lashes, and glossy lips. Whatever fragrance she was wearing smelled French and expensive.

Her iPhone on the table buzzed every few minutes, and each time, Maude apologized that she "had to take this." The calls were about supplies and deliveries, or this or that catered event. She seemed furious most of the time. "What do you mean the dinner rolls are late?"

In his peripheral vision, Darko saw Safo assessing Maude's appearance with both admiration and disapproval.

"I have no good reason or motive to see Katherine murdered," Maude resumed.

"Maybe you do," Darko said. "Perhaps her death makes your name on the house deed all the more legal."

Maude laughed. "Inspector, please. The document was and is legal."

"Kate received threatening phone messages," Darko said, pushing on, "some of them calling her a witch. Were you or your daughter responsible for those?"

"Of course not!" Maude exclaimed indignantly. "We don't do things like that."

Darko looked at Safo. "Do you have any questions for Mrs. Vanderpuye?"

"Em, Mrs. Vanderpuye, where were you on the Friday and Saturday of your daughter-in-law's death?"

"I was at home Friday night," Maude replied. "I went to bed around ten-thirty, and in the morning I left Accra early to come here. We had a wedding party planned."

"On Friday night or early Saturday morning, did you hear Solomon go out?" Darko asked.

"No, I didn't. Our gate squeaks, so I would have heard him. Can I make a suggestion, Inspector?"

"Sure."

"Have you spoken to James Bentsi-Enchill, the lawyer Katherine was hiring to sue us?"

"Not yet. Why do you ask?"

"I suppose you know his history with Katherine?"

"I've heard a version, but I'm happy to hear yours too."

"They were an item in school until Solomon came along," Maude said. "James was jealous even after Katherine and Solomon got married. Mr. Bentsi-Enchill often said nasty things about my son behind his back. Can you imagine how happy James must have felt when Katherine turned to him for help in suing Solomon? It was like the perfect revenge. He took advantage of the situation and began to show off by taking Katherine around town."

"How do you know that?" Darko challenged Maude.

"Oh," she said, tossing her head as if this was all common knowledge, "I hear the two of them were frequenting Il Cavaliere at the Polo Club and getting quite cozy with each other."

"What is Il Cava—whatever you said?"

"Il Cavaliere. It means 'The Knight,' Inspector. It's a restaurant at the Polo Club. It's quite exclusive, so I'm not surprised you don't know it."

Darko ignored the putdown. "When were Kate and James supposedly at the Polo Club place?"

"They were spotted there in February."

"You're saying Kate was committing adultery?"

Maude sighed. "Look, I don't like to speak ill of the dead . . ."

But you're going to, Darko thought. "Is James married?" he asked.

"No, he's divorced," Maude said with a dry laugh. "A divorced divorce lawyer. What an irony. Anyway, he kept demanding sexual favors from her in return for his services, and he went too far. She rejected him."

"How did you find that out?"

"I have my sources."

"Care to name one, madam?"

"My daughter, Georgina, has a friend who clerks for Mr. Bentsi-Enchill and knew what was going on. That's as far as I'll go."

"What are you saying about who killed Kate?"

"I'm just telling you what I know. You can draw your own conclusions."

"Thank you, Mrs. Vanderpuye. We appreciate your time."

"You're welcome," she said, beginning to text.

"One other thing," Darko said, turning back, "is Georgina here?"

"She's not around at the moment," Maude responded without looking up.

Darko exited the restaurant with Safo. The sun was bright, cleaner than in Accra, and a sea breeze kept temperatures pleasant. A second building nearby bore the name CLUB MAUDE in a looped font.

"Must be the nightclub," Darko said. "Let's go in."

Safo cleared her throat. "I don't think there'll be any dancing going on right now."

He smiled. "That wasn't my intention."

The door was open, so they entered without invitation. Recessed lighting threw shadows across the dimly lit space. Cozy booths surrounded the dance floor. Behind the bar at the other end, a guy was polishing shot glasses. "Help you?" he asked the detectives.

"Georgina Vanderpuye around?" Darko asked.

"Who are you, please?"

"We're from CID. Is she here?"

"Office, please," the man said, pointing with his chin. "Around the corner, first door on the right."

Darko opened it without knocking. A woman in a tight red dress hitched up to her waist, sat astride a man in an executive chair behind the desk. He let out a yell as he saw Darko and Safo enter, the woman shrieked, and the two separated as if a water cannon had blown them apart. The man jumped out of the chair and tripped over the pants at his ankles. Pulling down her dress and rearranging herself, the woman screamed and cursed in Ga. "Don't you know how to knock? Are you *idiots?*"

"Lock the door, next time," Darko said. "I'm Chief Inspector Dawson, CID; this is Lance Corporal Safo. You're Georgina?"

"Yes. What do you want?"

"We're investigating the murder of your sister-in-law."

"I don't know anything about it," Georgina snapped. "You can't just barge in like this." She looked at her partner-in-mischief. He'd managed to get his pants back up. "Get out, Hamlet."

"Yes, madam," Hamlet said, turning his face away in embarrassment. He was taller than Darko with twice the muscle mass. He shut the door behind him as he left.

"Your underling?" Darko said.

"The manager of the club," Georgina replied, shooting a surly look at them. She was tall and leggy with a tiny waist, and her buttocks strained her dress. She clearly didn't have Maude's polish.

"We've just finished speaking to your mother," Darko said. "She said you weren't around, so I came looking."

"So you've found me," Georgina snapped. "Now what do you want?"

"Any idea who killed Kate?"

"Why would I have any idea about that?" she said, taking a seat in the executive chair.

Darko made sure he didn't steal a glance at her legs as she crossed them. "Where were you the night of Friday the twenty-eighth?" he asked.

"I was here at the club," she said after a momentary pause. "I hosted some friends until four in the morning."

"Who can confirm that?"

She shrugged. "Hamlet or the bartender; they both saw me here. You can ask either one—or both."

"Who was making anonymous calls to Kate, telling her she was a witch?" Darko asked. "Was it you?"

Georgina rolled her eyes and sucked her teeth. "Please, Inspector—what did you say your name was?"

"Dawson."

"Inspector Dawson, I have no clue what you're talking about."

"I think you do," Darko said, walking over to the desk where Georgina sat. He leaned close to her. "I'll make a deal. You tell me who made those anonymous calls, and we won't reveal to your mother that you and Hamlet have been fucking in the office."

Georgina narrowed her eyes. "You're not serious."

Darko exchanged a look with Safo.

"He's serious," she said to Georgina.

Georgina folded her arms. "Do whatever you want. I don't care."

Darko nodded. "Okay, Safo. Go ahead and tell Mrs. Vanderpuye all about it. Give her all the details."

Safo was about to leave the room when Georgina caved. "Wait," she called out. "Okay, yes. I was the one who made those calls. It was me. Are you happy now, Mr. Detective?"

"Why did you do that?" Darko asked. "Did you believe she was a witch?"

"All I know is that there was something wrong with Katherine, and she was ruining my brother's life, okay? She was *never* right for him."

"Did you plot with your brother to kill her, then?" Darko asked.

"Don't waste my time."

Darko stood in front of her with his hands on the armrests and drove the chair back against the wall.

"*Stop!*" Georgina yelled. "Are you crazy?"

"Answer my question," Dawson said, his face inches away from hers.

"No, no, no!" Georgina cried. Her voice cracked. "I didn't plot anything. Please, it wasn't me, and I know Solomon would never kill anyone."

He released her. Georgina pressed her palms against her eyes and took heaving breaths.

"Your mother says you know one of Mr. Bentsi-Enchill's clerks has some information," Darko said, leaning against the desk. "Is that correct?"

Georgina, subdued now, nodded. "Her name is Victoria Hammond. I can give you her phone number if you like."

"Yes, please."

When Georgina had found the number in her phone, Darko had her text it to him.

"Thank you, Georgina," he said.

She didn't answer.

Outside, Darko questioned Hamlet while Safo tackled the bartender separately. Their statements matched: Georgina had partied all night on Friday, finally packing it up at four A.M. Theoretically, Darko thought, if you drove like a madman, you could cover the fifty kilometers from Prampram to Accra in time to murder Kate before Esi showed up for work. But it was too unlikely for him to seriously consider. Or was it?

CHAPTER THIRTY-FIVE

ON THE WAY BACK to Accra, Darko called Victoria Hammond, who said at first she didn't want to talk about her boss's dealings with Katherine Vanderpuye.

"I can have a police vehicle come for you if you prefer," Darko said pleasantly. "We can question you at CID Headquarters just as easily."

Darko wasn't being truthful. In fact he wouldn't have any access to such a vehicle, and certainly not for that purpose. But Victoria bought it, uttering a small gasp. "Okay, no, em, what about if I meet you in front of Nkrumah Memorial Park in about one hour?"

"Thank you."

Darko turned to Safo. "I'm texting you the numbers of two of John Papafio's contacts, who he says can swear he was at Baden Powell all night and never left the premises. Please give them a call and ask about the whereabouts and movements of John and Howard-Mills. Oh, and Atiemo too. We know he was there at one A.M. to take over from the bishop, but what about between eleven P.M. and one? Could he have slipped away then to kill Katherine?"

"Yes, I see what you mean. Okay, sir."

ON SCHOOL OUTINGS, Sly and Hosiah had visited the park and mausoleum dedicated to Nkrumah, Ghana's first president, but Darko never had. As he pulled up with Safo alongside the park's perimeter wall, he muttered, "I must see this place one day before I die." Then again, he had made the same promise to himself several times before.

Victoria Hammond was late, but after twenty minutes, she came running up to them from the courthouse, which was on the other side of High Street. "I'm sorry, Inspector Dawson," she apologized, out of breath. She appeared older than she had sounded on the phone.

"Mr. Bentsi-Enchill and Mrs. Vanderpuye went to lunch a few times," Victoria said in response to Darko's questions.

"That could be a legitimate business meeting," Darko said, "could it not?"

"Of course, Inspector," she agreed.

"What about dinners at the Polo Club? Did those take place to your knowledge?"

"I don't know about that," Victoria said.

"To your knowledge, did Mr. Bentsi-Enchill ever pressure Mrs. Vanderpuye for sex in return for his services or for any other reason?"

Victoria looked shocked, but Darko was past politeness now. "No, sir. Not to my knowledge."

"Knowing him, would that be his style?"

Victoria shook her head. "The only people who level that kind of accusation against Mr. Bentsi-Enchill are those with an ax to grind."

"Who, for example? Maude and Georgina Vanderpuye?"

Victoria pulled a face. "Exactly, Inspector. I don't have direct evidence, but I wouldn't put it past them."

"Is Mr. Bentsi-Enchill in court today?"

"Yes. He has a case this morning."

DARKO AND SAFO found a seat along the wooden benches in the packed, stuffy courtroom on High Street to watch Attorney James Bentsi-Enchill perform. Ghanaian lawyers still wore the long black robes and clownish white wigs dating from the British colonial era and addressed the bench as "m'Lord." Bentsi-Enchill was engaged in a back-and-forth with a female lawyer. It was a divorce case, and at times, humor ensued in the battle, and the lay audience burst into laughter.

Bentsi-Enchill was short, with a paunch and a retreating hairline. He was verbose, dramatic, and quick to pounce on the slightest misplaced word or misquote from the other side. In Darko's judgment, he had more skill and experience than the opposing counsel. By the end of the morning's session, he seemed to have left the other attorney in the dust.

The judge banged the gavel, and the court broke for lunch. From the rear where they had sat, Darko and Safo made their way down to the bar against the grain of people filing out. The lawyers and their clerks were packing up their binders and fat folders.

"Mr. Bentsi-Enchill?" Darko said.

He turned. "Yes?"

"Detective Chief Inspector Dawson with CID; and my partner Lance Corporal Safo. Can we talk for a moment?"

He was unruffled. "Of course. Let's go to my office where we can speak in private."

Bentsi-Enchill left his voluminous files for his clerks to handle. Darko and Safo followed him to the back of the court and up a staircase that led to a row of offices along an outdoor veranda. With an antique-looking desk occupying much of the space, Bentsi-Enchill's office was small but comfortable. He hung his robe on a hook on the door and propped his wig on a mannequin head. "Please have a seat," he said. "Would you like some water?"

After the stifling courtroom, Darko and Safo gratefully accepted. Bentsi-Enchill fetched three bottles out of a small fridge on the floor, gave out two, and took one. He got half of it down in a few gulps and then sat down in his office chair opposite the detectives. "Now, how can I help?"

"We're investigating the death of Katherine Vanderpuye," Darko said.

"Ah," Bentsi-Enchill said, shaking his head. "An unimaginable tragedy. I can still hardly believe it. Shall I tell you what I know,

Chief Inspector, or do you have specific questions you would like me to address first?"

"If you could start with what you know, sir."

"Very well. Kate came to me two and a half weeks ago stating that she intended to sue Solomon for fraudulently removing her name from the documents of the house the two of them jointly and legally owned—"

"Two and a half weeks ago?" Darko questioned. "What about in February? Did you have dinner with Katherine at the Polo Club?"

"Oh, yes," he said, not particularly bothered, "but it was about legal matters, and it wasn't a date, if that's what you mean. I invited some couples for dinner, and I included Katherine and Solomon. Look, we all know about our old rivalry, but I don't bear any grudges and have no problems extending an olive branch. They both came to the party."

"Can you prove it?"

"Absolutely," Bentsi-Enchill said, reaching for his phone. It took him a few minutes to retrieve the photo. "Here we are."

He showed it to Darko. Indeed, both Solomon and Katherine were in the group picture around a restaurant table. Bentsi-Enchill hit MENU and then DETAILS, which revealed the February date.

Darko had been unaware of that little trick. "So," he said, "you never went to the restaurant—or any restaurant—with Kate alone?"

"No," Bentsi-Enchill said.

"Do you mind sharing the photo with me?" Darko asked.

"Of course not," the lawyer said. "Give me your number." As he texted the image, he said, "I have a pretty good idea you've been speaking to Maude Vanderpuye or her equally odious daughter, Georgina. They run a well-oiled rumor mill, determined to shift any culpability for the murder away from themselves."

"Do you have any evidence that one or both of them is responsible for Kate's death?"

The lawyer leaned back and crossed his legs at the ankles. "Maude and Solomon mounted a vicious and sustained attack on

Kate. Maude, in particular, wanted to destroy her daughter-in-law in the most venomous manner possible. She recruited her son to the campaign and brainwashed him into believing his wife was a witch and was killing their baby in her womb and trying to kill Solomon as well. When Kate decided to strike back by coming to me to launch a lawsuit, Solomon was ripe for revenge, and he and Maude conspired to kill her. I doubt they included Georgina because she can't keep her mouth shut."

"You're a man of the law, sir," Darko said, "so you know it's all about evidence. Do you have any to back up your accusations?"

"Look," Bentsi-Enchill said, turning up a palm, "Solomon had the keys to the gate and the front door of the house. He let himself in, killed the watchman, and then butchered Kate. Or other way round, perhaps."

"But other people could have had motives," Darko pointed out. "Bishop Howard-Mills, for example. Did Kate talk about him?"

"I know she was going to him for solace and guidance. Personally, I wouldn't have gone to a religious fraud for any advice, but who was I to interfere?"

"Religious fraud?" Darko asked.

"All that healing and casting out of demons?" Bentsi-Enchill laughed. "A moneymaking con with thousands of victims—poor people making the man rich. He has four houses and owns a radio station. Did you know that? He flies his wife to London for shopping sprees. The bishop should be arrested, but then so should many others of his ilk."

"May I ask you where you were on the night of Friday the twenty-eighth of April, sir?"

"Ghana Bar Association annual dinner," Bentsi-Enchill answered.

"Until what time?"

"About eleven."

"And after that?"

"Home. I was exhausted."

"Can anyone confirm you were home?"

"I'm afraid not. I'm divorced now, and the kids were with their mother." The lawyer sounded wistful. "No one at home but myself these days. Ah, well." He slid his chair back a few inches. "Anything else I can do for you?"

"I think that's all," Darko said, preparing to leave. "Actually, just one more thing, Mr. Bentsi-Enchill. Are you willing to swear you didn't request any sexual favors from Katherine Vanderpuye in exchange for your services?"

"Yes, I am," he replied. "There was no quid pro quo. And now, if you would excuse me, lady and gentleman, I must prepare for this afternoon's session."

CHAPTER THIRTY-SIX

AFTER SAFO AND DARKO had returned to CID, he went through Katherine's mobile texts and phone logs. She had already done that, and he trusted her, but a second pair of eyes was always a good idea.

Darko's fingers stopped scrolling. "Wait a minute," he said. "Did you see this?"

He flipped the phone around so Safo could take a look at the screen.

"Oh!" she exclaimed, and clapped her hand over her mouth. "Please, I missed it. I'm sorry."

The text to Kate was dated 17th April, about three weeks before.

WE HAVE A RESERVATION AT 7, WILL PICK U UP 630

"A reservation where?" Darko said.

His phone buzzed with a text from Christine. She couldn't fetch Sly from school detention that afternoon, so Darko would have to do it. He only had about an hour.

"I want you to pay a visit to the Polo Club restaurant tomorrow," he said to Safo. "Ask the manager and staff if they remember seeing Katherine Vanderpuye with James Bentsi-Enchill on seventeenth April—or if there's a record of the two of them being there together on that date. If they were there, it means Bentsi-Enchill lied about his taking her to the restaurant only once, back in February."

"Yes, sir."

Darko stood. "I'm going to pick up my son from school."

HE WALKED INTO St. Theresa's concrete yard. Four boys were playing basketball around the hoop at one end of the playground. Two floors of classrooms surrounded the courtyard. As far as schools went in Accra, this was one of the best kept. Darko and Christine were glad Sly was here, and they hoped to get Hosiah in the next year. The difficult part was the hefty fees.

Darko turned onto the hallway leading to the staff office. Just outside of that was a nook where Sly and a couple of other students sat doing their homework. He looked up when he saw his father, smiled, and jumped up to start packing up his books. He didn't need any prompting to leave.

"Did you finish your work?" Darko asked him.

"Almost," Sly said. "I can do the rest at home."

Before they left, Darko put his head in Sister Aboagye's office. She wore a starched blue habit and had a motherly air. "Sly is doing better," she said. "He's a little bit of a daydreamer, and he loses focus, but I think he can work on that. Eh, Sly?"

Sly smiled bashfully and squirmed. Darko thought he pulled that off quite well.

"Thank you very much, Sister," he said. "We appreciate it."

Outside, Darko and Sly put on their helmets, and they took off on the motorcycle, the son with his arms wrapped around his father's waist.

"Where are we going, Daddy?" he asked against the wind.

"Achimota Forest."

Once they had cleared the jams at the Nkrumah overpass and George W. Bush Highway, the rest of the way was easier. Some stretches of the Achimota Road were open enough for Darko to open the throttle. He heard Sly laughing with glee behind him. They turned into the entrance to Sandra Simpson's lodge.

A watchman let them into the compound within the chain link fence and went to notify her.

Sly's face shone with the thrill of the ride. "That was fun Daddy," he said, removing his helmet. "Who are we coming to see?"

"A lady called Sandra Simpson," Darko replied.

The watchman emerged from the house. "Please, you can come."

Sly waited outside while Darko went in. Sandra was on the back veranda stretched out on a chaise longue with a novel. Her skin was pale, and her prominent dark eyes seemed to fill her face more than their share. She was too thin for Darko's tastes, but he could see why some men might find her attractive.

"Please," she said, gesturing to a chair after introductions.

Darko sat, telling her why he was there. "Mrs. Simpson," he continued, "I'm not interested in passing moral judgments. Your affairs are your business alone. Except where they could have a bearing on a murder investigation. I know you've been seeing Bishop Howard-Mills."

Simpson stiffened and blinked several times. "Who told you that, Mr. Dawson?" she asked. Her voice had iced over.

"I followed him here last Wednesday."

She chewed on her top lip, probably wondering if she had an out.

"I saw you open the door to him," Darko added to help her decide.

That did it. "All right, then," Simpson said. "Yes, it's true. I see him when my husband is out of town. Does he have to know? It will ruin me, Inspector. And the bishop, for that matter."

"No one else needs to know," Darko said, "but it's crucial I find out if he spent time with you early in the morning of Saturday, twenty-ninth April—around say, one o'clock."

She shook her head. "No, because my husband was still here. He left the following Monday and then Clem was able to see me on Wednesday. Saturday was when poor Katherine Vanderpuye was murdered, right?"

"Yes," Darko said. "Did you know her?"

"No, I didn't."

"Are you aware if Howard-Mills was involved romantically with her?"

"He might have been." Simpson pressed her lips together. "I know she and Clem texted each other."

"You know? How?"

She smiled. "I sneaked a look at his phone once while he was in the bathroom and saw a phone notification."

"It didn't bother you?"

"I have no right to complain," Simpson said. "I don't own Clem. He gives me his time when he can. I'm the lonely one; he isn't."

Darko rose from his chair. "Thank you, Mrs. Simpson. I appreciate your time."

"You're welcome, Mr. Dawson. I'll see you out."

OUTSIDE, DARKO CHECKED Simpson's story with the watchman. After some confusion over the dates, he confirmed she had been accurate. The bishop could not have visited her the Saturday of the murder.

"You have a fine boy," the watchman said, smiling as he opened the gate for the motorcycle to exit.

"Thank you, sir."

As they rode off, Darko felt no clearer about the bishop. Had he left Baden Powell Hall the night of the murder or not? If so, for how long, and where did he go?

AROUND ELEVEN THAT night, Darko was watching the nightly news with Christine sleeping on his lap when Cairo called.

"Papa's gone," he said.

Darko sat up. "What?"

"I thought he was in his room. I went to check on him to make sure he was all right for the night, but when I looked in, he was gone."

"I'll come over now." Darko shifted Christine off and rose

abruptly. Her head flopped back onto the sofa, and she murmured, "Ouch."

He shook her awake. "I'm going to Cairo's place. Papa has disappeared."

CAIRO AND HIS wife, Audrey, lived in Christian Village. It was no longer a village but a new middle-class enclave and an example of Accra's sprawl. By the time Darko got there, Cairo had done some searching in the immediate area of their home, and he directed Darko to meet him at a nearby gas station.

Cairo was distraught and furious with himself for "allowing this to happen." He had already gone to the local police station to alert them, in case any of their officers on the beat happened to spot Jacob wandering.

Darko had butterflies in his stomach. Anything might have befallen their father. That he couldn't walk very fast was small comfort. A car could have struck him, or he could have fallen into an open gutter along the road.

Audrey was driving Cairo. Darko split up with them, and they went in opposite directions in expanding radii. Darko paid particular attention to abandoned building sites into which his father might have wandered. Darko got out of the car several times with his flashlight and called out. He wished he could scour all the gutters, but at night that would have been an impossible project.

At minimarts and fuel stations, Darko slowed down and circled them in the hope that Papa had been attracted to the lights and decided to sit down and watch the world coming and going. The irony was that if Christian Village had actually been a village still, Darko could have stopped and asked practically anyone if they had seen his father.

He called Cairo. "No sign?"

"No, nothing."

"We'll keep searching," Darko said. "Don't worry. We'll find him."

The question was, dead or alive?

DARKO DIDN'T WANT to give up, but he didn't know where else to look, and he was starting to feel desperate. Should he go farther afield, or go back over territory he had already covered? He thought he noticed the car wobbling slightly, and then it became more pronounced. He pulled over, switched on his flashlight, and saw his back right tire was flat.

"Shit!" he cursed—one of the rare moments he used that word.

He called Cairo to tell him what had happened. His brother cursed too but used a far milder version as a courtesy to Audrey in the seat beside him.

Darko went a little farther to a small fuel station that was closed for the night but still had good lighting. He began to change the tire as quickly as he could. A shadow passed over him, and Darko jumped and turned.

Jacob had somehow lost his shirt. His pants were sagging, and he had only one shoe. There were leaves in his hair.

"Papa," Darko said. "What are you doing all the way out here?"

"Where's Beatrice?" Jacob asked, confused. "She said she was going to Ketanu, but she never came home."

Gooseflesh rose over Darko's body. Beatrice, his mother, had mysteriously disappeared during his childhood. Ketanu was the village in the Volta Region where she was last seen alive.

Darko went to his father and put his arm around his shoulders. "Beatrice will be back soon, Papa—don't worry. Let's go home and wait for her there."

"All right." He squinted at Darko. "Who are you?"

"My name is Darko. I know Beatrice well."

Jacob nodded. "Good."

Darko surveyed his father to check for any injuries, but the old man seemed okay. Where Jacob had gone and how he had got here, Darko would never know. He got his father into the front seat of the car, strapped him in, and called Cairo. "I found him. Or rather, he found me. Yes, he's about as good as can be expected. Confused as hell, but otherwise okay."

CHAPTER THIRTY-SEVEN

FIRST THING IN THE morning, Darko called Dr. Quainoo, the psychiatrist who had evaluated Peter Amalba.

"Peter is not mad as in schizophrenic," Quainoo told Darko in a high-pitched voice that sounded like a child's squeeze toy. "Paranoid personality disorder is probably his diagnosis, but some of the religious grandiosity is a little difficult to pigeonhole. That might just be a cultural addition to his underlying disorder."

"So, what should happen to him now, sir?"

"Putting him on one of our state psychiatric hospitals will turn him outright psychotic. No, if he's going to prison, then he's going to a 'normal' one with 'normal' prisoners, so to speak. He's been sent to Central Jail, and he'll be there until remand."

"Thank you, Doctor."

SAFO WAS CARRYING out her assignment at the Polo Club, so Darko went to Central Jail by himself. This part of town, the Tudu commercial area where a serial killer had lurked a few years ago, was one of the oldest in Accra, and Central Jail had changed little to none, especially on the outside. Inside, some new fixtures and a couple of computers had modernized the place somewhat, but its age still showed.

Darko flashed his credentials to the sergeant at the desk. In the background, the jail was as dark as a cave.

"You have Peter Amalba?" Darko asked.

"We do, sir. Do you need to speak to him?"

"Yes, please."

"Okay, we have a small room."

The sergeant lifted the hinged partition of the counter so Darko could pass to the other side, and then went to the bars and yelled for Amalba, who came forward to peer out. "Yes, sir?"

"You have a visitor. Your wrists."

Peter stuck them out, and the sergeant slapped cuffs on faster than Darko could blink, before unlocking the door with a giant set of large keys. A constable marched Peter to the interview room at the far end of the counter, and Darko followed. A bare, pockmarked wooden table and two chairs sat in the middle of a room that hadn't seen a fresh coat of paint in years.

"Please, do you need me to stay here?" the corporal asked.

"No, I'm okay, thank you," Darko said. "I'll call you when we've finished."

Peter's hands were in his lap. His eyes were down as if he were studying the table.

Darko sat. "How are you, Mr. Amalba?"

"I'm fine, sir. How are you too?"

"Are they treating you all right?"

Peter shrugged. "The food is terrible."

Darko nodded. He'd never tasted prison food, but he knew it was pretty awful. "You met with the psychiatrist," he said. "How was the experience?"

"He asked me so many questions. After a while, I wanted to get away from him."

"Understood," Darko said.

Peter looked up tentatively. "What did that doctor tell you?"

"The bottom line is you're not crazy," Darko said.

Peter seemed unmoved by the news.

"And because you're not crazy," Darko said, "I now view you differently. You may think these stories you've told about being in love with Katherine Vanderpuye and seeing Bishop Howard-Mills around her house at three in the morning are funny or entertaining, but the law of the land does not, and neither do I. The consequences of lying are serious. You understand?"

"Yes, please."

"That's why I'm here today. To have a frank, honest, and, above all, *truthful* discussion with you about what happened and what did *not*."

Peter looked away. For several minutes, he said nothing at all. Darko saw his jaw tensing in and out.

"Okay, Mr. Darko," Peter began, "I want to tell you that I have suffered for years from demons. They control my thoughts and make me do things that, on my own, I would not do. I have been to exorcists, and I have been to deliverance services with pastors and bishops, including Bishop Howard-Mills's Qedesh. Sometimes the demons seem to flow out of me, but then they return.

"Michael knew of my troubles. Sometimes he took me to see a psychiatrist, but they couldn't help me get rid of these evil thoughts. And some of the medicines they gave me made me feel terrible."

"What are the evil thoughts like?" Darko asked.

Peter rested his forehead in his palm. "That people want to hurt me, or destroy me, or curse me. And that makes me want to hurt them too. At times I have been desperate, afraid of myself. Michael told me to seek salvation at the Qedesh.

"I met Kate end of last year at the Qedesh," Peter continued. "She was studying her Bible before the service. We talked, and she was very nice, and we had a good time. And the following week we met at the Qedesh again and sat next to each other at the service. I fell in love with her.

"When I found out Kate was hosting one of the *bussells* at her home, I accompanied a church member to a prayer meeting there. John Papafio was very abusive to me when I arrived, telling me I wasn't on the attendance list, instead of welcoming me like a genuine Christian would do. So what if I wasn't on the list? Is that a crime? After that, I know for a fact he prevented me from ever attending another meeting at her house.

"Toward the end of last month, after I had met with the

bishop, I was about to leave John's office when Kate walked in. She greeted me, but she was cold, as if she barely knew me. She ignored me and began to converse with John. At first, I thought maybe Kate was in love with him, but when the bishop came out of his office and was standing next to her, he began to touch her back, and then I understood it was the bishop she loved. John had been keeping me away from Kate for the *bishop*, not himself.

"I left the office, but I saw Mr. Howard-Mills come out with Kate, and they went to the back of the building, so I followed. There are two doors there. One door on the right was locked, but the one on the left was not, so I went in. There's another door between the two rooms." Peter's voice dropped in volume and pitch and gave Darko the shivers. "I heard what the bishop was saying to Kate. He said he wanted to see her outside of the church, this so-called man of God who always preaches against fornication.

"Kate told him she regarded him with respect, and now was not the right time because she was going through so much trouble with her husband. Bishop Howard-Mills said he could come to see her late at night during his break from the prayer vigil at Baden Powell Hall the following Friday. He said he would go to her house around two o'clock and call her from outside her gate. I couldn't hear if she gave him any reply. Maybe she was speaking too softly."

Peter rested his head on his cuffed hands, appearing exhausted by his account.

"Do you want a break?" Darko asked.

Peter shook his head. "I'm okay. That week from Tuesday all the way to Friday, I was thinking of what the bishop had said about visiting Katherine early on Saturday morning.

"On Friday, Michael traveled to Takoradi, and that left me alone in the house. I slept a little and woke up after midnight. I took a cab to Kate's area, but I couldn't remember the exact location of her house. At that time too, there was *dumsor*, so it was very dark. I walked around, lost. When it was getting close to three o'clock, I started to think I should go home. Then, just as I found Kate's place, I saw Bishop Howard-Mills walking away from the house."

"I thought you said it was *dumsor*," Darko interrupted. "How could you see if the street was dark?"

"Please, her generator was on and a bright light at the top her house shines into the street, so I could see the bishop—but only from the back."

"How was he dressed?"

"He had that light blue suit with the long top."

"You said before he was holding a machete," Darko reminded him.

Peter looked down. "That wasn't true. I never saw that. Maybe he had it under his clothes, rather. He hurried to his car and drove away."

"What vehicle?"

"A saloon car."

Why not his SUV? So people at the vigil would think he was still there, Darko speculated. "Did the car have some writing on the side?"

Peter frowned. "I think so—and also on the back window, but I couldn't see very well."

Casting back to the Independence Square event on Wednesday night, Darko remembered seeing decals on the windows of the Power of God Ministry vehicles.

"What happened next?" he asked Peter.

"I wanted to make sure the bishop had not done Katherine any harm. I tried knocking on the gate and ringing the bell, and I called out Gabriel's name, but he never answered. I decided to wait until morning. I found a place on the ground to rest in the empty building across the street from Kate's house, and I slept a little. Around five, I woke up when I heard the house girl unlocking the gate. And you know the rest."

Darko leaned forward. "Peter, tell me one thing. After you saw the bishop walking away from Kate's house, were you so jealous, so angry, that you decided to kill her? Did you go away and return with a machete, which you used to kill Gabriel and then Katherine? Peter, did you kill her? Tell me now. Free yourself from the burden of guilt."

Peter shook his head stoically, but unexpectedly, his face crumpled, and he began to cry.

"Tell me what's in your mind," Darko pressed. He was hoping, praying, for a confession. He wanted this to be over and done. "Come on, Peter. The truth."

Peter was shaking his head as his tears fell on the table. "I wish I could have saved her from the bishop. But, I arrived too late. Kate, I'm sorry, I'm sorry."

He clenched his fists as if trying to hold on to his last reserves of fortitude, and then he looked up, eyes reddened but his expression no longer contorted. He heaved a sigh and was silent.

"Okay," Darko said, getting to his feet. "Stay here for a moment."

He left the room pulling the door shut and calling for the constable, who came up. "Are you done, sir?"

"Yes, I am. Thank you."

WALKING OUT, DARKO was ninety-five percent sure he knew who had killed Katherine Vanderpuye. He got a hold of Dr. Kwapong on the phone. She told him she had concluded Kate's autopsy earlier in the day. "As you know," she said, "it was gruesome and brutal. Nothing much changes from our observations at the scene. The killer almost certainly used a machete or an ax. Now, one hopeful finding is that fragments of Kate's nails had broken off, so she might have scratched the assailant in a struggle. I sent nail swabs and samples to the lab for DNA, but of course, it will be some weeks before we get the results."

Darko wished he had them now, but long-delayed DNA findings were the reality of Ghana's CID. He sighed in resignation and frustration. "Thank you, Doc."

CHAPTER THIRTY-EIGHT

"PLEASE, SIR," SAFO SAID, when Darko had returned to the CID detectives' office, "the manager at Il Cavaliere checked in the reservation book and confirmed Katherine and Bentsi-Enchill had dinner there together on seventeenth April."

Darko blew out his breath harshly. "Bentsi-Enchill," he said shaking his head in disgust. "What did I tell you about people lying, Safo?"

Safo smiled. "That they do it as easily as breathing oxygen."

"Correct."

"Also, sir, the two contacts John Papafio gave us—I called them. They both say they saw John off and on throughout the night at Baden Powell, and if he did leave the premises, they were not aware. I pressed them to give me more exact times during the night, but they couldn't be any more specific. The same goes for the bishop and the reverend. Sir, I think the problem is there's so much going on at the same time at these vigils. I'm not surprised these two guys were so vague."

Darko grunted. This attempt at nailing down alibis hadn't yielded much.

"Please, what happened at your meeting with Peter Amalba?" Safo asked.

Darko told her about it.

"Do you believe him, sir?" Safo asked.

"Let me ask *you* that," Darko responded.

"I'm not sure," she said.

"Commit yourself. What do you *feel*?"

"He's lying."

"Why?"

"The story is too neat, too convenient." Safo sucked her teeth, a gesture Darko had never seen her make. "Peter and the bishop were around Katherine's house on the same night; he saw the bishop walking away from the area, and all that. No. Peter is trying to frame him. I believe the part where he says he discovered the bishop's involvement with Katherine. I think Peter became so jealous and full of rage that he wanted to kill them both."

"My wife feels the same way," Darko said, reflecting. "Is this a male-female thing?"

Safo giggled. "I don't know, sir. Maybe."

"Or is it because you and my wife love the bishop so much that you can't believe he would kill anyone?"

"Oh, *sir*!" Safo protested, laughing.

"Don't 'oh sir' me," Darko said. "I know the way you women stare at him and his light brown skin and wavy hair. Isn't that true? Confess."

Safo was in hysterics.

Finally, she's loosening up, Darko thought. "You're laughing because it's true, and you're too embarrassed to admit it," he said coolly.

While Safo recovered from her laughter, Darko called Chief Superintendent Oppong. "We'd like to speak with you, sir."

"I can see you in an hour, but you will have to make it quick. I'm taking my wife to a function this evening, and she doesn't like me to be late."

Neither does mine, Darko thought. "Very good, sir. We'll be up."

OPPONG SHOOK HIS head after Darko had presented his case against Bishop Howard-Mills. "It's not enough evidence to bring the bishop in," he said. "This man Peter Amalba is an unreliable witness, and frankly, I don't trust him. And I don't find the psychiatrist's diagnosis of paranoid personality, or whatever, to be an exoneration, as you seem to believe. Amalba is not right in the head. We can't hang a prosecution on his testimony."

"Sir, John says Mr. Howard-Mills attempted to *rape* Katherine."

"It doesn't necessarily mean the bishop later murdered Mrs. Vanderpuye. We can't make the so-called attempted rape the basis of a murder charge, especially now the would-be victim is no longer alive to back up the rape accusation. And John's account is only one version of what happened. We don't have the other side."

"Then let's make the bishop come in and give the other side," Darko said, exasperated. "I don't understand why we can't have him here for questioning."

"I do. Get more evidence."

"Isn't it sometimes a process of elimination?" Darko questioned. "Out of the people we have considered as suspects, the three most plausible are the bishop, Solomon, and James, in that order of importance. I say we start with number one."

"You left out Peter Amalba," Oppong said. "You have more work to do, Dawson. Get to it."

DARKO WAS ANNOYED as he left Oppong's office. At times like these, he hated being under the thumb of his superiors. Did they lose all their sense when they passed rank of chief inspector?

Darko called it a day for himself, but asked Safo to go through Katherine's belongings in the exhibit room one more time. He explained they were looking for a diary or journal, as Aunty Nana had suggested. Had the malarial attack not set him back two days, Darko would have done this last week.

He rode out to Christian Village. Jacob was sitting on the veranda of Cairo's house with Franklin, who was watching a video on his tablet. Cairo and Audrey were still at work.

"How are you, Papa?" Darko said to Jacob.

"I'm fine." He squinted at Darko. "Who are you?"

He's getting worse by the day, Darko thought.

"Have you seen Beatrice?" Jacob asked. "She said she would be back soon from Ketanu."

"I expect she'll return any day now," Darko said.

Jacob seemed satisfied for the moment.

Turning to Franklin, Darko said, "Is he eating a little better?"

"He cleaned his plate today at lunch," Franklin said.

"Good. Thank you for what you're doing, my man."

He and Franklin slapped palms and finished with a finger snap. Darko sat and chatted for an hour or so, every once in a while trying to engage Jacob, but the man simply wasn't there.

"PAPA WAS QUIET," Darko told Christine as he washed dishes, and she cleaned off the kitchen table. The kids had gone to bed. "When he's like that, it's sad. When he's agitated, it's distressing."

"Yes." Christine sighed. "Lately I've been worrying, what if Mama becomes like your father at some point? I never used to think that."

"It's frightening sometimes when you try to look into the future," Darko said. "Although I must say there's absolutely no sign of any dementia in your mother right now."

Christine smiled. "She told me that the two of you had a good talk the other night and that she appreciates your apologizing for the pushing episode while you were sick."

"Oh, cool," Darko said without much feeling.

"And the investigation?" Christine said, leaning against the sideboard. "How is it going?"

"We might have some DNA under Kate's fingernails," Darko said, "so that will be helpful if we find something other than her own DNA. Then we can test the bishop, Solomon, Peter Amalba and James Bentsi-Enchill. Those are really the only suspects we have left."

"The DNA takes time, right?"

"Yes," Darko admitted. "They have a backlog at the Accra lab, so I believe they're still sending samples out to South Africa."

"It's the twenty-first century, and we still have to send DNA samples to another country," Christine said. "It's embarrassing. And it's not as if South Africa doesn't have its crime plate full already. So is that all you have pending? The DNA?"

Darko didn't like her tone much. "My prime suspect is the bishop, but Oppong doesn't agree."

"Neither do I," Christine said. "Because it's Peter Amalba who did it. For some reason you refuse to believe it. It's frustrating."

"I'm not refusing to do *any*thing," Darko said. "I just suspect the bishop more than I suspect Amalba."

"Why?" Christine said. "Because for some reason, you're obsessed with the bishop. You're determined to nail him at any cost."

"And you are determined to defend him. I have nothing personal against the bishop. Look, I *know* Kate was your cousin, I *know* you want to see someone go to prison for her murder, but you have to stop trying to tell me how to do what I was trained for. Let me do this, okay? I'm as committed to solving this as anyone else—you, your mother, anyone."

"I'm not so sure," she muttered, turning away to go to the sitting room. He followed. She sat down and picked up the day's *Ghanaian Times*.

"What does that mean?" he asked.

She put the paper down. "Usually you come home, and you're excited about a case. You have all sorts of questions, and we discuss it. But on this one, you're like an old car that won't start."

Darko stared at her. "What are you talking about?"

"This is all about your feelings toward my family," Christine said. "You can't seem to get close, just like you pushed Mama away from you when she was trying to take care of you. You know my mother, Uncle Ransford, and Aunty Nana, but apart from them, you know almost nothing about my extended family."

"Because you never talk about them."

"And you never ask," she shot back, her voice cracking.

"But you don't even have get-togethers with your family," Darko said. "That would be a good way for me to get to know them. Why don't you invite some of them over? Don't try to put your family issues on me. I have no objection to getting together with your family."

"You are always busy. When am I going to have family over?"

"Oh, come on," Darko said.

"Okay," she said, tossing the paper away. "I'm not going to trouble you anymore about the case. Go ahead and solve it all on your own. And by the way? Don't expect me to help you. You need to know anything about my cousin Kate, you ask someone else." She got up. "I'm going to bed."

"Why are you behaving like this?" he called after her. She didn't answer. Darko watched her leave. What was wrong with her?

He needed to escape from all this stress. He'd had enough. Christine was hounding him, and Oppong was on his neck. The case was in shambles; he didn't know where to go next. Too many loose ends were fluttering around in his mind like strings. Maybe Christine was right—he *didn't* know what he was doing. That irritated him—that she actually could be right. Darko's thoughts skipped to his father's chaotic dementia. For a moment, Darko became teary and pressed his palms into his eyes. He felt suffocated. He had to get out.

He got up and went outside to make a call.

THE DISTRICT OF Nima bustles with activity until late at night. It seems neither traders nor customers care to sleep. Music blared. Unreliable street lamps and a patchwork of florescent, LED, and candlelight from the vendors' kiosks helped guide the way of pedestrians zigzagging at their peril between cars winding their way along the streets.

If Darko had wanted to buy a TV, microwave, live sheep or chicken, stovetop, kitchen sink, prostitute, or an iPhone or engine block, he could have, but his mission at the moment didn't involve any of those.

He hadn't seen his friend Daramani Gushegu in seven or eight years. He was an ex-con whom Darko had busted for *wee* possession back then. Unable to keep his hands off the stash he had found in Daramani's room, Darko had taken some of it and smoked it. It was good stuff.

Daramani had served his time, and as far as Darko knew, he had stayed out of trouble since then and now had an honest job. The reason he hadn't seen Darko in so long was that Darko had been trying to stop smoking—albeit with dubious success—and Daramani was clearly detrimental to the efort.

But now, Darko needed relief. He still had Daramani's telephone number—what did that say about his decision to give up the habit—and he called him. Daramani was overjoyed to hear from Darko again and invited him over.

"But not to smoke, oh," Darko warned him.

Daramani guffawed. "You are funny."

CHAPTER THIRTY-NINE

DARKO HAD ARRANGED TO meet Daramani at the Nima lorry park, so Darko wouldn't get lost trying to find the place.

"*Ei!*" Daramani exclaimed when he saw Darko. "Big boss, how be?"

They embraced, laughing.

"*Chaley*, what is this?" Darko teased, pinching Daramani's paunch. He had filled out.

Daramani giggled. "Too much beer, oh. Make we ride to my place?"

"Sure, let's go."

Darko got on the motorcycle and Daramani sat behind him and gave directions to his lodgings. Darko parked outside the door. The alley was dark, and foul water was trickling along the ground. When they went into Daramani's home, Darko was pleasantly surprised by how much of a step up it was from before. It was tiny, but not a mess the way Daramani had once lived. He now had a small kitchen area, a stove, a microwave, a refrigerator, and of course, a flat screen TV. With his network of wily contacts, Daramani would have picked up every item dirt-cheap, and he was probably stealing electricity from the main lines along the street the way many Nima residents did.

"*Chaley*," he said to Darko, "make you sit down, relax small. I dey get some Malta for you."

Darko laughed. "*Na gode*," he thanked him in Hausa.

The drink wasn't as cold as he would have liked, but Malta was Malta.

Air-conditioning was what lacked in the room, which was steamy hot. Daramani and Darko took their shirts off and drank some cold water out of a *sachet*. Daramani took out his *wee* and rolling papers from a spot under the bed, which Darko reflected was not an effective hiding place.

Daramani created a substantial joint, lit up and took a couple of deep drags. Darko began to salivate. He got up and sat next to Daramani, who passed the joint to him. Darko drew on it like a thirsty man finding water in a parched wilderness. He had forgotten how good it was. He became mellow and found Daramani's bad jokes hilarious.

"So how be?" he asked Darko again. "And your woman?"

"Fine," Darko said. "Everything cool."

"Your boy?"

"Oh, yeah." He passed the joint to Daramani. "Cool. But I get two boys now, oh."

"Wow!" Daramani exclaimed laughing. "*Ei*, my boss Dawson! I'm happy to see you."

They slapped hands and snapped fingers again.

"Where your wife dey?" Darko asked.

"Navrongo. With the chil'ren. They go come back next two weeks."

"Oh, nice," Darko said, stretching his legs out. Fluid images and thoughts came into his mind, bounced around and swayed back and forth like water sloshing in a bathtub. For a moment, Darko thought about how he'd warned Sly against hanging around *wee*-smoking boys, and here Darko was carrying out the same act.

Gifty. Meddling Gifty. What was Darko going to do with her? Kill her, he thought. No, not really. That was a joke. Pray for her, instead. But she might be beyond repair by now. God might have given up on her.

Peter Amalba. Maybe he *did* kill Kate. No. Darko still didn't think so, no matter his wife's opinion.

Solomon. And his mother. And Georgina. The Three Devils. They all could have plotted it and Solomon executed it because what Kate was about to do to him through the courts could have ruined him.

What about James Bentsi-Enchill? Darko was undecided where he stood with him. He was one of those fifty-fifty suspects. The same went for John Papafio—well, probably less than fifty percent in favor. Reverend Atiemo—less than ten.

And now. The Bishop. The Big Fish. Peter's story about how Howard-Mills had made indecent advances toward Kate agreed with John's. If Peter's claim was true that he witnessed the bishop lurking around her house at three that Saturday morning, then Darko was certain the bishop was his man. But how to tie Howard-Mills to the murder directly? Through a pleasant haze, Darko imagined a bloodstained machete with the bishop's prints all over it. A detective's dream.

Darko leaned over to get the joint back from Daramani, who smiled crookedly at him, heavy-lidded eyes now bloodshot. The irony, Darko thought with the clarity of an eagle's vision, was that all these suspects were pious to varying degrees. So much for the virtues of religion.

It struck Darko that if Kate had kept a diary or journal, her killer might have it now. Although that meant the killer would have known about it and known where to find it. Even if it were just lying around, he would need to have known its significance.

He opened his eyes. *Solomon*. Maybe between January and April he had discovered her writing in her journal. He read it and saw what she was saying against him, or what she was doing with James. He killed her for it and took the diary. He might have destroyed it, or he might have hidden it somewhere.

Darko closed his eyes, floating. Being high filled him with confidence he would solve this mystery in the next forty-eight hours. He didn't know how, but he knew he would.

He was beginning to feel hungry. Sexual too. Lots of *ashawo* outside in N-Town, he pointed out to himself. But then they probably all had *gono* and AIDS. Forget about that.

• • •

DARKO WOKE WITH a start, panicking. *What time was it?* My God. It was almost two-thirty in the morning. His partner-in-weed had slumped against his shoulder fast asleep. Darko pushed him roughly away and scrambled up, looking around for his T-shirt.

"Hey, *chaley*," Darko yelled at Daramani, when he found it on the floor, "I'm leaving. Lock the door."

Daramani half sat up, looking like a dead man revived. "Okay, boss," he muttered. "Bye."

Darko left, angrily banging the door behind him. He felt foolish, riding home fast and taking corners at impossibly sharp angles. Whoever said marijuana slowed one's reflexes didn't know what they were talking about.

At home, Darko felt famished and looked in the refrigerator for something to eat. He grabbed a mango and sliced it up, stuffing the juicy pieces into his mouth and licking his lips and fingers afterward. Then he hunted for *banku*, but none was left from the day before. He kept poking around in the refrigerator for more food.

"What are you looking for?"

Darko jumped and turned. "Oh, it's you."

Christine was up and had just walked in. "Yes, it's me," she said. "Any objection?"

"None at all."

"Why are you so hungry?"

He shrugged. "I'm like that sometimes."

"There's *omo tuo* and groundnut soup. I'll warm it up for you." She spooned some of the soup into a small pot to heat it up. "Where were you?"

"I went to think. Expand my mind."

"With natural herbs?" she asked with a smile.

Darko didn't respond to that. "You couldn't sleep?"

"No," she said. "I was worried about you, that's all. It's been a long time since you left the house without a word."

"Yes." He leaned against the counter near her. "I owe you an apology."

"I think I owe you one even more."

"All right, then let's call it even and forget about it."

Darko sat and ate like a starving person as they talked, strenuously avoiding the subject of Katherine's murder.

IN THE MORNING, when Darko had arrived at work early, Safo had texted him.

NO DIARY N THE BOXES PLS, I CHCK ALL

He called the IT people to see if they'd found anything on Kate's PC. They hadn't even gotten to it yet. Darko closed his eyes and buried his head in his hands.

Two knocks on the door and Safo came in.

"Morning," he said. He knew he probably looked a little bleary-eyed. "How are you?"

"I'm fine. And you, sir? Are you okay?"

"Yes, I'm fine. Why?"

"Oh, no, nothing," she stammered.

"Thank you for the work looking for the diary," Darko said. "Good job."

"You are welcome, sir. So today, will we check Katherine's house for the diary?"

"Yes," he said. "We'll take one last look before releasing the scene."

CHAPTER FORTY

AFTER AN HOUR OF searching Kate's home, neither Darko nor Safo found any sign of a journal or diary.

"What next, sir?" she asked.

Darko was thinking. It took him some time to answer. "A trap," he murmured finally. "Let's go visit some people."

SOLOMON VANDERPUYE APPEARED surprised to see Darko and Safo at his law firm on Switchback Road.

"Inspector," he said, a question in his voice. "Good afternoon. Can you give me about fifteen minutes to finish up with a client?"

"Of course," Darko said.

He and Safo sat in the small waiting area. Through the door to the next room, Darko could see someone filing large folders. After twenty minutes, a burly man with a dense beard emerged from Solomon's office and departed.

"Yes, Inspector," Solomon said, after Darko and Safo had entered and taken seats. "How can I help you?"

"Something has surfaced, and we need your assistance," Darko said. "Your mother-in-law has informed me that Katherine was keeping a diary—like a personal journal of all that was going on. It might be the key to our discovering the events leading up to her death."

"A journal?" Solomon raised his eyebrows and pulled his head back in surprise. "Really?"

"You weren't aware of anything of that nature?" Darko asked.

"No, not at all. Is Nana sure of this?"

"She's positive," Darko said.

"Kate was writing a diary without my knowledge?" Solomon muttered, as if no one else was in the room. He seemed stunned.

"That might have been the whole point," Darko said. "A diary is often private. Why should it matter so much to you?"

"Of course it matters!" Solomon said heatedly. "Hiding things? Keeping secrets? That's what she was doing?"

Darko sat back and stared at him as if burning holes into the lawyer's head.

"What?" Solomon demanded. "Why are you looking at me like that?"

"Is it possible," Darko said, "that you discovered this diary full of these 'secrets,' as you call them, and that something in there made you so furious that you killed Kate for it?"

"*No*," Solomon said, scowling. "I don't know anything about this diary. And I did not kill Kate."

"Maybe she wrote she was seeking the counsel of James Bentsi-Enchill? I think that would have troubled you, no?"

Solomon's eyes clouded. "Inspector Dawson, have you come here just to torment me? Why are you doing this?" His voice shook.

"I'm sorry if I'm causing you distress. You know what, though? Kate was in a state of torment as well. People telling her she was a witch? How do you think she felt?"

"I never told her she was a witch," Solomon said. The veins in his neck stood out like tunnels under his skin. He seemed to be holding in fury like a pressurized container. He gasped and leaned against the desk with his elbow, his hand covering his eyes.

"Are you okay?" Darko asked.

Solomon shook his head slowly. "I miss her very much now," he whispered. "I do."

"There's a table at the side of the bed in your room," Darko said. "The bottom drawer is locked. Do you have the key?"

"A locked bottom drawer?" Solomon said, mystified. "I don't know anything about it. I mean, I never even noticed it."

"That's a shame," Darko said. "It would save us trouble tomorrow."

"What's happening tomorrow?" Solomon asked.

"Final search of the house before we release the crime scene," Darko said, standing up. "After that, you'll be able to get all your clothes back."

Solomon didn't move. He stared intently at Darko up to the moment the detectives shut the door behind them.

Outside, Darko and Safo got back into the Tata Jeep CID had provided for their rounds, something akin to striking gold. Today was their lucky day.

"Now he misses her," Darko said with disgust, slamming the passenger door shut. "The hypocrisy of it."

"Where now, sir?" the driver asked Darko.

"Courthouse."

"SHE MIGHT HAVE written down details of the lawsuit when she got home," James Bentsi-Enchill said, "but I certainly never saw her with a diary or notebook or what-have-you."

They were in the parking lot behind the courthouse. Darko and Safo had intercepted James as he was halfway to his vehicle. The afternoon sun was ferocious.

"Why? What is the significance of this?" the lawyer asked impatiently.

"The diary might hold some clues to her murderer."

"How so?"

"She might have talked about which man in her life was pursuing or harassing her, or threatening her life."

"Yes," Bentsi-Enchill said, sounding doubtful, "I suppose so."

"Or maybe about how a certain lawyer wanted to rekindle his high school relationship with her."

The lawyer swung around and looked as if he was about to plant a fist in Darko's face. Instead, he shook a finger. "Stop this, eh? I tell you, *stop* this harassment, or I'll have Chief Superintendent Oppong suspend you, or worse. This is ridiculous!" His shoe crunched on the gravel as he whirled on his heel.

"Is it?" Darko said, following him. "Then why didn't you tell us about taking Kate to dinner at the Polo Club on seventeenth April?"

Bentsi-Enchill stopped and turned slowly. "What?"

"We ascertained that with the manager of the restaurant," Darko said.

"I forgot," the lawyer said. "I simply forgot, that's all. It doesn't make any difference anyway. I didn't kill her."

"We'll see if her diary indicates otherwise when we search her home in the morning."

"Do whatever you want," Bentsi-Enchill said, turning away again. "You won't find anything on me."

SHADOWS WERE ELONGATING as Darko and Safo arrived at the Qedesh compound. John's front office was locked, so they went around to the rear of the church building and knocked on the two doors. Darko tried both, but they were locked. He had the bishop's number and tried calling him, but the network was down.

Just as Darko was wondering what to do, Howard-Mills appeared around the corner. He was dressed elegantly in a pale green tunic with black embroidery.

"Ah, Chief Inspector Dawson and Lance-Corporal Safo!" he said, with a broad smile. "Nice to see you both. How are you? I hope you haven't been waiting here long."

"Not at all," Darko said. "We checked at the front office, but it was closed."

"Yes, John is away on an errand, and I was in the main chapel where they are refurbishing the stage." He unlocked the door. "Please, come in, and welcome."

Darko and Safo sat down while the bishop turned on the air conditioner.

"Whew!" he said, sitting down and mopping his forehead. "That's better. Now, what can I do for you?"

"Bishop, you told us that during the break starting about one in the morning you usually stay at the prayer vigil site?"

"Yes, that's correct," Howard-Mills said, but he was a little wary.

"I wanted to give you a chance to modify that statement."

The bishop angled his head. "Why is that, Inspector?"

"The vigil of last week Wednesday, you did leave the premises."

Howard-Mills looked away for a split second, during which time he composed the lie to follow. "Oh yes, you are right," he said brightly. "My wife called me on a rather delicate matter, and so I rushed home."

"Bishop," Darko said, leaning forward, "I know you are a man of God. You do good deeds, and you perform miracles, but somewhere in the Bible it says, 'for all have sinned, and come short of the glory of God.' There are two sins that concern me at the moment—the sins of murder and of bearing false witness. Now you face a choice whether to sin again or not, because I'm about to ask you a question, which I would like you to answer truthfully."

Howard-Mills made a gesture to Darko as if clearing the way to proceed.

"Did you," Darko said, "leave the Baden Powell Hall a week ago last Saturday morning to—"

"I did not kill Kate," the bishop interrupted swiftly. "She was dear to me—to all of us—and I would never have harmed her."

"Yet you tried to rape her, isn't that true?"

The bishop exploded, jumping up into Darko's space and shouting at him. "How *dare* you accuse me of this? Who told you that, or did you make it up?"

"You wanted to see her outside of her counseling meetings with you," Darko said. "You even told her you would come to visit her that Saturday morning."

"I did not go to her," he growled through clenched teeth.

They eyed each other for a tense moment.

"Perhaps you can help us with something else," Darko said.

"What?" the bishop snapped.

"When you met with Katherine a number of times, did she mention that her mother had suggested she start a personal diary or journal?"

Howard-Mills leaned back and opened a desk drawer. "Like this?" He removed a book and handed it to Darko. It was a dark blue hardcover with the title, OUR DAILY BREAD in gold letters.

Darko opened it and found it to be a diary with a daily biblical inspiration. "You gave Katherine a copy?" he asked the bishop.

"No, I didn't have one on me," Howard-Mills said, "so I asked Kate to get one from John. I don't know if she did."

"She did," Darko said. "Nana confirmed it. We want that diary because Kate might well have written about the man who was to kill her."

Howard-Mills eyes seemed to light up for a moment, but he appeared weary. "You could be right."

"May I keep this diary?"

"Yes," Howard-Mills said. "Of course."

"Anything to tell us, Bishop?" Darko prodded.

But he shook his head. "No. Nothing at all."

CHAPTER FORTY-ONE

DARKO WAITED IN DARKNESS in Kate's bedroom. It was still soiled and splattered with blood, and it was not a comfortable place to be.

This is a risky experiment, Darko thought. If it didn't work, it would be a long and fruitless night with hell to pay when the Chief Superintendent found out. Darko had not informed his boss he would be carrying out this operation. He was certain Oppong would not have approved it. For that reason, Darko hadn't involved Safo either. It would have put her in an uncomfortable position of choosing whom to disobey: Chief Inspector Dawson, or Chief Superintendent Oppong.

AT FIVE TO one, Darko heard the outside gate squeak. After a while, someone tried the front door. Darko had left it locked because he hadn't wanted the "visitor" to catch on to the lure. It shouldn't look *too* easy. Instead, Darko had provided an alternative way to get into the house.

He moved into the hallway and listened. After six or seven minutes, the intruder found the access point: the sitting room window was open about a centimeter. All that was needed was to pry the mosquito screen loose. That took four minutes at most, and then Darko heard the window sliding open.

He backed up to the door of the bedroom. A flashlight beam swept around, catching the hallway for a moment. But it didn't stay. Darko moved out carefully into the hallway again and saw the silhouette of a man searching with his flashlight. He shone it behind the sofa and pulled out the cushions to run his hand along the back. He turned to one of the armchairs and did the same.

Darko put his hand on one of the light switches in the hallway, and, praying that *dumsor* wouldn't strike at that very instant, flicked it on. The sitting room flooded with light. The man jumped and whirled around. It was John Papafio. He stared at Darko in shock. "What are you doing here?"

"I was waiting for you," Darko said. "What are *you* doing here?"

John was rigid as he struggled to compose himself. "It's a private matter, Inspector," he said. "You need not be concerned."

Darko held up the diary. "Perhaps you were looking for this?"

"What is it?"

"Don't you know?"

"Oh," John said, craning his neck forward. "That must be the diary the bishop told me to come and look for."

"The bishop sent you here?"

"I confronted him about trying to rape Katherine," John said. "He broke down and confessed he killed her. When I told him I had given her a copy of *Our Daily Bread*, he begged me to come to the house and look for it because it might have information that could incriminate him."

"Why didn't the bishop come for it himself?"

"He couldn't," John said. "He's away."

Darko smiled. Even without the tingle in his palm, he knew John was lying. "Why didn't you report Mr. Howard-Mills's confession?"

"I wanted to find the evidence and then hand it over to you," John said. "It would make things easier for you. Where did she hide it?"

"In a good spot," Darko said.

John stretched out his hand. "Give it to me, Inspector, please," he said.

"No," Darko replied. "This is evidence for court. You don't get to see it."

"What did she say about the bishop in the diary?"

"It's what she says about *you* that matters. It points directly to you as her killer."

"Nonsense," John said with disdain. "I can't have killed Kate because I was at the Baden Powell vigil all night."

"Even at the point the woman in the congregation wrapped herself around Reverend Atiemo, and it took several men to peel her off?"

John's eyes moved off center for a second. "Of course," he said. "In fact, I helped get her away from the reverend."

"No, you did not," Darko said. "I asked Blankson, the security guy, and he said you were not present duing the altercation. That's because you were here in this house butchering Kate to death."

John shifted weight uncomfortably. He was an animal in a tight corner with nowhere to go.

"How could you have done it, John?" Darko said. "Did Kate deserve it?"

"You don't even know how she treated me," he said with contempt. "Who arranged the prayer meetings and Bible studies at her house? I did. Who kept that madman Peter Amalba away from her? I did. Who texted her beautiful poems? I did. And her response to my texts? She told me to stop, and that she was deleting them all from her phone. Why so cruel? And then, do you know what she did? She reported me to the bishop. *Reported* me! He asked me why I had been troubling her and told me to stop. Katherine no longer came to the front office. Instead, she went to the back to meet him."

"I put it to you that you made up the rape story to make the bishop look guilty. You wanted to ruin his life after you had taken Kate's away."

"The wages of sin is death, Mr. Dawson."

"So you say," Darko said. "After you had killed Gabriel, you went to Kate's door, but instead of announcing yourself as 'John,' you said you were the bishop. Once you had murdered Kate, you put on one of his outfits in case someone spotted you leaving the house. That's why Peter mistook you for Mr. Howard-Mills."

"I didn't want to kill Gabriel, but I had to do it to get to Kate."

"You feel no pain at all, John? No remorse whatsoever?"

"After what she did to me?" John said in surprise.

Darko stepped forward and put his hand on John's arm. "Mr. John Papafio, I'm arresting you for the murder of Katherine Vanderpuye and Gabriel Saleh. Turn to face the wall, please, and bring your hands behind your back."

John did turn to his left, but instead of stopping at ninety degrees, he continued the motion as nimbly and swiftly as a dancer, his elbow coming up to strike Darko in the face. Darko blocked with his left, which exposed his side. He saw a brief glint of the knife John brought around in an arc propelled by his momentum.

Darko stepped back to evade the weapon, but John now had him in a deadly embrace. Darko felt a strange, intense burning in his chest. He and John crashed to the floor and rolled. Uppermost in Darko's mind was that he must get the knife away from his assailant, and he struggled to grab John's right hand.

But the knife wasn't there. Darko looked down to see its handle protruding from his ribs and blood quickly soaking his shirt.

John stood up, chest heaving, and staggered to the table to retrieve the diary. He opened it up.

"What is this?" he shouted at Darko. "It's blank! This isn't Kate's journal! Where is it?"

Darko was struggling to catch his breath. He had just enough to tell John he had no idea where Kate's diary was, and perhaps no one would ever know.

John threw the book across the room in fury. He turned and moved in on Darko, a harsh smile transforming his face. Straddling his dying prey, John reached down to the knife handle. "I'm going to kill you, Chief Inspector Dawson."

Darko screamed in agony as John wrenched the knife out and raised it high over Darko's chest.

Darko saw Safo appear behind John with a rusty length of rebar she must have found at the construction site across the street. She raised it to her right shoulder and swung it. John's skull burst open with a dull crack and a bright flash of red. He flipped over to the side and lay dead still.

Dropping the rebar, Safo cried out and bent over Darko weeping. "No, please sir, don't die. Stop bleeding. Please, *no*."

"It's okay." He smiled slightly. "Tell my family I love them. That's all that matters now."

She tried to turn him toward her. She couldn't see the source of the blood. All she knew was that it was pooling beside and underneath him like a lake. She ran outside screaming into the night.

Dawson felt tired and wanted to sleep. He didn't feel pain anymore. He had always questioned whether God existed, and now he understood why man needed God: to assuage the fear of dying and the torment of the abyss. But if Dawson could go back to the living for just a moment, he would tell the world how, when he had stood at the precipice, he felt no fear at all.

GLOSSARY

Agbogbloshie (*ag-bog-blow-she*): highly polluted section of Accra.

Ashawo (*ah-sha-WO*): prostitute(s).

Awura (eh-WU-ra): Madam, Mrs. (Twi)

Awurade (eh-wu-ra-DAY): God. (Exclamation, Twi)

Banku (ban-KU): proportionate mixture of fermented corn and cassava dough cooked to a smooth, consistent paste and shaped into balls.

Cedi (SEE-dee): monetary unit of Ghana.

Chaley (cha-LAY): buddy, pal, bro. (colloquial)

Cutlass: machete.

Dumsor (doom-saw): literally, "off-on." Expression used in reference to the frequent power outages in Ghana.

Ete sen? (eh-tih-sen): How are you? (Twi)

Fufu (fu-FU): yam, cassava, or plantain pounded to a glutinous mass; usually accompanies soup of some kind.

Ga: language and people of the Accra Metropolitan area and several coastal communities.

Gari (ga-REE): popular West African food made from cassava tubers, consistency similar to couscous.

Garden eggs: eggplant.

Gono: gonorrhea. (slang)

Harmattan: dry, dusty, northeasterly trade wind blowing from the Sahara Desert over the West African subcontinent into the Gulf of Guinea between the end of November and the middle of March.

Hip-life: style of music fusing Ghanaian culture and hip-hop.

Jollof rice: West African version of pilaf or paella, and possibly a progenitor of the Louisianan dish jambalaya.

Juju: related to magical powers, particularly malevolent ones.

Kayaye (*KA-ya-yay*): girls and young women, often from Northern Ghana, who earn a living carrying staggering loads of different kinds on their heads.

Kelewele (kay-lay-way-lay): chopped ripe plantain deep-fried in ginger and other spices.

Kenkey (KEN-kay): balls of fermented corn dough.

Kente (ken-TAY): a woven fabric with an interlocking pattern of colors; originated by the Ashanti (Asante) people of Ghana.

Kofi Broke Man: roast plantain and peanuts, a cheap but filling meal commonly sold at roadsides.

Kwaseasem (*kwa-see-ah-sem*): foolishness.

Makola Market: one of the largest traditional marketplaces in Accra.

Malta Guinness: lightly carbonated, non-alcoholic malt beverage, brewed from barley, hops.

Mepa wo kyew (mih-pa-wu-CHEW): Please. (Twi)

Omo tuo: rice balls.

Paracetamol: Acetaminophen. (chiefly British)

Plaster: bandaid.

Sachets: small plastic bags of water sold on the streets in Ghana, usually 500 ml (1 pint).

Sakawa: relating to magical powers, particularly in connection with Internet money scams.

Red-Red: ripe plantain and black-eyed peas cooked with spices and palm oil.

Tro-tro: minivan transportation for customers paying a fare along the route.

Truck pushers: young men who transport scrap around the city on four-wheeled carts.

Twi (*chwee*): one of the Akan languages.

Wahala: fuss and trouble.

Wee: marijuana.

Ye fre wo sen? (yeh-freh-woo-sen): What is your name? Literally, "We call you how?" (Twi)

ACKNOWLEDGMENTS

I MUST THANK MY dear friend J.O. in Ghana for graciously allowing me to fictionalize the real-life traumatic events surrounding her infertility, including her acrimonious divorce.

Thanks also to Bishop Bonegas, founder of Great Fire Pentecostal International Ministry, Ghana, for answering my many questions and permitting me to observe one of his deliverance services.

And finally, many thanks to Ignacio Pena Licona for assistance with Bible references.